DEEPEST
ROOTS

DEEPEST ROOTS

SHEILA MOON

ILLUSTRATED BY SUE RENFREW

Guild for Psychological Studies
Publishing House
Fall, 1986

Published in the United States of America by
The Guild for Psychological Studies Publishing House
2230 Divisadero Street
San Francisco, California   94115

Illustrations: Susan Renfrew
Cover Design: Dorothy Nissen
Typesetting: Pan Typesetters
Printing: Braun-Brumfield, Inc.

This book is the third title in a trilogy. The other titles are *Knee-Deep in Thunder* and *Hunt Down the Prize*.

Library of Congress Cataloging in Publication Data

Moon, Sheila 1910-
  Deepest Roots.

  Summary: Fourteen-year-old Maris returns to the Great Land with her dog and her friend Zeke, where they join an animated tree house and talking animals in resisting renegade Beasts and evil Worms.
  [1. Fantasy] I. Renfrew, Susan, ill. II. Title.
Pz7M.778De 1986   [Fic.]   86-19578
ISBN 0-917479-10-6 (pbk.)

Gratitude to Elizabeth Howes and Luella Sibbald for lifelong roots.

Where will the end of pain be found
and the laughing light
that spills on the hills
when storms have blown away?

Some follow deepest roots,
some climb the air,
whoever we are, however we go,
friendship is fair.

from Hunt Down the Prize

CHAPTER 1

I had not wanted to leave those wonderful green and white mountains and clean water of my earliest years. But my father's work sent him—and therefore our whole family—to the West Coast. It was not as bad as I had anticipated, although the first year I missed the harshness of winter and the excitement of golden spring. I missed Jetty, my dearest friend in school. I missed my old cat, Nicky, who was too old to come on the journey and stayed with my aunt and uncle. Scuro, my small black dog, had come along and that helped. Also, it helped that the family next door had a son, Zeke, just my age and in the same class at school. Furthermore he was friendly, we liked the same kinds of things, and my family trusted him. We went lots of places together.

Like today. Zeke had been wanting to share some mystery of his for a long time. He had never said why, just hinted at some strange thing that would be there. He had talked with my parents, and had told them that we were visiting a very special friend of his, that we would not be out long, and that they were not to worry. They wouldn't have, anyway, because they trusted both of us. And also they knew Scuro would go along.

I had been sure that we were really visiting an old friend. So when Zeke led me and Scuro into a sort of large forest of oak trees about eight or nine blocks from our homes, I felt a bit uneasy.

"Zeke, where are we going? Nobody lives in this place."

"Now, Maris," he said in his reasonable voice, "Just trust me. I know where we're going, and who we're going to see, and we won't be late, and so please don't fuss."

We came at last, quiet as cats, to the foot of a particularly huge oak. Resting briefly against the tree, Zeke took off his worn sneakers—left foot, right—tied the shoes to each other by the laces, and hung them around his neck.

"Now do what I just did, Maris. Take off your shoes and tie them as I did."

Even if it sounded like a command I was used to this from Zeke, and had learned that he didn't mean it the way it came out. So I did what he said. Then I told Scuro to stay right there until we came back. He flopped down on the ground at the tree's foot, and looked up at me as if to say that all humans are crazy but that of course he would stay and guard.

Zeke took my hand. "Now you must hold tight to me and follow where I lead. You'll be OK, even if it seems scary at first."

Grasping the lowest limb with his free hand, he put one bare foot carefully and surely on some part of the trunk, and pulled me up after him into the shadows.

We went very slowly into the great tree—mostly, I think, because I was an awkward climber. It was late September, and night was by now almost total. I could see little except stars glittering occasionally through the massed blobs of leaves. I kept quiet, clutching Zeke's hand and trying to put my feet one after the other in the same places he put his. I almost slipped several times, but each time Zeke steadied me.

For Zeke the tree was so old and well-known a friend that whatever the goal was that we were moving toward was so compelling that our getting there was never in question. Zeke's hands and feet, like animal paws, knew where to take hold. And his fingertips seemed to stroke the living wood of the tree before his fingers closed around it.

We stopped to rest where two large branches of the tree provided a kind of ledge. "Zeke, what is it really that we are going to see?"

"It is—well, it's something very different—and that doesn't say anything—and, oh Maris, you'll just have to wait until we get there!"

I assured him that I would. So we talked no more and continued our climb. Suddenly, with a faint whisper of sound as his body brushed against leaves, he let go of my hand, wrapped my arm around a comfortable branch, and disappeared. I clutched the branch, frightened and trembling.

"We're here, Maris," his voice said from somewhere slightly above me, but very near. "I'm going to put my hands down, and you hold tight to them, brace your feet against the big trunk, and I'll pull you in."

I had no idea what he meant by "in." Were we going into the tree? But what else could we go into? My heart was pounding, partly from the exercise and partly because I was afraid and excited all at once.

His hands reached down and touched mine and closed around them.

"OK. Now—push your feet against the tree trunk and up you come."

It worked. I did come up, bumping my head against some hard object as I was pulled quite unexpectedly onto a solid floor. It was very, very dark, so I could see nothing.

"Sit where you are, Maris, and I'll make some light."

There was nothing else I could do or wanted to do, so I sat. My hands felt a rough floor of boards. Also, my eyes found a small and odd-shaped opening through which I could see stars through a sky hole. Then a match flared, and then a candle in a holder. Zeke stretched out on his back, a smile on his face, his eyes closed. I had only just taken that in when the floor gave a sharp shudder.

"Zeke! What was that? Was it an earthquake?" Being relatively new to this part of the country, I was certain that anything that shook had to be an earthquake.

"No. Now be quiet, Maris. Stretch out as I do, and wait."

After a few minutes of waiting, during which my fear grew larger, I felt the floor tremble very slightly. I thought I heard a very thin and reedy voice. The place began shaking in earnest. "Zeke!" I was now beginning to feel angry with him for not saying more about this place. "What are you trying to do? You bring me here and we lie here with earthquakes, or whatever it is that is shaking us! I think you're just trying to upset me!"

"Maris, I'm scared too, and . . ." At that point a tremendous shaking of the tree began. Zeke blew out the candle, stumbled to his feet, and put his arms around me. "For sure, Maris, it *is* an earthquake! And a big one! Hold onto me and maybe—"

"Maybe" was cut off by another rumbling jolt. The floor under us pitched and tossed. Sounds of splintering wood and crashing trees filled the air. We were flung downward in a black chaos of boards and leaves and branches and monstrous noise. Slipping from Zeke's grasp, I lost consciousness.

I floated into and out of a long, empty, echoing darkness, hearing sounds and trying to understand them but never quite succeeding. Eventually, I heard voices I could neither recognize nor understand. I felt paralyzed, suffocated, betrayed, alone, and hurting. My voice was gone. Was *I* gone? This was a terrible thought. I think I screamed, reaching into the darkness to find something that was alive and with me.

"My goodness and badness! It is upset, isn't it?" The voice out of the darkness was strange, reedy, and gentle. "Cat, help it to be less afraid. Zeke has a knock on his head but he's coming round, you tell me."

A long and lightless nothingness followed, in which I struggled to comprehend. It felt rather like when I had had my tonsils out and had woken from the anesthetic with a terrifying sense of having been lost and abandoned. I regained my voice but not my sight. "Help me! Help me!" I kept crying in a blind panic. Darkness moved around me and under me, as if some very large bird, or stretcher, or surface, was holding me.

"Cat," said the odd, reedy voice. "Cat, are your washing its face? Is it ready to get up?"

At this point a rough tongue began to wash my face as it had never been washed before. My forehead, my cheeks, my nose and mouth, my chin, my neck, and, at the very last, my eyelids. Then it began going over my hands. I found I could open my eyes.

I was nose to nose with a very large, rough-haired alley cat, one eye slightly closed, its hair a gray-brown mixture, its tail kinked from some past encounter.

"Well," said the cat, "I think you're going to be all right, even if your eye is funny-looking. Got clobbered with a bit of tree, I think. Looks like a tree clobber to me. Anyway, it doesn't matter so long as you're all right. And your friend got it harder than you did—whatever the two of you were into. His head has a real big lump on it and his arm—"

But Cat's speech was cut short by another voice—that strange, reedy, gentle voice I had heard—or thought I heard—some time earlier. "Dear Cat," it said lovingly, "Please let our friends be quiet and recover themselves. A lot of talk never helps difficult situations."

I had been slowly looking around me to see where I was. Surely it was someplace I did not know. I was able to consider it from my prone position, and decided it was not familiar surroundings. Overhead was earth, as in a gigantic cave whose dimensions went in all directions. From somewhere there was a gentle light. Because I lay on the ground I could not see very far, but I knew that on all sides—above, below, right and left—there was earth. No sky anywhere. I began to cry.

"There, there," said Cat. "You'll get over this soon. Let me help you." He began to wash my face again.

"Cat," said the reedy voice. "Are you looking after all who need help?"

I raised my head and looked around to see who "all" might be. To my horror I saw Zeke lying only a few feet away from me, his head bloody, his limbs every which way. He did not stir. "Oh, Zeke! You're hurt!" I stumbled to my feet and went toward him.

"Maris!" The voice was sharp and strangely familiar. "Maris! Let the rest of us help Zeke and you. We're lucky we all came out alive."

I looked around. Suddenly I realized that Scuro was near me and speaking. "Scuro! Are you all right? How can you speak? What happened? Where are we? Why can't I help Zeke? Why—?"

"Maris," snapped Scuro. "We are all doing what we can for Zeke. We need help and not words. When we have brought Zeke around there will be time enough to ask questions."

There was nothing for me to do but to accept whatever was going on. That cats talk, and that Scuro was talking, and that some reedy voice was coming from somewhere—none of these could I comprehend. And yet something in me did not question. Zeke needed help and I had hands and feet and human things that were necessary. I went shakily to Zeke and knelt beside him. I looked at Cat, then at Scuro. "One of you see if you can get me something to put under his head."

Cat took off at once and quickly came back with a large bulky piece of something that looked like an old ragged shirt.

"It'sss ahh I cood fine," he said through his teeth, his mouth filled with stuff.

"Thanks, Cat." I took it and carefully slid it under Zeke's head. The bleeding seemed to have stopped. Gently I tried to straighten his arms and legs. He moaned a bit. Then he sighed. I said, "Cat, maybe now you could wash his face some more?"

Suddenly, Scuro was beside Zeke and, while Cat washed away, Scuro took Zeke's sleeves—first the right and then the left—in his teeth, and carefully straightened Zeke's arms. Zeke moaned a little, but did not pull back or complain. Then Scuro took Zeke's pant legs and did the same for the legs.

"We must all go gently." The reedy voice was concerned. "Why don't we gather together so I can see you and find out where we are."

Cat and Scuro ambled slowly away from me. I followed them, after seeing that Zeke was breathing. Not more than ten feet away, if that much, they walked into a tiny, unbalanced, askew little house. "Come on," said Cat over his shoulder, "into my friend Domar."

As soon as we stepped inside I had the feeling that I had been here before. The floor trembled lightly and a soft, reedy voice said, "I am glad to have you, but is Zeke with you?"

"He's resting. His head got hurt in the fall but not too much. I hope."

"Is there something more we can do for him?" It was impossible not to act as if a real being was speaking.

"We're doing all we can," said Cat, matter-of-factly. "We really are, Domar. And how did you come out of the fall?"

"Thank you, Cat. The fall made me tilt more than ever and one of my corners is wobbly. And is my window all broken, please? I can barely see out, I cannot really see since we fell. Just blurs."

"Your window is busted but not gone, Domar. And it's got stuff in it." He spoke gently, "I'm sure we can straighten or repair anything that is really hurt. Zeke can, as soon as he is better."

"Cat, who is with you here, please? I can't ever see anyone unless it is outside my window—and, as I said, it isn't working right anyway—so please tell me."

"Well, there is a girl here, a friend of Zeke, who is called—?"

"Maris," I replied to Cat's obvious question.

"And there is a four-legged, a dog, bigger than me and different but also with fur, whose name is—?"

And before I could answer, Scuro said, "Scuro."

"I am glad to meet all of you. Could Zeke be helped in now?" Her oboe voice sounded so worried and sad that all three of us went outside at once to see Zeke, who was sitting and rubbing his head.

"The house wants to see you," said Scuro.

Zeke looked at Scuro with amazement. "Since when have you talked? How did you get here? What's going on anyway?" His eyes were almost fearful.

"Look," I said, "Zeke's just come to. Scuro, you and Cat go over there and rest a bit and let me talk to him."

They moved away and I sat down beside Zeke. His head had a huge welt and a cut on it, but it wasn't bleeding any more. He was able to move both arms and both legs, though he winced a bit.

"Maris," he said finally. "What's going on? We were in one big earthquake for sure. It felt as if the whole world was shaking apart. But this isn't earth where we are. It's either under the earth or somewhere strange."

"Why isn't it earth? I've been in caves before—not as big as this—but caves are part of the earth, aren't they?"

"Yes. But this isn't any usual cave, Maris. Not the earth we know. Scuro can talk. And a cat can talk. And this cave has a strange look about it somehow. Where are we?"

"Zeke, I don't know. Nothing is like it was, with talking animals and all that. And a little broken-down house over there that talks and—"

Before I could say any more, Zeke staggered to his feet and looked wildly around him. "Where is she? Domar, I mean. Where is the little house?"

"Take it easy, Zeke." I put my hands under his arm. "She's right near. Come on with me." I helped him stumble toward the little house, stopped a bit while he fought off his dizziness, and then supported him over to and into Domar.

He looked around the small room. There were tears in his eyes and a smile on his face. He sat down heavily, and groaned. "Come and sit, Maris." Which I did.

For quite a time we sat there in the unbelievable stillness. There were none of the sounds we were used to. Wind did not blow. No birds called. Nothing creaked or banged or clattered. No motors were heard. No voices. I knew I would have to break this silence or scream, when the little house trembled.

"Zeke? Zeke? Is that you, Zeke?" The voice was as small as a baby woodwind.

"Yes, Domar. I am here. I am all right except for a bruise or two."

"And you are talking with me, Zeke! You never have done this before!"

"Yes. I know. I don't know what's happened. I've talked to you a lot from inside me. I found you—it was—let's see—it must have been three years ago—when I was eleven—yes, that's right. You were a sort of birthday present when I climbed the oak tree on my birthday and found you. And I dreamed your name. Dom Arbor. Lady tree. Domar."

Zeke patted the floor of the little house and it trembled. "You helped me to understand what my name, Ezekiel, meant. I never liked it until you told me about the prophet. I heard you when I lay on your floor and dreamed. I dreamed all the helpful things you told me. And I talked with you inside. Whenever you trembled I thought you were talking. You heard me and gave me courage."

At that moment I was sure that the little house trembled again.

Boldly, I joined in. "Zeke, of course she speaks. I have just heard her. Unless we are both crazy, or dead, or something worse, Domar is speaking."

"I guess that's right. Even if it isn't possible. I think we have been dumped into another world, Maris. Look around. What do you see?"

"A little crooked house. You, Zeke. And me, Maris."

"And outside? Describe it."

"Well—it seems sort of underground—like in a cave—but also there is a strange kind of light—not sunlight and not what would be in a cave. It's like—like—something I feel as if I had seen some other time and place. But I can't remember."

"And the others?"

"Well, there's a talking cat named Cat, and my dog, Scuro, who talks. (I've a funny feeling that he did that once before.) And a talking house. And there aren't any signs of a big earthquake, and yet we were in one. And . . ." I couldn't take this any further because it was too unbelievable.

"OK. So we *are* in another world. Is there any other answer?"
I shook my head.

"So what do we do, Maris? We had better find out the reason we're here, don't you suppose?"

We sat silent for a time. Both of us were puzzled, it was clear, and yet both of us wanted to know what was happening. At this moment Scuro walked in the door.

"Are you two going to sit here all day? Why don't we do something about finding out where we are? Cat and I would like to explore, but as we are part of a pack, we would like to go and see where this hole in the earth leads to. We'll be careful. But we want to know."

"As long as we are a pack, then, let's get Domar into the discussion along with the rest of us." Zeke's voice had a bit of humor in it, so I knew he was feeling better. "Domar, did you hear what Cat and Scuro are asking?"

With her little tremble, Domar replied. "Yes, I heard. We cannot just stay here forever. I could, but I would be lonely. And the rest of you couldn't because you all have to do what you call eating. And so far there doesn't seem to be anything to eat."

Domar was nothing if not sensible and reasonable and all those things that my mother admired so much and did not get from me.

"Yes," I said. "If Cat and Scuro could explore this place—and we could get some rest and know better what to do next—and where to go from here."

"I guess so," Zeke replied. "I guess I do need to rest so that I will feel up to whatever comes next."

Zeke stuffed the old rag under his head and closed his eyes. I shook dirt and splinters out of my jacket and put it over him, and without a word he slept. I went outside where Cat and Scuro were waiting. "Well," said Scuro, "are you going to let us go?"

"Yes. But please go very carefully. We need you back here."

"We'll be back soon," said Scuro. He and Cat walked calmly away towards the dimmer part of this strange earth. I was uneasy. But I soon fell asleep.

CHAPTER 2

When I wakened I felt as if I had slept for several weeks. I was rested and very hungry, and curious. For some reason I did not feel afraid. When I looked over at Zeke he was still deep in sleep. His face was bruised, but the swelling seemed to have gone down. He twitched as if he was dreaming, but his face did not look troubled. I was glad about that.

I got to my feet hoping not to rouse either Zeke or Domar. I succeeded in tiptoeing out of the tiny room as slowly and gently as an ant. When I stepped outside I was overwhelmed both by the size of the huge cavern and equally by my hunger. At the moment there was nothing I could do about the second problem, but I could do a bit of looking around if I didn't wander too far and kept Domar always in sight.

For the first time I could concentrate on looking at where we had landed. I walked about twenty yards away from Domar and stopped. As far as I could see in all directions the cavern stretched into darkness. It was enormous. As I looked upward from where I was I could almost make out a ceiling, but not quite. And above the place where we had landed—very high up—there was a vague sense of open dome, although I could see no opening. How we had managed to fall that far—if fall we had—and not be killed or at least seriously injured was almost more than I could believe.

At that moment I heard a loud bark and then Scuro came rollicking up to me. Cat ambled slowly behind, and went into Domar. "Maris," said Scuro in a fever of excitement, his tongue hanging from one side of his mouth, "Maris, Cat and I have found out a lot of things—including where there is something to eat."

"Inside this cavern?"

"Yes, inside it. It's a big, big, big cavern, believe me! It goes on and on and on, with curves and bends and low places and high places and—oh, yes, I forgot—we met a friend of ours. He reminded me that he had helped us once—when I said who we were. He came out of a side tunnel, and he said he would lead us out when we wanted him to. Also he said he would come over later and tell us what is going on. He—"

At this point I interrupted him. "Scuro! Slow down! Please tell me who this friend is. What is his name? What is he? When did he know us?"

"Sorry. He is a bat, and his name is Ears. He says he knew us quite a long time ago. Or he knew you and heard of me. Or something. I'm all confused and tired."

Suddenly, a shadow came swooping down over us in a wild and apparently directionless flutter. And then a small thing landed on Scuro's back. Scuro stood very still, half fearful and half helpful. I looked down and there, very near Scuro's head, was Ears. His large, furry hearing trumpets were pointed in my direction, his tiny eyes above them, and his soft velvet wings were outspread to balance him. I could see that his mouth was open—and I suddenly was flooded with memories of the past when I first met Ears and learned how to understand him. I bent my head down very close to his open mouth. "Maris!" he said in a tiny squeak. "It is good to have you back in the Great Land! When did you know that you were needed?"

For a few moments I was paralyzed and voiceless. The Great Land? We were in the Great Land? How wonderful! Now I realized why I kept feeling I knew this place! How terrifying and exciting! What did the Great Land need from us? Something, or I was sure we would not have been sent for. In the Great Land I had learned that I came because I was sent for in some strange way. And now in this unexpected meeting with Ears I was flooded with memories of the other journeys—memories of the Guardians, of the Beasts, of battles and deaths and triumphs and disasters.

"Ears," I said, leaning down to him again where he rested on Scuro's back, "Ears, can you say what the need is? Just briefly, so I can tell all of our comrades."

I took him on my hand and transferred him to my shoulder. He fastened his tiny feet firmly and lifted his tiny face. I tilted my head towards his mouth. Because it was so still in this cavern, I could hear him quite clearly.

"Maris, the reformed Beasts worked very hard to change those Beasts who remained captives. Mostly they succeeded. But three of the more negative ones got away and joined the few that escaped. They have been working hard with all sorts of negative creatures in the Great Land to win them over. Including the Worms. They have picked those who were out of sorts with all other creatures, including also a great lot of odds and ends of creatures who are angry with the land—such as snakes, birds, fire ants, lizards, crayfish—not that all of them are against us. Only those who want to be something more powerful than others. You know what I mean."

I felt very sad. "Yes, I know what you mean, Ears. It's the same in our world. No matter how good life is, some want it to be their way rather than all beings' ways. So we will help as we can. As we did before. I guess that's why we were dropped into here."

"We need you as soon as you can travel, Maris. The Old Ones need you. Scuro tells me that you're a bit banged up right now. But could you come as soon as you can? Please! Scuro and Cat know the way to our place, and we will wait for you there." Ears disappeared silently into the cavern's vastnesses.

For a long few minutes I stood motionless. I was feeling the Great Land, its beauties, its beloved Guardians and friends, and its new perils. What could we do—a boy, a cat, a dog, a tree house, and me? And then I knew that we couldn't do anything unless we ate, and unless we could get Domar in some sort of mobile state.

"Scuro, where is this food you found?"

He scratched his ear thoughtfully. "Well, Cat saw some fish in a little pool we passed. And we did see a few trees that might have had something on them. And that's the best I can think of."

"You didn't ask Ears where we are in the Great Land?"

"No. I was stupid! I was so busy trying to remember that I forgot! Fooey on me! I'm sorry."

"Don't blame yourself, Scuro. We didn't know that we were in the Great Land. Zeke and Domar and Cat won't know what we're talking about at all, poor dears."

"I wish Nicky was here," said Scuro sadly. "He was stubborn and stuck-up sometimes, but he had real guts."

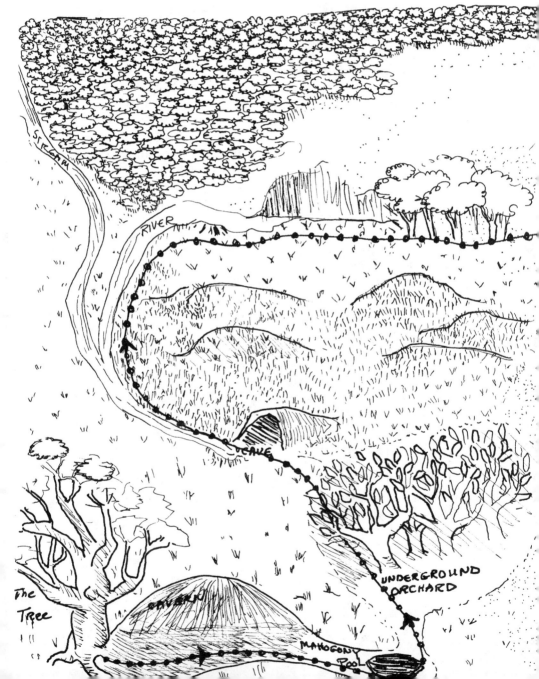

STREAM

RIVER

CAVE

The
Tree

SAVANN

UNDERGROUND
ORCHARD

MAHOGON
Pool

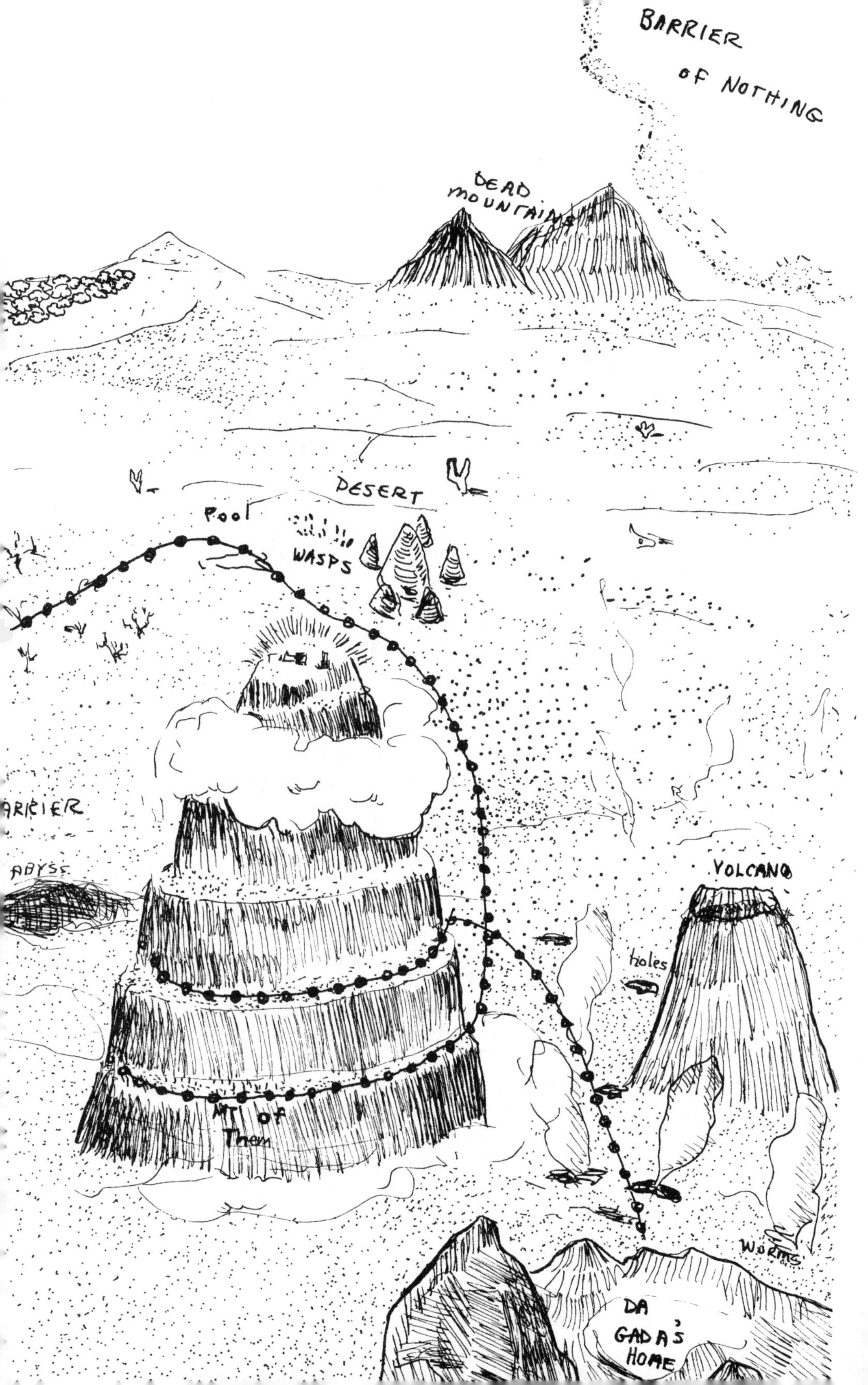

BARRIER
OF NOTHING

DEAD
MOUNTAINS

DESERT

Pool

WASPS

BARRIER

ABYSS

VOLCANO

holes

MT of
Them

WORMS

DA
GADA'S
HOME

"Maybe Cat will be a helper, Scuro. I miss Nicky too. But he isn't here. Cat and Domar will be our company. And, of course, Zeke."

At this moment Cat strolled calmly out of Domar. He yawned widely. "I'm starved. I should think everyone was. Except Domar—and she never eats. Doesn't have to."

"How is Zeke, Cat?"

"Don't worry about him, Maris. He's been snoring, and rolling over, and muttering about food and earthquakes. Here he comes."

I turned quickly toward the little house and, sure enough, Zeke was limping in our direction, yawning and stretching.

"Zeke! Zeke!" I ran to him. "You are better! You look it! I'm so glad!" He raised one hand as warning to me. "Don't worry," I said, "I won't hurt you. And I know where we are—sort of, I mean—and I'm beginning to get an idea of what we have to do and why we're here and—"

"Maris, stop talking! I'm starved—and I'm very mud-dled—and somehow I sense you know a lot more than I do—and—"

"Zeke!" It was Domar's voice. "Zeke! You're all talking and I can't see you because my eye isn't!"

Despite hunger and bruises, Zeke began to laugh. "Dear Domar, your eye isn't and my disposition isn't! And it seems like both of them need to be fixed." He turned to me, his eyes with life in them at last. "I'm sorry I was such a grump, Maris. All of us have had a hard time. Not just me. And you and Scuro and Cat have been working. I haven't. I'm truly sorry, friends."

"Don't be." I put my hand out. "Let's all help Domar."

"And Cat and I will go for food," said Scuro.

"Wait, Scuro. Let's get Domar on her feet if we can, and then all go together. Because if we have work to do in the Great Land we need to stay together, don't we?"

Everyone assented. Zeke led the way and we all went into Domar. Her roof was low. Zeke could just stand upright and not bump his head. Domar's floor width varied from two of Zeke's paces to two-and-a-half. The great tree from which four of us had fallen in the earthquake had obviously dictated Domar's shape to whoever had made her. And I was sure it hadn't been Zeke. There was an opening to enter through and a smaller one to look out of, and the smaller one had some of the tree and some splintered boards hanging across it. We went outside.

"There's the problem," said Cat, pointing his nose toward the window. "Some of the tree walloped the window on Domar's way down. Sounded like the whole thing was going, but it didn't. We bounced, sort of, and then we kind of halfway floated. When we lost sight of the good old tree Domar and I just sort of spun around leafishly in darkness until we landed. I guess you two people got thrown out somehow."

"I hit the tree when I fell, I think—but somehow—I wonder where the rest of the tree went—except those pices that hit Domar's 'eye'—as she calls it." Zeke rubbed his bruises thoughtfully. "Cat, you did best, I guess. How did you escape?"

"First, because I'm a cat. Second, because I was outside—on Domar's head. And how about you, Scuro? You weren't in Domar."

"No. I was waiting at the foot of the tree—as all well-trained dogs should wait at the command, 'Stay!'" He looked at me to see if I would react. I didn't. He went on, his eyes laughing with me. "So all at once the ground began shaking, tree branches were falling, noises of all sorts were around me, and before I could decide whether to disobey Maris and run off or to stay, I was in a space filled with flying cats and flying people and then we were here, some in better shape than others. Cat was best, Zeke worst, Maris and Domar in between."

Zeke was grinning when Scuro finished. "It's great that we all made it, isn't it? And we know from Maris and Scuro that this Big Land—"

"Great Land, Zeke! Not Big! Great and Big are not the same thing!"

"OK. Sorry. This Great Land, whatever it is, is in real trouble and needs us. So let's fix Domar's 'eye' and then get going toward food. I'm starved!"

I surveyed the absurd little tree house. No two lines in her were the same. No sides matched. Her roof had holes in it. Her one window was sort of 2 by 2¼ feet wide and 1½ by 1 foot high. Her "door" was similarly misshapen, but on a scale large enough so Zeke and I could get in without bending our heads too far. Her foundation resembled a badly designed skateboard without wheels.

There was a diagonal tilt from the S.W. edge and another tilt from the N.E. edge—so her floor was wavy. She was the oddest house I had ever seen, for sure.

First of all Zeke—with Cat's help—cleared Domar's eye-window of the splintered wood and the tree branchlets. This had to be done first because Domar kept asking to be able to see. As soon as the window opening was free, we all went and stood outside it.

"Oh, my slats and sides, how nice to see you all!" Domar's voice, as always since our brief acquaintance, delighted me. "And now I can talk to you while I look at you! Cat, I know you. And Zeke. Maris I have heard about from Zeke—but only just seen. And the curly black one must be Scuro. What a fine company! Greetings!"

"*Greetings, Domar!*" We all shouted at once.

"Now we can go, can we not? To be hungry I do not understand. You are all that—whatever it is. You say you cannot do anything about it here. So—let us go."

I was learning that Domar was definite and very, very direct. Zeke already knew that. So did Cat—who, I had learned from Scuro, had lived with her for a long time—since he had been abandoned some years back.

Cat was first to answer her. "Domar, what makes you think you can walk? You never have. You have no legs or feet. Just how do you think you'll do it?"

There was a long silence.

At last the oboe voice said clearly, "I can rock."

"What do you mean, Domar—rock?" Zeke asked.

"Watch me. I learned it from my tree."

We watched very skeptically. For quite a few minutes nothing happened. Then, slowly and uncertainly, Domar began to move—her shortest side lifting ever so little and settling, lifting and settling. And surprisingly enough, each time it lifted and settled the little house moved—very slightly, but moved.

"Domar, it's a good idea—but it's not enough. Try the other side also. Shortest side then the opposite, next shortest side, then shortest side, then next shortest opposite." Zeke explained. "Or I could say—rock the side right next to the door, then the side right next to the window."

It sounded confused to me—but obviously it wasn't so to Domar. In a few minutes, with Zeke calling out like a sergeant,

"Right side, left side, right side, left side," Domar was rocking herself slowly but surely behind Cat, Scuro, and me, headed toward where Cat and Scuro had seen possible food. Domar's gait was rather like that of a person with two stiff legs rocking from one to the other in a clumsy forward movement. Or like a child's toy I had once—a small, roundish person of some kind, and if I started it rocking back and forth it also began slowly to move forward as well as from side to side. I never understood the principle of the thing then, and I was equally unintelligent now. All I knew was that it worked for Domar. If she had been a people being, she would have been terribly tired in a short period. But as a house being she could keep going just as long as we could and she never got weary. Her only complaint was, in all our journeyings, that she saw everything in a wobbling way and had to stop sometimes so that the world would be a little quiet.

For a while as we proceeded forward along—or under—this enormous cave, nothing seemed to change. The all-pervading and dim light was everywhere and the same. The sides of the great cave were most certainly earth—as we had thought from the first. And, as we had already seen, the cave was enormous. The first indication of change was when the earth beneath our feet began to slope very, very slightly downward.

"We're getting nearer to the pool I think—aren't we, Cat?" Scuro asked.

"I think so. Only a few paw lengths further."

After more slow minutes of progress Cat suddenly speeded up. "I think it's just a bit further ahead. The ground seems to be familiar."

Sure enough, Cat was right. The earth underfoot began a slow descent—one that we would hardly have been aware of had not Cat told us it was coming. Then I discerned a turning of the earth walls of the cave, a turning towards us, bringing the walls nearer. And then, at our feet almost, was a small, lovely pool the color of mahogany, not from silt in it but from the color of the stone in which it lay. It seemed to be carved out of the earth's stone. It was a beautiful bowl shimmering with clear water, which seemed to be trickling into it from a source as yet unseen—and the trickling gave to the water a very slight ripple as if it were made of satin.

"Isn't it one of the most beautiful things you ever saw?" I asked of anyone near me. "Isn't it?"

"It sure is!" said Zeke. "Can you see it, Domar?"

"No, Zeke, I cannot. Please help me to turn with my eye in the right direction."

So Zeke and I pushed the little house around, foot by foot, so that she could "see" what we were seeing. This eagerness on the part of Domar proved to be both a rich joy and a difficulty from here onward. A joy because she so deeply wanted to participate in everything we did and saw and found and experienced, and difficult because it required always a great deal of patience, and often of time, in order to get her in the right position for looking. However, it was always worth the effort.

The pool, as I watched it, was ever-changing and ever the same. The diminished light in this great cave was caught in the water's small ripples, and it even reflected on the nearest walls with occasional shimmers. Domar, Zeke, and I were enchanted by the pool, and we got so absorbed in watching it that finally, with a voice of exasperation, Scuro said, "Look, you three. Cat and I are hungry, even if nobody else is. Zeke, would you be kind enough to give us permission either to fish in this pool, or to go somewhere else to look for food?"

"Oh, for everyone's sake, I'm sorry, Scuro and Cat! Of course it is time to get food. Isn't it?" And he turned to me with the question.

"Of course it is. I'm sorry, too, Scuro and Cat. Please go ahead while we go in and talk to Domar." I said this purposely because I did not enjoy seeing Cat catch fish—and yet I knew we needed food.

After we were inside and had told Domar what we were about, I said to Zeke, "Do you know how to cook fish without a fire?"

"For gosh sake, no! What do you think I am—a wizard? We've got no matches, no fire stick—even if I could use it, which I can't—and even if we had those things and I had those skills, we've nothing to cook anything either on or in. So we eat raw fish, if Cat gets any."

"Ugh! I don't think I could do that!"

"OK, Maris, then you just go hungry. There isn't any other way."

It turned out that Cat did get four middle-sized fish, and Zeke cleaned them somehow, and fixed them so that they didn't look so much like fish, and I was able to eat part of one. I ate very fast and didn't look at what I was eating.

Zeke and I rested inside Domar after we had eaten, while Scuro and Cat evidently stretched out beside the pool. That is where we found them when we came out, ready to go on.

"Where was that orchard place you and Cat found, Scuro?" I asked as we set out.

"That's the direction we're going. It's not too far off."

Before we left I tried to see where the source of the lovely pool was, and in what direction. Somewhere behind these rocks was a water source. That much we learned. As to where the water went from the pool, that was disappointing. I found a lip of the pool over which the water was dripping. But it went all directions and in no direction and very soon it just seeped into the underfoot earth. So much for the pool.

Our raw fish did give us a lift. So we set out for the "trees with something on them" —a bit refreshed and a bit more at peace. At least we didn't seem to be snappish with one another.

"Zeke," I said, after we had been going along for quite a time. "Do you see that the surroundings are changing? Not much, but enough to make things different."

He stopped. Domar, Cat, and Scuro went marching onward at Domar's slow pace. I stopped and stood beside Zeke. He was gazing upward and then downward and then forward and backward. Then he began nodding his head. "I see what you see, I think, Maris. The roof of this cavern is getting lower. The light is getting less—or at least it is changing. And we have been going over a few patches of earth that is more like earth—less rocky. Is that what you've been seeing?"

"Yes," I said, and started to say something more when Scuro came running back to us.

"It's just ahead—this tree place—and it does have things hanging on the trees. And it smells good in there. I guess Cat and I went so fast the first time that we didn't really see what it was like. It feels good, Maris. It really feels good. Homey-like, somehow."

I almost got irritated with Domar because her rocking gait was so very slow compared with how I would want to go. But I held myself in and realized that we would all have to go together most of the time, and that I had better acquire some patience because there probably was a long journey ahead of us. So Zeke and I ambled along, watching the walls change and the ground under us become softer and more like real earth.

I looked overhead. The ceiling of the cave through which we had been traveling had lowered even more. And the light had changed too. It was—well, it was warmer, closer to what a pale sunlight would be at home. Suddenly, ahead of us I saw what looked like trees—and not only that but they looked like fruit trees! I grabbed Zeke's hand as I broke into a run. I think he saw what I saw because he ran willingly with me. When we got to the grove of trees—which bore fruits of various kinds similar to the fruits I knew—we were greeted by Cat. "We can't reach those things up there. Give a hand."

Zeke and I immediately began to reach up and pick the fruits, which resembled apples and pears, mostly, and yet were not the same. Neither of us could resist biting into a fruit. It was sweet, not as juicy as the ones we knew, but good. Zeke and I realized how hungry we were because neither of us had eaten much of the raw fish. So we ate until we were satisfied.

Cat and Scuro had nibbled at a fruit or two and then had stretched out on the ground under the trees. Domar was just standing there quietly, and I realized that we had all forgotten her in our excitement.

"Dear Domar," I said, going inside. "We are very impolite to think of our stomachs before we think of you."

She gave her little shake which, I had now learned, meant that she heard us and was glad that we were present. "Maris, I do not mind. I know that animal beings and people have to do what you call eat. So I am patient. I have learned to be so from Zeke and Cat. So what have you found?"

"Can't you see any of it?"

"Not really. I can see Zeke, but not anything else."

So I called Zeke, and we turned her so that her "eye" was facing toward the trees with fruits on them, with Cat and Scuro asleep under them.

"It is very strange," she said in a low voice. "I was made—or, you might say, I was born—high up in a tree with lovely leaves that became many colors for part of the year and then disappeared for the cold times and came back again when the days got longer. That much I saw for myself. But these are different. Smaller. And filled with these things you call fruit. Interesting. But not as fine as those colored leaves on my trees. I am glad you can eat them—whatever eating feels like."

I was just about to reply when Zeke said, "Listen! What's all that terrible noise? And where is it coming from?"

I listened. It was terrible. Then I remembered from the past. "It's a Beast! It's a Beast! We've got to get Domar turned so that both her 'eye' and her door are hidden! And then we must be inside! Quick!"

How we ever managed it none of us will ever know. But we did. Very quickly we had Domar partly against the wall of the orchard cavern and partly in the orchard trees. And we did manage to climb or crawl into one of her two concealed openings and to lie down on her floor before the roaring reached us. It was terrible. It took me back to that sound of Beasts when I had first come into the Great Land. Now, as then, Beasts screaming in the darkness was one of the most awful of the sounds of things that are terrifying. I was sure that the others were feeling as I was. Scuro and Cat came close to me and curled beside each other. Zeke said nothing and made no sign of what he was feeling. What Domar was feeling I could not guess.

It seemed forever that the sounds went on. It wasn't, of course. After a very long time of silence, Cat volunteered to go out and see what could be seen. We let him go because he was by far the quietest and the lightest in weight, and could get in and out the easiest. He came back before very long to say that nothing was in sight, and no sound could be heard in any direction. With that comfort, we all went to sleep—more or less, that is.

CHAPTER 3

I had expected to have nightmares after that terrible presence of the Beasts. But I didn't dream. I awakened the next "day"—although I could not tell night from day in this cavern.

"Zeke?" I spoke softly. "Zeke?"

"Yes. What is wrong?"

"Nothing. I just wondered if we'd better get moving before anything more comes at us."

"Yes. Although getting started doesn't mean that there will be no Beasts around, does it? You know their habits, I guess, and I don't."

"I don't think they will come right now. I don't know why I think this, but I do. So let's get started."

I looked around the room to find the others. But Cat and Scuro were not there—which did not surprise me because Scuro was always an early riser, except when it was raining. And Cat probably was ready to go along with Scuro. Zeke and I went outside and looked around. Sure enough, there they were, side by side, crunching away at what could only be some fish caught this morning. We waved at them and left them to their meal.

Our food was the fruit that hung on the trees near us. We gathered as much as we could and put lots of it in Zeke's voluminous jacket pockets. As soon as we had eaten all we could, Zeke and I pushed Domar around again so that her door and her eye were both pointed toward us.

"Good morning," she said when we had turned her. "You are all eating, so you must feel safe again."

"As safe as we can be, Domar."

"That doesn't sound very safe."

Zeke laughed. "I doubt that we will be really safe at any time now, from what we know from Ears. So we just have to go along and try to get to the ones who are waiting for us as soon as we can. And keep trying to avoid trouble."

'That is very good, Zeke. And couldn't you always be ready to turn me around and get inside me? At least I can be a temporary hiding place, can I not?"

Domar was usually right—like now. "Yes. You are our hiding place, Domar. But for now, I think we should move."

It took Domar a short time to get herself coordinated into her weaving and wobbling gait. We asked Scuro and Cat not to get too far ahead of us, and Zeke and I walked alongside of Domar. For a time nothing changed except for the almost imperceptible narrowing of the walls of the earth cave and the definite lowering of its ceiling. Soon we had passed beyond the trees and the stream. All we could see around us—above, below, at the sides—was plain earth.

"Look ahead!" said Zeke suddenly. "I see light!"

"So do I," Domar said.

Scuro and Cat were already stepping up their gait, and Zeke and I started running also. Perhaps we were all unwise, but it had been so very long—or had seemed so since we were dropped into this alien place—that light seemed to mean home and civilization and all those things. Scuro reached the incoming light first, with Cat close behind, and Zeke next. I held back in order that Domar might not feel abandoned.

What we saw was a wide and rather pleasant sweep of valley with some distant hills and, beyond them, a mountain. The valley had trees in some places, and what seemed to be cleared land in other places. Judging from the winding line of trees to our left as we faced the valley, it was likely that there was a stream in the valley. It seemed peaceful and without threats, but as I recalled the terrible Beast screams of the night, I was not willing to act as if there were no dangers.

Zeke obviously had the same thoughts because he said, "Cat and Scuro, let's go together and stay together. We've no idea of what is ahead of us."

Cat grumbled a bit but stayed near Scuro and the rest of us. It was very still in the valley. At first there were no sounds except Zeke's and my footsteps and Domar's scratches and squeaks. The sky had color in it. There was vegetation underfoot. For the first time since we arrived in the Great Land I began to have a sense of its particular meaning to me. It is strange how you can be homesick for something that you have forgotten about altogether. And I began to see within my mind and heart scenes from the past—muddled and mixed scenes of Beasts and darkness and dangers and, above all else, of Them, the Guardians, the beautiful ones.

Deep in such remembering, I was startled to hear a raucous but friendly voice screeching, "Hello, hello hello! Welcome, welcome to all! Hello, hello, hello!"

We all stopped as down swooped a very large woodpecker, with a reddish and brownish body and a head striped very much like a clown. It made a landing on top of Donmar, its head bobbing about in obvious excitement. Its eyes were dancing with good humor.

"Again, welcome, welcome, welcome! And my name is Antic. And what are your names?"

Such a creature was irresistible and totally friendly. All of us, including Domar, loved Antic from the beginning. For a while we chatted about how we got here, and about the food, and about where Antic lived—which was not far from here, he told us. Domar, of course, asked Antic to come before her "eye" and each of them praised the other lavishly. After the first getting-acquainted time, Antic preened his feathers carefully, in silence.

"Now, friends," he said unexpectedly, "Let me give you my messages from other friends." He hopped into Domar's "eye" so that she and all the others of us could see and hear him.

"Ears had been sent, and I was sent by the Guardians to find you, and to be sure that you were the ones that They were waiting for. That's why I asked your names and stuff like that. Silly but necessary. So here's how it is. Bad. Slithers has really stirred up a terrible trouble, making things worse and worse. And—"

"Antic, please don't go so fast," I said. "Who is Slithers?"

"I'm sorry. Of course you don't know how much trouble there is. Slithers is a most dreadful and terrible being. He is the head of the restored Grey Worm colony—living deep underground beyond the Barrier of Nothing and the Beasts' Volcano, the dead mountain. He has gotten the Worms convinced that they must grow bigger and bigger and bigger if they are ever to succeed in being more powerful than the Beasts. So they are killing every weak and small Worm that is hatched. This has been going on for a long time—and now there are more and more young worms growing to monstrous sizes. My own opinion is that even the Beasts are upset by this. I know the Guardians are—not that I know Them personally, but the word gets out, you know. Now, let me tell you about—"

At this point I interrupted. "Antic, please slow down. We can't take it all in at once. You go too fast."

Antic hopped about on Domar's roof, and then back into her "eye." "Oh, dear! I'm sorry, I really am sorry! I'm talking too fast and too much and too loud. I'm always being told that. I am always sorry and apologetic. And I always do it again! What do you suppose makes me like that? I still don't have any answer. I am sorry, really I—"

At this point Zeke began to laugh so happily that I joined him and we laughed and laughed, while Scuro and Cat—and probably Domar—were wondering what was going on. Finally we stopped, tears of laughter on our faces. "Oh, Antic!" Zeke exclaimed. "Now I see why your name is what it is! Now perhaps you can slow down and tell us some facts. Please."

"Well, it's only recently that the Worms have listened to Slithers, and he's the biggest, meanest, and smartest of the lot. You ought to hear him! He goes on and on and on with great big words like 'pride' and 'most powerful' and 'leaders of the world' and things like that—and then he tells others—Worms, that is—to save the strong and big and sturdy and to get rid of the small ones in every family. The Worms already know that they can only lick Beasts if they are more and bigger than Beasts. They're getting there, believe me! That's one fact. The Old Ones say that Brawn and Potens are louder and meaner than any Beasts have been for a long time. Good Beasts like Quatro and Tusks and some of the others are doing their best to stay related to the Old Ones and to serve them. But Quatro has disappeared. No one seems to know about him. Everyone is worried. He is our very finest Beast!"

"Quatro! I remember him. He was wonderful. He was to serve one of the Guardians, if I remember."

"That's the problem. He just up and disappeared one day. Hasn't been seen for a long time."

"Quatro wouldn't ever join the rebel Beasts!"

"Agreed! Everyone agrees! But no one knows what could have happened to him. Anyway, that's one of the problems that are pushing us around. And one of the reasons that you all are needed. Oh, and I forgot to tell you that Dark Fire said you were to come just as fast as you could without endangering—was that the word he used—yes, I think it was—he is always using big words—anyway, I guess you get the message, don't you?"

I would have laughed if it hadn't been so serious. But I didn't. I only said to the others that if the Old Ones needed us as badly as Antic was telling us they did, we'd better start moving fast. The next period of time was so filled it was hard to see what our surroundings were. I know that we passed a place where a small river began running alongside us. I had expected that we would probably find water—from the green of the land when we left the cave—but I had not anticipated it would be so lovely and meandering and singing. Even with the solemn news from Antic, this river valley encouraged and refreshed us as we hurried along it.

Eventually, we found a wide and slow piece of river where Domar could be near the water and have her eye see it and us as we sat along the bank. We nibbled some of our fruit and some cress that Zeke found. Cat and Scuro went fishing, of course.

"This—this river—is that what you call it? This river—does it always move this way?" Domar's voice was delighted and curious. "I wish I could move like that. How nice it would be. Could I, do you think?"

"Not unless you were a houseboat, Domar," Zeke replied.

This opened a whole new and complicated conversation, in which Zeke tried his best to describe a houseboat to Domar, and they got in deeper and deeper, and Domar got more confused as they went along. And, much to Zeke's annoyance, I couldn't help laughing.

I had just about decided that this discussion—if that's what it was—was getting us no further on our journey and that I had better get us moving, when I heard a tiny voice somewhere in the region of my left hand, which was touching the water of the river's edge and playing with a stone that I couldn't see.

"Please, that rock belonged to me! Or rather, I was sleeping on it a few minutes ago. Could I have it back, please?"

I looked everywhere around me but could see nothing alive. And then it occurred to me that I had better look at the stone I was pushing around. Which I did. And to my surprise and delight I saw a lovely little snail with a pinkish-green shell peering at me from a place only an inch or two from the stone. "I am so sorry, little one," I said. "I didn't mean to push your resting place around. Here it is." And I put the stone close to the sanil. I also leaned toward the stone and snail and put my face as near to them as I could without bumping my nose.

"Oh my," said the small voice, "I hadn't anticipated anything quite so huge!"

I pulled back a bit, enchanted by the face below the two waving "horns" —or whatever it is that snails have in front. "I didn't mean to frighten you. Do you have a name?"

"What is that? A name?"

"Well, I am Maris. A human being. You are a snail. I'll call you Molasses. And what are you doing out here in so large a landscape?"

"I heard the Beasts coming past last night, making the loud noises they always make, and I was afraid. So I decided that I would find some quiet little pool someplace else. Is that what you're doing?"

"Not really, Molasses. We're trying to find some way to help the Great Land, which is in trouble. We don't know just how we can help. We're going to the Great Ones to find out."

"Can I go along?" The voice was little, but very bright and intense. "Can I, please?"

I turned to Zeke, who had been watching and listening. "What do you think? Could she be of help? Would it be safe?"

Zeke had a bit of laughter in his voice when he said, "Why not? I don't see why a small one cannot be just as helpful as a large one—perhaps in some circumstances more so." He turned his attention to the snail, putting his face down nearer to her. "But just how do you think you can keep up with us, Molasses?"

Molasses lifted her head with its two horns and pointed her tiny face toward Zeke. "I've been looking at that big thing with holes in it. Couldn't I have a bit of water put inside it as my place? There are things that snails can do which no one else can."

What could we say? How could we know whether we would have any need, in the days and nights to come, for an insignificant little freshwater snail now named Molasses? I looked at Zeke. Zeke looked at me. And Molasses peered hopefully at us.

"Why not?" said Zeke. "Who knows who will help with what, in this mysterious business. Why not?"

We all agreed. At least none of us protested. Zeke and I searched along the river until we found a stone with a fairly deep hollow in it. We also found some moss and put it inside the hollow. And then we soaked the moss with water. Molasses settled into it happily.

"But how will Molasses keep moist if we have to go away from this stream? We've nothing to carry water in." Zeke shook his head.

"Don't worry," said Molasses. "We snails can seal ourselves into a stone for quite a long time. Usually there's some water somewhere to be had before we dry up."

Antic spoke up loudly. "I can always fly and find some water. I mean I usually can find some water, and bring it back in my beak if it isn't too far."

"Why I always thought big birds were dangerous to snails. At least my mother taught me that. But I guess you aren't one of those. Thank you."

"I'm only dangerous to acorns and other seeds and fruits, little snail. I'll not hurt you."

On that note we set out again. Soon we realized that the river was going downward into a canyon. Scuro and Cat went ahead to see how the canyon looked. They came back quickly, saying that it was dropping downward fast, and that if we stayed with the river we would soon be isolated between steep walls with no exit.

We decided to stop where we were for the night—because there was, very near, a small grove of richly green trees with broad, protective leaves. We could hide Domar in there, with us inside, and hopefully be protected until morning. Zeke looked over the ground very carefully and did not find any signs that large creatures had passed this way recently.

With all of us inside Domar, and with her openings concealed, we felt peaceful. And almost unafraid. Zeke and I rolled up in our jackets. Molasses was in one corner in her rocked moss covered over with a bit of branch to conserve the moisture. Scuro and Cat rested nose to tail in another corner, and Antic perched in Domar's "eye," his head under his wing. We were truly an unbelievable company, I thought to myself, just before I drifted off.

No sound of Beasts came to disrupt our night. Wakening early, I tiptoed outside and wandered to the river. It was beautiful at this moment of silence, and I wished deeply that we could keep on this river path because of its richness and color. But this would not be right. We had work to do, probably fighting to do, and we needed to get to the Old Ones as soon as possible. The only alternative was to go on the flat land to the left of the river. Zeke and I stood and looked.

"What do you see?" Zeke asked.

"Well—it looks like there is a kind of level plain after the trees thin out. And way beyond there I think I see a sort of mountain—but there's too much mist or haze or something to be sure.

"Yes, I see what you see. Maybe the haze comes from a lake or something out there."

"Or maybe it comes from the work of the enemy Beasts. They can do that, as I remember. But then, so can the Old Ones. And so can just plain nature, I guess."

We stood for quite a time watching the distances. Neither of us saw anything further that we could define. Antic and Scuro joined us, and they could not see anything unusual either. Cat had gone for a short wander.

We decided that as soon as Cat returned we would go in the direction of the haze and take our chances. Meanwhile, Zeke and I ate what few fruits we had saved. We commiserated with Scuro—who said he didn't mind and could wait until later. Molasses, when we went to put more water in her rocked moss, muttered that she was quite comfortable where she was, thank you very much, and would stay there until whatever was coming next had come.

At last Cat returned, apologizing for his delay but bringing a large piece of something, which he shared with Scuro while we all ignored them. And after that we set forth again.

Before too long we were moving into a mixed desert and scrub-growth land. The earth underfoot was not really sand, but very little grew on it except tiny flowers with almost no leaves. From time to time we found a small gray bush, quite lovely, which reminded me of what back home we used to call desert holly. Fortunately, the levelness of the ground made it possible for Domar to get along with her odd gait. Had it been real sandy desert, she could never have made it.

Nobody talked much as we went. I'm sure we all felt that somewhere ahead there was danger and need and that we had no idea of what danger (except that it was at least partly from Beasts) and of what we would be called on to do.

At our first rest point—really quite a desolate spot, except that there was a tiny pool seeping up into the sandy soil—we met a most important member of our company, although we did not know that when he arrived out of nowhere. We were all sitting on the sand and Molasses was investigating the pool's edge. Suddenly, there was a buzzing sound, as of a wandering hive of bees. It grew louder and louder. We were all looking every direction and seeing nothing when suddenly Scuro said, "Here it comes, whatever it is!" He ducked his head as a large dark oval creature like a miniature bombing plane sailed in over us, not touching us but circling around loudly until it finally came to rest on the ground an arm's length away.

It was the largest and most impressive bee that I had ever seen in my entire life. It was as big as Cat, of a warm honey color, with enormous eyes, unlidded, and a face that, despite its insectness, was not threatening. In fact it was quite benign, I realized, once I got past the initial shock.

"Pleaz-z-z I am z-zorry if I frightened you, my friendz. I uz-z-z-ually do, you z-z-ee. My name is Waff—It is spelled with s'z-z-z-s. You z-z-ee what I do with s'z-z-z. I try to avoid them."

He stood silently near us, wings tight against a round and shining body, the great eyes watching us intently.

Since I had previous experience with the strange beings of the Great Land, I stepped forward toward Waff. "We welcome you, Waff—I and all of my friends. Can we do something for you?"

"No. You can do something for the Great Land. Already you know that. Earz-z told you, and Antic told you. And now I tell you. Dark Fire and Grandmother told me to come to you."

"How wonderful to hear from them! But are they in danger? Are they—"

"I beg of you, do not give me idle queztions, pleaze. The Old Onezz are all right so far. The Land izz not. The Land izz being hurt all the time by Beaztzzz, like Brawn, and Potenzzz, and others. And by certain non-Beaztzzz, like Cuckoo the robber wazzp, and other beingzz related to them. And above all, by the Wormzzz, who, under the rule of Slitherzzz, are growing in size and in number, and are friendly with the Beazztzz. It izz not a good picture at all."

We stood there—or sat there—silent in our dismay. We needed our silence in order to absorb the awfulness of the picture, knowing that we were to try to be saviors to the Great Land. Once again I glanced at our company. It was not possible that we could do anything! Not at all possible! We were odd, and weak, and awkward, and not prepared for battle—and, in fact, altogether unsuited for any such enterprise.

But Cat said in a loud voice, "Personally, I'd be willing to take on one of those Worm things all by myself. Unless it was as big as Domar. Then Scuro and I would have to work together." He stopped suddenly, as if he realized what he'd said and almost wished he hadn't but really didn't.

Zeke reached down and patted Cat. And Scuro said, "I'll go right with you, Cat."

"Me-e-e to-o-o," cried Antic, from the safety of Domar's "eye."

"Waff," I said, "I believe all of us want to go with you right away. But can you prepare us more? How far is it? Are there threats and dangers almost at once?"

"Mine izz the early danger," said Waff, turning his large gleaming insect eyes directly to me, each facet shimmering in the light. "There are zeveral wazzpz waiting for me between here and there. We've battled before. They hate me. They hate the Old Onezz. They work for the Beaztzz. I want to get rid of them. They want to get rid of me."

Cat had been listening carefully to Waff, his eyes glinting. "Look here, Waff. I'm good at catching wasps. I admit that if they are as big as you—probably skinnier, though—I'd have a fight on my paws."

"Cat, you *are* a comrade. They are like me but thinner, and that makezz them vulnerable. Yezz. I'd be proud to have you with me." He turned his gaze from one to another of us.

"The big one I do not underzztand. The dog, the cat, the people, I do. The big one—but you know, zo it must be OK."

There was no reply from Domar. But from her "eye" Antic said loudly that the "big one," Domar, just might be a splendid place from which the battle of the wasps could be launched. "We could hide inside—or trap them there—or something."

"I truzzt you, Antic. You don't need to get mad at me. If you like Domar, then I do. Happily I would hide inzide. Happily I would fight from her—and for her azz well. But I believe we need to go now."

After a few moments of being sure that everything and everyone was ready—especially Domar—we started off into the desert. If that is what it was. I felt a sort of loss when we left the tiny pool behind, and saw before us seemingly endless, dust-colored, dry, level ground. We had to proceed more slowly than ever because the ground was soft dust and severely hampered Domar's going. But, as Waff said, "Zzzlow izzz better becauzzz we are more ready."

"I don't see why," said Cat, who was marching along just under the buzzing body of Waff. "As I see it, the longer I think about a danger the worse I feel. The sooner I can grab it the better I feel."

"I think about it in my head," replied Waff. "And the more I think the more I zzzee what I need to do and then the more ready I am to do it when it izzz time."

"Well, we're different, that's all," said Cat. "We ought to make a good team in some way or other."

For quite a time we moved silently—and, I suspect, thoughtfully—into the unknown, dun-colored land. It was very, very still. There was not the slightest breeze, not anything that a breeze could stir if a breeze existed. I was just about ready to break into this nothingness with a shout or a song or something, when Waff said, "Watch yourzelvez now. We are coming to the little hill where the wazzpzz are. Juzt ahead there, to the right."

We stopped. Less than a quarter of a mile off was a strange looking hill, shaped like a pointed hat, dust-colored, thrust up into the sky. It must have been five or six feet high, and it had several peaks around the central point of the "hat."

"I think we would be zafer if Domar ztopped and we put her where her openingzz were away from the hill." This we did quickly.

"We will walk toward the hill and let the wazzpz come. We will fight them. When the fight iz going on, Antic, Zcuro, and Zeke can come running, and yelling, and barking, and diving at them. I really believe we have a chance."

And with those words Waff zoomed into the higher air. "Come on, all of you!" At these words Scuro took off with Cat. Antic, from the top of Domar, launched himself. Zeke stopped long enough to shout, "Maris!" You stay inside Domar!"

And then I could see nothing because Domar's "eye" was facing away from where the others had gone. I felt it was unfair for them to leave me, just because I was a girl! After all, I had, in the past, probably fought as many battles as Zeke had—if not more! I was getting angrier as I thought about this. But I knew that this was not what I needed to do. It never helped, and nursing might be needed. So I wakened Molasses, told her what was happening, and put her back in her little rock-room stone. Then I told Domar carefully and slowly, so that she would understand what was happening—or about to happen. And told her that we who had been left here must be ready to provide shelter and whatever help we could give if it was needed. I could talk with Zeke later.

"Thank you, Maris," she said. "I am glad to be a part. Could you maybe go outside very quietly and see if there is anything to see?"

I could. I knew I shouldn't. I wanted to. So I did. I went very cautiously around the corner of Domar to where I could look towards the wasp's hill. It stood out sharply against the sky. At first I could see nothing except the hill. And then I realized that several objects were in the sky near it, and several on the ground. And from the look of it, the battle was on. Suddenly Antic appeared, dove towards me, and screamed. "Waff got the main wasp! They're real mad! Zeke got stung—and maybe Cat—but we've got them scared! Get ready for us!"

And he swooped away.

CHAPTER 4

There was no way to get ready for whatever was coming except to wait. We had no medical supplies, no bandages if anyone was hurt, no beds except Domar's floor, no weapons of any kind. And there was nothing, at least around where Domar was, that would serve in any of these ways. There was no grass, no branches of trees, no water . . . Yes, there was that little pool—no, that was where we were earlier, the place from which we left! We had absolutely nothing. Well, we did have Zeke's worn shirt and jacket that he had taken off when leaving with the others—and we had my jacket that had come all this way with me. I said to Domar as I ran out of the door, "Be ready for anything!"

Everything was what we got very promptly. When I again looked toward the wasp's hill I could see running figures coming our way—I was sure I could make out Scuro—and perhaps Cat—and Waff would be in the air if he could be seen at all from this distance—and Zeke, yes, I was sure I could see Zeke. And then Antic hurtled himself into the space where I stood. He whizzed past, crying out, "Get ready for them! Get something to strike at the wasps with! Hurry!"

I ran in and out of Domar so fast I hardly knew what I was doing. But I did grab both the torn shirt and my old jacket, one in each hand, and when the huge wasps descended I began thrashing and beating at them with shirt and jacket and shouting, "Girls can fight!" The wasps got tangled in the clothes, tried to get free, got confused and more tangled. I saw two of them fall to the ground, unable to get up. So I kept striking at whatever was buzzing about me—until Waff's voice was sharp in my ears saying, "Ztop! Ztop! Marizzz! Now you're hitting me and Antic, and we don't need it!" I paused, and looked down at the desert ground near me. Three wasps lay there, one looking very dead and the others only feebly struggling. Also I saw that Waff was hovering above them but near to the ground, and must be saying something to them which I could not hear. Then all but the very still one began to crawl away from us in the direction of the Wasp Hill. I looked toward Waff where he hovered, to see if he wanted me to hit them. But he only watched them as they crawled slowly away on the sandy ground. He waited until they were almost out of sight.

"Now, Marizzz, we have work to do. Cat needz help. Zeke needz help."

I looked wildly about me, and then realized that Cat and Scuro and Zeke were all lying on the ground in the Shadow of Domar, obviously exhausted. I rushed to them and knelt beside where they lay. It was clear that Zeke had been badly stung. One eye was swollen shut, and his left hand had a huge welt on it. And Cat was licking and licking at his own right forepaw. Scuro just seemed done in.

Cat looked up as I came beside them. "Wow, what a fight! We got about six wasps all together, three chased us, but we scared the rest of them so that they flew away! I knocked one of them out—that's how I got stung. But it was worth it! It was worth it!"

"But what about Zeke, Cat? We need to do something for him."

"Of course. But my idea is that the best help for him would be cat spit and dog spit. Anyway, it's all we've got."

"But we need medicines and things."

Cat replied, "Some of the best medicine there is, is in cat spit and dog spit. Haven't you seen us washing and washing and washing wounds when we get them? That's not just because we haven't got anything better to do. It's because our spit has healing things in it. Stretch him out comfortably so we can get at him. I'll get Scuro."

I knelt beside Zeke. He muttered something as I turned his head so that the stung place would be accessible. He groaned and opened his good eye. "Wow, what a battle that was! You should have . . ." but his voice trailed off into a groan. I explained to him what we were doing, or about to do, for his healing. He managed a one-sided grin and the words, "Well, now what about that!"

While Zeke was being worked on, and while Antic sat atop Domar and went over himself feather by feather, I watched and worried for awhile and then went inside Domar to tell her what was going on. I gave her as full an account of the battle as I could. Antic added his story. He said how vicious the wasps had been, and how scornful of the Old Ones and the Great Land, and how sure of the ultimate power of the Beasts and Worms. "Until we bashed into them! You should have seen them then! Cat and Scuro and Zeke were terrific! And that Waff—now he's really something! In all my living I've never seen such flying! Straight up! Straight down! He zooms in on enemies so fast that they don't know what has hit them!"

We were very quiet for a few minutes—during which I heard the wee voice of Molasses. I looked toward her corner and realized that she was half-way to where we were. She had left her damp rock and was creeping across the dry and bare floor to come to us. I lifted her into her rock again and brought the rock to where Antic and I were.

"Thank you," said the little voice. "My Grandsnail told me once that there was healing in the substance that we put out to slide forward on. So can't I help? I want to help where I can."

So I picked Molasses up again and started to take her outdoors to Zeke. Then I thought that maybe indoors would be better for everyone. Then I remembered that Waff and Antic were air beings and probably preferred outdoors and . . . "Pleezzz izz it all right if I come in?" And suddenly Waff was hovering in Domar's inside. "Am I intruding?"

"Of course not," Domar replied.

"Thizzz izzz a place I could be happy in. Almozzt the right place to hatch a family. Really. Two or three—or more—could be brought up here. I like it."

"Thank you," said Domar. "Children would be nice here. You may when you wish."

"May what?"

"Bring up your family. I would like to have a family in here. Mostly I've been alone."

"I too. I came from a group known as zzolitary beezzz. Azz zzoon azz they are mature, our children depart. And your children?"

"Tree houses don't have children of their own."

"Please take me to Zeke so I can work!" Molasses's little voice was insistent.

Zeke was delighted when we came out to where he was. He grinned as I told him what Molasses had said. "Good grief, Maris! I must be important! To be treated by a cat, a dog, and a snail all on the same day is really something."

Molasses asked him where he hurt the most and he said, "Just above my shut eye." So I deposited her there, staying just long enough to see her elastic little body begin its slow movement across Zeke's swollen forehead. I wanted to stay and watch the healings, but there were other things to do. Like, first of all, to go and talk to Waff and Antic. Both of them knew about the troubles ahead of us, had recently seen and talked with the Old Ones, and both surely had some idea of what we needed to do next.

"What I have to zay," Waff announced when I sat with him inside Domar, "I have held until now—until the time came. The time has come. A friend will come to you here—an old friend, he told me—and will go with you—with our company—on the next zztage."

"Who is it that is coming, Waff?" I found myself very excited, and I tried in my mind to guess who it might be.

"I cannot tell you, Marizzz. That wazzz a promizzz that I made."

"All right. I won't ask you any more. What I will ask, though, is what are we going to eat? And when? And where will we get some more food?"

Waff looked at me fixedly for a few seconds, as if he was wondering what to say, or whether to say anything, and then he said, "I do not believe that we will zztarve. We could go much longer and yet we would live, Marizzz. I believe that it would be important to prepare for the one that will come. We do not know when, but would it not be good to be ready?"

"I suppose that you're right. If everyone is OK, we can get together here." I went about checking on all my comrades. Zeke looked much better. He had returned Molasses to her rock hole, which rested in the shade, and was sitting and talking with Cat. Cat seemed to be doing very well with his stung paw—walking about on it with only a slight limp. Scuro, still half-asleep and half-not-asleep, was stretched out near Zeke, who had an almost normal forehead. Antic was perched above Domar's "eye," looking out at us.

"OK, friends," I said, "We're going to gather inside and get ready."

"Ready for what?" Zeke asked.

"Ready for whoever is coming to us. And that we don't know. But Waff says we should be ready."

When we had all assembled on Domar's floor we were really a crowd. I moved Molasses and her stone into the midst of us—sort of like the center of the circle—and the rest were sitting or standing around the stone. Let's say our names. Maris—"

"Zeke."

"Cat."

"Domar."

"Scuro."

"Antic."

"Molasses."

Waff."

"All right, friends. We are all here. And I don't know what to do now."

"Marizz, I am sure that, when you have been in the Great Land or with the Guardianzz before, you have focuzzed on a place, a face, zzomething."

I pondered for a minute or two—and then I did remember how hard we had always concentrated in order to move Thaddeus through space. Could the one who was coming to join us be Thaddeus? I could try. So I closed my eyes, breathed in and out as deeply and evenly as I could, and tried to picture him as I had last seen him after he had been made a Guardian. I shut out everything and everyone and held his ridiculous and wonderful self before my closed eyes. Nothing else existed. My world was silent, dark, empty. I held on to his image with intense concentration. Wonderful, awkward, living, willing, helpful Thaddeus, his salamander self lumbering along, always with a sense of humor about himself. "Thaddeus! Thaddeus!" I said to myself. "Thaddeus!"

Suddenly, Domar shook so that we all rushed outside to find out what had happened. As I reached the ground another violent convulsion shook us and all at once there before us in a cloud of disappearing smoke stood Thaddeus, pot on his head, a bizarre load on his back.

"Oh, Thaddeus! Thaddeus!" I began to cry very wet and welcoming tears of almost intolerable joy.

"Maris! Dear Maris!" Thaddeus—the salamander magician, in all of his gorgeous, rich brown body with its red-orange stripes, walked slowly toward me. "How good to be with you again." He nodded his head slowly, rattling the great black magic pot that he always wore like a hat because there was no other place to put it. "I am so glad the Old Ones chose me to come!"

I put my arms around his neck, gently, so as not to disturb or displace any of the piled up magic equipment on his wide back. "I'm glad they chose you, Thaddeus. Very, very glad! And here are our comrades."

He bowed to each one as I presented them. Scuro he knew, of course. And must have known Waff. Each one of them—Cat, Antic, Molassses, Zeke, Scuro—when he bowed to them each bowed back. Except Molasses, who pulled her tiny head in and out. And then I introduced Domar. I told Thaddeus about her and how we were becoming her family. He stood before her eye window while I presented her. When I finished, he gave the deepest of Thaddeus bows, almost losing his magic pot in so doing. "Domar," he then said in his most impressive voice, "if I were not one of the Guardians I would ask to become one of your family. But at least for the time of our journey together I hope I may become one of this company, even if I must stay outside most of the time. Not from choice but from size, you see."

I really believe that Domar chucked—very softly—and then she said, "Thaddeus, perhaps when we gather to talk, you may be able to at least have your head inside. Without what's on top, of course. And I welcome you as friend and as rescuer and as Guardian—whatever that is."

Rarely had Domar made such a long statement. Thaddeus gave Domar an exceptionally deep bow. He also did a most wonderful thing after that. He had us take the bundles off his back—Zeke and I—and asked me to get the black feminine prayerstick. Fortunately, I remembered what it was from my past work with him, and after removing all his bundles from his back and after searching through all of them, I found it and gave it to him.

He stood very still before Domar's door. He closed his eyes. For a very, very long period he stood so. Finally I said, "Thaddeus? Are you all right? Can I help you?"

He opened his eyes. "Thank you, Maris. I was wool-gathering, I'm afraid. Yes, you can help me. Please put my pot as near as possible to Domar's door. Put the black prayerstick in the door, half inside and half outside. Then come and stand opposite me."

We stood facing each other. Thaddeus carefully removed the black pot with my help, and stood it between us. Then I placed the prayerstick in the door, half in and half out, as he had asked. And there we stood facing one another.

"Close your eyes, Maris."

He closed his and I closed mine.

"Now keep remembering Them, the Guardians, and the need They have for this company. And that we must make ourselves secure against the enemy for this next stage of the journey."

All these things I did. Against my closed eyelids I could see the Guardians at the Place of Them. Not quite, but almost. And I could imagine a warm fire burning, and friends gathered around it, and the lovely music of a spinning wheel and many beings singing and—

"Whooosh! That does it now!"

I looked, and a tall, slender, golden flame was burning from the wand laid in Domar's door. As we watched, a very delicate and lovely golden green sheen began showing around all the dimensions of the door's opening. We all kept silence while the color came slowly to every inch of the doorjamb, until finally the little door, heretofore so plain, shone like the entrance into some enchanted place.

"Well, that is better than I had hoped. Indeed it is." Thaddeus was always, I suddenly recalled, more surprised at his magic than was anyone else. He reached over and picked up the wand from which the flame seemed to be coming. The flame continued, but it did not seem to burn. Thaddeus proceeded calmly around to the small window and placed the wand there. The same thing happened. The wonderful green-gold color soon was glowing softly from Domar's "eye" as well as from Domar's door.

"Can you see what is happening, Domar?" Thaddeus asked.

"No. I cannot see unless something or people are standing quite a few spaces outside my eye."

Thaddeus walked back a few paces from her now golden glowing window. He held the wand in his right front hand. It continued to glow. "Domar, can you see this?"

"Oh, yes! Yes! It is a lovely glowing thing!"

"Domar, that is what both your door and your eye window are like now. Lovely glowing things. And more than that, no one who does not belong in this company can pass through this golden glow."

I ran to Thaddeus. "Dear friend! You are so wonderful! So dear!"

"My goodness, Maris. This is nothing out of the ordinary. It might be, if I had to secure a whole castle, or move a whole mountain, or change the course of a river (which I have not yet mastered). But for such a lovely lady as Domar, and for such a splendid company of friends, I find it a very delightful occupation."

As always, whenever anyone told Thaddeus something nice he was apt to break into speech which was never quite explanatory. Probably because he didn't know the explanation anyway.

"Now," he said, in his serious and let's-be-about-it voice, "we need to be going along to our destination." He looked around at our assorted shapes, sizes, and capacities. "Dear me, we are not all cut to the same mold, are we? Even if I were twice as good a magician as I am, I could not transport any of you with me. And even if I could, I'm not sure it would be a good idea. The Guardians are convinced that we need to try hard to take ourselves by ourselves. 'Help each other but do not expect miracles.' That's what Arachne says."

"Is Arachne well, Thaddeus?" I had to ask about this incredible spider spinner who had sung us forward on so many many journeys. "Is she?"

"Of course, Maris. You will see when you get there. But you won't get there unless we start. Will you?"

In a chorus of yeses and pleases, Thaddeus got his answer. To guide us. And he told us his plans.

"Domar and I are surely the slowest, so we should go first. Our flyers—Antic and Waff—can keep us notified if they see anything unusual, either harmful or helpful. Cat and Zeke can go on one side of Domar and Scuro and Maris on the other. And Molasses can go in my pot—and I'll even conjure up a little water."

Thus we set out into the unknown—a vulnerable, slow assortment that no sane person would ever put together. Yet we were together, all involved in the Great Land and its future.

Before very long we drew near to the Wasp hill. Close up, it did not seem as big as it had when I had seen it from a distance. Waff went ahead to look it over, and reported that the two injured wasps were there nursing their wounds, and afraid of us, and resolved never again to fight over anything. Thaddeus said he intended to bring them some healing from the Guardians. So we all rested while he paid them a call. We were too far to hear what was going on—but we could see Thaddeus's tail moving back and forth. That usually meant an argument.

"Well," he said on his return, "they are a bit more ready to let go of their attachment to the Beasts. They said you had been kind not to kill them—thanks to Waff for that—and that Beasts would never have spared them. So I gave them some healing stuff. Right now they are grateful to us. How long it will last, who knows? They did give in without too much argument. We shall see."

We set out again in the same sequence. Suddenly, Scuro said, "I think it's changing."

"What is?"

"The land, what else? Look ahead. I can see rising ground, maybe even hills, maybe even big hills."

I realized I had been wandering off in my mind—as I often did—to places I could never quite define. So I took Scuro's advice and looked ahead. There were big hills—quite a distance away yet, to be sure—but big ones rising up from lower ones rising up from level ground.

"You're right, Scuro. Let's ask Thaddeus."

So I called out, and everyone moved toward Thaddeus and Domar. When we all were clumped near Domar's "eye," I said we wanted to know what was ahead—and also needed a bit of rest. The second reason was not quite honest—but I didn't want Thaddeus to feel I was bossy. However, he saw right into my conniving, and said, "Maris, sometime you've got to learn to be really, *really* honest."

"Yezzz Marizzz. Thadeuzzz izz right. Zzpeaking true iz very important."

All I could do was to agree and apologize. And I really meant my apology. Thaddeus turned his bumpy reptile head towards me, and held my eyes with his. "Apologies will not do it! Not ever! How do you think you can help the Great Land—and the Old Ones—unless you are truthful all the time? Lies can manipulate—can have great and evil power. How do you think the Beasts win others to their side? With lies. Nice, convincing, fine-sounding lies! That's how they do it."

I was deeply ashamed—truly and deeply. I think I've not since then (or hardly ever) manipulated anyone with untrue or partially true stories. Of course I've told little fibs—but not often and never in important situations. Thaddeus had done it by saying I could not aid my beloved Guardians with lies. After my apology I cried, right in public, and no one comforted me. And then Scuro licked my tears.

Finally, Thaddeus said, "Enough, enough. Let us stop for food and rest and nightfall."

For the first time since we toppled into this world, the sky looked like a proper sunset and obviously a proper night was coming soon.

CHAPTER 5

Supper was a strange mixture of forgotten fruit (half squashed from Zeke's and my jacket pockets), and some wonderful cold water, and an incredibly tasteless but stomach-satisfying mess that Thaddeus made in his black pot. It was an honest meal, and elegant—not for the quality of its menu, but for the quality of its guests.

Thaddeus had always been able to bring out the very best in everyone. I never understood how or why, but some sort of warm inclusiveness was part of it, and also his own unmatchable absurdity in almost any situation. Above all, there was his wise and loving and courageous and honest self. During this meal all of us were inside Domar except Thaddeus. But his black pot—from which we each selected our own food—sat in the room's center and our host's head and front feet were inside Domar while the rest of him was outside. Domar's golden door was filled with Thaddeus. Most of the conversation during and after dinner was between Waff and Thaddeus. Occasionally, Antic spoke, because he too had knowledge of the Great Land and its troubles.

"Why do you think Quatro has disappeared?" Thaddeus asked. "Have you talked to others, Waff? Antic?"

Waff replied first. "By way of the Wazzpz—some of the fence-zitting onez that zay 'yezz' and 'no' and 'maybe' to Slitherzzz'z 'join-uz-Beastzz' argumentz—I heard that Quatro had been put out of hiz high pozition with the Old Ones becauze he wanted more power."

"I do not believe that." Thaddeus was very definite. "Never. Dark Fire—whom he carries—chose him. You know that."

"What could it be, then, Thaddeuz? Haz he been abducted? Murdered? Zent on a zecret errand?"

"Truly, Waff, I do not know. I serve Dark Fire and all the Old Ones when they need magic, but I am not told their personal knowledge. Only those who are totally Old Ones are present at all the discussions. I can't do any guessing."

"I hear what you zay, friend. Do you, Thaddeuz, or anyone here, have zome ideaz about what we are needed to do? Or some zpeculationz?"

After a pondering silence Antic spoke more seriously than I had heard him. He was impressive in his flashing colors. "I have been doing a lot of inside sort of wondering. One of my wonders is—what's the sort of stuff that hides some of the mountains between the Place of Nothing and the Dead Mountain? I've heard the Worms live around there, somewhere underneath. Who is making the mist? It's different from the Barrier of Nothing, because that's just—just—well, nothing. You've seen it, Maris?"

I nodded. "Has anyone flown over or into this mist stuff, Antic?"

"No. I considered it once but then I unconsidered it. I mentioned it once to Ears, and he shrugged and went wobbling away. And once I was about to ask Great Owl, but he hooted at me before I could say anything, so I didn't—say anything, I mean."

Waff spoke up suddenly. "Izz it maybe that we have to explore that mizzzt? With maybe help from otherzzz? Like the eagle King Featherzzz, or the vulture Gada? They are both great helpers to find."

"Dear friends," said Thaddeus. "In all truth I am certain that we must first go to Them on Their Mountain. They will tell us what comes next. They wish to see us first. Let's all step outside into the night."

I remembered other times I had gone with comrades up the Mountain of Them. Each time it was different. Sometimes dark. Sometimes with weather changes—quite unexpected ones. Sometimes in fear, sometimes in joy, always in excitement. What could we expect? But how could Domar possibly climb Their Mountain? I said nothing, however, remembering for once that matters had a way of making themselves very evident when the time was at hand. So we went out into the darkness. Except for Molasses staying inside.

We remained silent for quite a period during which night grew thick. The sky was almost a purple black. (There were no stars in the Great Land. Occasionally—and unpredictably—a moon climbed into the night sky, as I recalled. But more often than not the sky was, as now, a deep mystery.)

Thaddeus broke the breathing stillness. "Look! There! There!"

It took a few seconds for the rest of us to solve where "there" was, because Thaddeus was pointing with his nose—which he always did and which I always forgot. As he stood beside us, his tail moving back and forth excitedly, I sighted, as best I could, along his nose's direction. I stared into the dark sky—stared until my eyes hurt—and then suddenly I saw a small point of glowing light. I turned my eyes away and back three or four times, to be sure I wasn't imagining. At last I was certain.

"I see a light, Thaddeus! I see a light on top of Their Moutnain! I hope its Theirs. I know it's a light!"

"You are correct, Maris. They are telling us that They are waiting for us. Come, friends. We must go."

"Now?" Zeke sounded shocked. "Now? In this black night? We couldn't even see each other—not to mention a path—if such a thing exists at all. It's crazy! It's . . . "

"Zeke," said Thaddeus, "you cannot know what They know. And They know we can get there. Once They know we've seen the signal and have really started—They will send a messenger, be sure."

"And how will They know when we have started? Please?" Domar spoke softly but urgently.

"Domar, my dear friend," said Thaddeus, "someone will go to Them and tell them."

"Antic can't see at night, Thaddeus, can he?" said Domar. And we don't want to risk any of our family unless we must, do we, Thaddeus?"

Domar was beginning to sound like the old woman in the shoe. But Thaddeus went on amiably. "Don't you worry now, dear Domar. We won't risk anyone. I'll give Antic a homing pigeon feather from my magic stuff—and I'll set it for the Place of Them. After all, Antic comes from Them."

Everyone gathered around Thaddeus as he stood near the free-gold light of Domar's door. All of his equipment was in a muddled pile on the ground and he was poking into it, pulling at an item, returning it, poking some more. "Maris, do come and help me!" (He had long ago taught me to identify different things.) "I want the striped stick and I can't find it!"

I began going over, in a somewhat more orderly way, all his bewildering assortment of sticks, feathers, stones, little packets of colored sand, shell, dried flowers and leaves, pieces of wood, and unidentifiables. At last I found the lovely golden prayerstick of polished stone.

He nodded his head as if he had known all the time where it was. "Now, Maris. Hand me the black one."

I knew he meant the black prayerstick. I found it.

"Please put the two sticks across each other and then find me some black sand."

When I handed him the sand he made a careful circle of it around the crossed sticks. "Now give me a feather—I guess any feather will do." At last I found a feather that seemed almost to have a silver glow to it. I handed it to Thaddeus.

"My goodness, Maris—are you planning to be a magician some day? This is exactly what is needed and I forgot I had it! It is a feather from the Snowy Owl—so much better than a homing pigeon feather! I remember my great uncle telling me that! My goodness!" He stood holding the feather and gazing into the darkness.

"Dear Thaddeus," I said. "Shouldn't Antic be on his way to Them?"

"Of course!" With that, Thaddeus took the owl feather, laid it on the crossed sticks inside the black sand circle, leaned his head down, and breathed onto this arrangement. For a few moments a golden flame seemed to flicker on the silver feather. The flame vanished. Thaddeus turned to Antic. "Take the feather in your claws and do not let go of it for any reason! Not for any reason! It will speak to your wings and take you to the Place of Them and return you to us (unless They send another)."

Antic bowed his head in assent, took the feather in his left claw, and was gone into the night. I shivered as he became part of the darkness, and I heard Thaddeus saying some charm over and over.

"When will we know if Antic gets there, Thaddeus?" Zeke asked. "And how will we know when to start?"

"I think that the light They are using to reach us will go out and on and out and on and out and on as soon as Antic arrives. That shouldn't take very long if the feather is set right—and I'm quite sure it is. We must be prepared to start the moment the signal comes."

"What if it doesn't come?" Zeke asked.

"It will. One way or another." Thaddeus was usually composed, but occasionally forgetting. "Help us get ready to travel, Zeke."

We all went to work. Thaddeus provided an eerie light so we could see what we were doing. I was getting Thaddeus's things ready for departure as he wanted them. Zeke was turning Domar in the direction for departure—which wasn't easy in the strange illumination we had. Waff had gone inside Domar and settled down beside Molasses on her tiny rock. Cat and Scuro said they would walk on either side of Domar because they could see in darkness. Thaddeus would lead because his magic—he hoped—would keep us on course.

So we stood silently watching the tiny point of light high in the black sky. It felt to me as if we had been standing for endless time when Zeke and Thaddeus at the same moment said, "Look!"

Then I too saw that small light go out, then on, then out, then on, then out, then on—just as Thaddeus had said.

"All right," said Thaddeus. "Here we go. Zeke, you go with Maris just behind me and just ahead of Domar. Cat and Scuro will go on either side of Domar. And please don't be anxious. My magic will help keep us on the path. There will be a guide—or perhaps guides—before too long."

With that we started.

Cat and Scuro had worked out a ridiculous but very simple way to keep Domar on course. Cat was at front right and Scuro at front left. Once they learned the pulse of Domar's rocking gait, they began guiding by "Meow" and "Woof," sounded first on one side and then on the other. Domar was wonderfully cooperative and accurate, and obviously had complete trust in their guidance. We all "woofed" and "meowed" along in the darkness for quite a long time, it seemed to me, but Thaddeus knew where he was going. He moved slowly and confidently. Zeke and I could just barely see his bulky shape ahead of us.

After quite a time—almost hypnotized by his confidence—Thaddeus suddenly stopped. I would have bumped into him if Zeke had not grabbed my arm. Domar stopped because Cat and Scuro had seen us stop and had acted accordingly.

"Yes. Yes, of course. Yes. As soon as we can. Yes." Thaddeus was talking into the darkness.

"What's wrong, Thaddeus?" I asked. "Are you all right?"

"Of course I am! Antic and Ears are here from the Old Ones. They want us all—including Domar—to come to the Place of Them."

All of us—I, Zeke, Cat, Scuro, Antic, Ears, Molasses (who was so small we almost forgot her, but didn't)—gathered inside Domar. Thaddeus's head, forefeet, and black pot were inside.

He cleared his throat, blinked twice, cleared his throat again. "What can I do to help you do whatever you intend to do?" I asked.

"Well now," and he opened his eyes, "I should think we need to get Domar to the Place of Them first. And then the rest of us can proceed on foot to learn whatever we can."

"How can we? She can't fly or burrow or—well, she can't do anything that would get her there fast." Zeke was earnestly perplexed. "How can it be done, Thaddeus?"

"Magic, Zeke. Magic. Let me explain—especially to Domar." He cleared his throat. "Will you trust me, Domar?"

"And why should I not trust?"

Thaddeus chuckled. "Why not, indeed! Let me explain. If my magic works, I will make you very, very small, Domar. So small that Ears or Antic can fly and carry you to the Place of Them. And when the rest of us arrive I will make you your own size again. If my magic works in reverse."

"But suppose I could not be changed into my real size again? I would not want always to be so little."

Thaddeus gave one of his rare chuckles. "They would love you in any size, Domar. But I am quite certain that I can not only make you small, but that I can restore you to your normal size again. Are you willing, Domar?"

There was a considerable pause, followed by a slight tremble of Domar's floor. Her voice, clear and confident, said, "I am willing. I trust you. Yes, I truly do. Even if I become forever tiny, I trust you." A silence come over us all. Zeke looked solemn. Cat rubbed his head gently against Domar's door sill. I had tears—only a few, but needful—and Scuro nuzzled my hand sympathetically.

Ears and Antic had been patient during our conversation. But Ears, who was hanging upside down in Domar's door, said in his tiny voice, "I'm supposed to go back to Them before day comes. So shall I go now, and say that you are all en route? And that Antic will come very soon? Carrying a tiny house that talks?"

"Yes." Thaddeus spoke firmly. "Carry those messages, Ears. Just carry those messages. We will all get there."

Ears departed soundlessly into the night. Thaddeus said, "Maris, will you assist me, please?" Suddenly, I remembered Molasses. "Thaddeus, should we take Molasses and her rock out of Domar? She's so tiny already that—"

Domar's voice broke in. "Please! We can shrink and grow together."

"That is a very good idea," said Thaddeus reassuringly. "Now then, Maris, let us get ready."

And that we did—in the usual disorderly procedures that seemed to work for Thaddeus. I sorted and searched and rummaged, found things he wanted and things he didn't know he had, or was not sure of their powers. But, strangely enough, through all the apparent confusion his mastery of magic never seemed to diminish. As always, he had me put all his magic equipment in a huge pile in front of him. He poked in it, took items out, put them back, combined things, changed combinations. He often just stared at the confusion as if he couldn't make sense of it, then suddenly he would move one item and everything was ready.

It was like that this time. He had asked me to remove some items, to put them back, to add this to that and subtract that from this, to put a prayerstick here, then to move it to there. I was tired. I knew he must be. And the others—especially Domar—were bound to be edgy.

"We are ready, I believe." He spoke calmly and certainly. "We must all move outside. Maris, please take the items I point to. Then, Zeke, please take everything else outside and make a neat pile. Please put the pot three paces from the door."

I picked up various things as he pointed. There were four feathers—white, black, yellow, blue—which he had me place at Domar's four sides. Various rocks of various shapes and sizes made a ring around Domar. I trickled black dust that shone faintly in a wide circle outside the rings of rocks.

"Now we are ready," he said calmly. "Maris, you stay beside me, here before Domar's door, with Antic on your shoulder. Zeke, please stand facing Domar's back. Cat, you stand on Domar's window side, and Scuro on the opposite side to Cat. Each one of you must stand outside the circle of glowing dust, stand very still. Don't move until I call your names. Whatever happens, don't move."

We took our places. The night seemed darker than ever. It was so silent it was scary. Suddenly, Thaddeus said, "Give me the black prayerstick." I gave it to him. He pointed it downward and then upward and then he began to spin. Faster and faster he spun. The black stick began to glow brighter and brighter and suddenly Thaddeus bent down and touched the faint circle of dust. It grew brighter and higher until I could not see Domar at all. I wanted to protest but I knew I must not. And others, praises to them, did not move nor speak.

Slowly the flames fell, and as they slowly died out, I saw in the middle of the glowing circle a tiny house. It was Domar, with a minute door and window shining in the darkness. It was a Domar to be held in cupped hands.

"Take her up gently, Maris," Thaddeus whispered. "Tell her all is well and we are now going to the Place of Them. And that you and Zeke will take turns carrying her. And that she will be her full self again before too long."

She was a glowing jewel as I knelt beside her. I bent my head and whispered her name. She moved, and a very tiny but clear voice piped. "Maris! I am here! I feel like me, but everything looks so big! I hope I do not have to be like this always—but I am glad I am with all of you."

I lifted her as gently as I could in my cupped hands. Zeke came and helped me to my feet, as gentle as I was being to Domar. He stood beside me, then reached out his hand and touched the tiny house. "Domar," he whispered. "It's me, it's Zeke."

"Oh, Zeke!" I felt Domar stir in my hands as she spoke. "Zeke, we are still all together. I am very glad."

Out of the darkness came Thaddeus's voice. "Come now. We must be going on. The Old Ones await us. Ears has gone to tell Them we are coming. Antic will go now and tell Them we are bringing Domar with us rather than sending her. And, Antic, if you can get back before daylight, please come with any news you can gather. Off you go, and off we go."

For a while the traveling was relatively easy. It seemed to be level ground underfoot, even if occasional rocks met our feet—mine and Zeke's mostly. Scuro and Cat had night vision, of course, and Waff had asked if he could travel with Thaddeus because, as he said, "My zeeing was made for daylight." Thaddeus invited him to ride in the black pot—which was in its usual place on Thaddeus's head. It must have been a disagreeably bumpy ride, but Waff never complained.

Domar was in my hands and Zeke's hands alternately—so neither of us would get fatigued and risk dropping her. From time to time we whispered to her to reassure her, and she would reply with a small stirring that said she was all right. We were going quite well when suddenly Scuro said, "Did any of you bump your head? I just did! I can't go any further! There's a blockade of some kind!"

Then Zeke spoke from somewhere. "Me too. There's a smooth wall. I can feel it in front of me. you'd better stand still, Maris, if you've got Domar!"

I stopped at once, not wanting to risk dropping Domar. She stirred in my hands and I whispered, "Don't worry, Domar. We will know in a moment what happened."

The night was deeply silent. For a while I could not hear anything. Nothing indicated that anything existed. It was frightening. Then I heard a scuffling sound and before I could react in any way Zeke's voice—very near—said, "Are you here, Maris? Let me know where. Thaddeus must be about, somewhere."

"I'm near. At least your voice sounds near. But this is the blackest night I've ever been in. Scuro and Cat must be somewhere in it."

"We are." It was Scuro's voice, a little farther away than Zeke's. "At least I am. Cat, are you there?"

"Of course." Cat sounded quite relaxed. "We've met a smooth wall—like Zeke said. It seems to go straight across everywhere. At least everywhere I've tried it. Let's all get together. Maris, since you're carrying Domar, why don't you stay where you are and hum a little hum so we can come to you and Domar?"

So I sat, my back against the wall—or whatever it was—and began a humming sound. It was not at all a bad sound, as I expected it to be because I wasn't a singer. It sounded quite pleasant as it echoed against the unseen wall. I kept it going. Zeke stumbled into me soon and, with a bit of space between us, also began to hum. Before long I heard a sniffing sound and suddenly Scuro's wet nose touched my face, and then came Cat and rubbed his head against me.

Something was missing. Of course! "Where's Thaddeus? And Waff? Has anyone seen them or heard them or touched them? Shall we call?"

"No!" Zeke commanded. "Better we should be quiet and try to hear."

We went into a deep stillness. The dark was dark and the silence silent and Domar was totally still. It went on and on—this silence. I am certain that each of us was swept by fear, although no one spoke of it. It seemed forever that we stayed there. It seemed to me to be growing colder and darker and more threatening all the time. I held Domar close to me, whispering to her from time to time—which probably helped me as much as or more than it did her.

The silence was catastrophically broken by a loud sneeze, a banging of metal, a noise resembling a buzz saw, and finally the sound of some heavy substance crashing to the ground. I jumped to my feet, jostling Domar enough that she squeaked at me. And what I saw, in the dim but definite illumination, was Thaddeus waving a sparkling wand and pushing his head against a wall that had already broken in several places. And Waff was buzzing fervently in and out of the space where a piece of wall had fallen.

"It izz down, Thaddeuzz, it izz down!"

"And what is on the other side, Waff?"

"Nothing."

"What do you mean—nothing?"

"There izz a big deep hole. Not really a hole, though. It hazz no bottom at all." Waff's voice had awe and fear in it. "It izz black and nothing. Nothing at all."

"Well, now," Thaddeus said calmly, "we'll put a bridge over it. You see, Waff, I am quite certain that the wall and the hole were put here by the Old Ones."

"Why? Why would They do that?"

"Because it could catch Beasts and Worms—whereas others, like us—would find ways to resolve it, to get around it."

"I zee, I zee. You are very wize, Thaddeuzz. And are we near to Them, now?"

"We will see. We will see after we make a bridge."

By the time this conversation was finished we were all clumped together around Thaddeus and his lighted wand. His black pot sat before him, but all his belongings were scattered about and he was gazing at the mess unhappily. "Maris, do come and help! I can't make a bridge without your help!"

I gave Domar to Zeke—explaining to her what was happening—and went to Thaddeus. He was standing at the edge of the hole where the wall had collapsed, eyes closed, tail moving slowly to and fro. He was readying himself for magic. I could tell that. I could not tell—nor could he, I'm sure—what magic was needed. So I did what I knew he wanted. In the dim wand light I began sorting out his things which had spilled all over—putting like things together, colors and shapes and sizes and qualities—which I knew could help him to decide what to do.

After I had his items sorted and arranged, he opened his eyes and said amiably, "Thank you, Maris. You do help me." He gazed off into space. "Now then, how can I make a bridge, I wonder? Perhaps you could give me . . . " His voice trailed off. On a hunch I gave him the black prayerstick and the gleaming one of many colors. "Of course! The feminine one and the masculine one! How else can an abyss be crossed!" He placed them about a foot apart, upright in the ground. "Let me see. I am sure I had some red wire somewhere."

I hunted through all his things in the poor light, did not find it, was about to say either it was lost or he'd never had it, when suddenly he turned away from me and I saw it curled around the end of his tail.

"Thaddeus, it is on your tail."

"Well, get it for me please, Maris. Somebody put it there sometime. I don't remember."

He took it. He studied it and the two prayersticks for quite a time. At last he took them and the wire and began to play with them. When he finished he had a beautiful and delicate bridge about six inches long. "Now," and he looked at me directly, "now I've got some spinning to do and I need you to assist me actively. So put some black sand on my head and some white sand on my tail, let me spin until you can't see me and at that very moment shout 'Bridge.' Just once. That should do it."

Thaddeus's "should" always upset me because it was too much like "if." However, there was nothing to do but to do. So I put black sand on his head and white sand on his tail. He sneezed. Then he began to spin—holding the miniature bridge in his forefeet. Slowly he spun then faster and faster and faster until he was a spinning spool, and at last I could not make out Thaddeus at all—only a large blur with a dot of red in the middle.

"BRIDGE!" I shouted with all the voice I had.

Thaddeus collapsed—as he always did after a spinning time—and I went to him at once and in the dim light of the wand stroked his head until his eyes opened.

"Well, well," he said as he struggled to his feet. "I wonder if it worked. Go and look, Maris. I'm too tired." And he closed his eyes.

I beckoned to Zeke to come, with Domar. Scuro and Cat came along. I walked to the hole in the wall and lifted the burning wand. We all gasped because there, across the empty abyss, was a lovely and delicate bridge of red, suspended between two towers—one white, one black.

"Oh Thaddeus! It is so beautiful! It—"

"Don't talk about it! It's life is very limited! Go across at once and I'll follow! Go!"

We knew he meant what he said, and we rushed to obey. Zeke carried Domar. Then Cat and Scuro went. I followed as soon as I'd gathered up Thaddeus's things and put them in his black pot and balanced his pot on his head. Waff clung to my arm as I went across. Thaddeus came last. He moved slowly. I knew he was tired so I waited at the bridge's end and reached out for his foreleg as he neared the other side.

I was just in time. The moment his tail came off the bridge the entire lovely structure collapsed and disappeared silently in the abyss.

CHAPTER 6

Then we all collapsed. We had moved back from the great emptiness so we could not see it, but the terror of it clung to us. Thaddeus was stretched out flat, his chin resting on the ground and his eyes closed. Waff was a brownish bundle on top of Thaddeus's pot. Zeke lay flat on his back, arms outstretched, with his right hand still carefully cupped into a valley where Domar rested. Scuro and Cat lay side by side. I was near Zeke.

I suspect we would all have fallen into weary sleep had not Domar's wee voice peeped, "Is everyone here, please?"

"Domar dear," I said, sitting up, "we're all here, and all right. I'm sure we'll be moving soon. I guess we should." And unwillingly but urgently I spoke each one's name.

Scuro and Cat responded at once. Zeke yawned and grumbled but got to his feet—being very careful of Domar. Waff buzzed his wings, and then buzzed softly at Thaddeus. Slowly Thaddeus's head lifted and his eyes opened.

"My goodness!" He spoke slowly. "My dear goodness! Being a magician is very tiring! Very very tiring . . . " Looking at us he said, "You all seem healthy. Now get yourselves ready to proceed, because I'm going to end the light and we travel in darkness. I have a sense that the Old Ones may want each of us—or at least some of us—to come alone. That is, on our personal path. No matter what happens, Zeke, you will care for Domar. Waff will stay in my magic pot. Let us go forward."

So suddenly that I felt blind, all light vanished. I'd not realized what a subtle aura of light Thaddeus had set around us until it was gone. I stood quite still for a few moments.

"Remember," said Thaddeus's voice out of the nothingness. "Remember that you are going up, *up*. If your feet feel down, turn around at once and go *up*."

Carefully, I took a few steps. The ground under my feet felt upward. From then on for a seemingly endless time I shuffled along at a painfully slow pace. It proved to be not too difficult to find "up" because it obviously was a very steep mountain, and the instant my feet erred in a down direction I lost my balance. At first I heard others—or thought I did—and then endlessly only the slow shuffle of my own feet.

Once I was so afraid and confused that I cried out, "Zeke! Scuro! Somebody! Find me!" No answer came. No sound from anywhere. So I plodded upward, foot after foot after foot endlessly upward. Finally, I collapsed—exhausted, frightened, almost in a state of panic. I lay face down on the rough and invisible ground trying to get my breath, wanting to call and knowing that I must not. When I felt a bit rested I rolled onto my back. The sky was ink black. No stars. No planets. Black. How awful this Great Land could be when it was dark!

Then my eyes caught a blink of light—on and off and on and off! They *were* there, the Old Ones, awaiting us, beckoning us onward! And that light was near, I was sure. I staggered once more onto my weary feet and headed upward toward that beacon. I don't know what happened after that. I only remember my lungs hurting, my feet faltering until I lost consciousness. The next thing was a light shining in my face.

I was lying on the ground, face up. Over me was the face of Scuro—very close, because he was licking me with his rough tongue. Above his face were the faces of Zeke and Thaddeus, with Cat peeking in between. And above the faces was one of Thaddeus's wands—held by Zeke, I think—casting a warm glow over us.

"Are we there?" I asked weakly.

"No," Zeke replied. "But it's not much further, Antic says. He just arrived. The Old Ones are waiting for us eagerly, he says." He patted my hand. "You must have passed out. I stumbled over you and called the others. It took some time to get us together—because we sure were going on our own paths." He patted my hand again. "Do you feel like sitting up?"

I did. And, although I was was a bit shaky, I was ready. Zeke helped me up, Thaddeus put out the light, and each of us started out once more. Suddenly, I felt a touch on my shoulder. Startled, I turned my head. Right next to my eye was a dim form.

"It's me, Antic. Just wanted to say, keep on as straight as you can toward the light. You'll get there." He vanished.

The only way I could do it was to fix my eyes on the light and then shuffle forward—sliding one foot ahead of the other, keeping them close together and hopefully in a straight line. I was no longer fearful, so the lonely going was easier. Very slowly I came nearer the signaling light. Then suddenly I was there. Earth was flat as I moved forward. I could hear footsteps, and I almost called out. But I didn't.

All in a moment of time the light went out and the noises ceased. I stood as still as a tree, waiting. I felt no fear. I was quite certain that some of the Old Ones were near. Then from this almost touchable darkness I heard the wonderfully familiar sound of a spinning wheel.

"Arachne?" I said into the dark. "Arachne? Is that you?"

"Of course! I'm inside a hollow tree stump, which you're almost running into! Move to your left. Come in! Come in!"

Filled with joy at the sound of my spider friend's voice, I moved to the left, stumbled into something, fell over it, lost my footing and landed awkwardly and a bit shaken beside Arachne sitting at her spinning.

"Well, I should have known you would arrive this way." She peered at me over her wheel. "You've always been an awkward girl." She put out two of her many feet and patted me on the head. "It is good to see you, Maris. Once again the Great Land needs you."

I tried to stand, bumped my head on a root-like thing in the tree hole, and sat down next to Arachne.

"Your various friends have each found—or been found by—one of us Guardians. The Old Ones will come soon."

We sat quietly together. The sound of the spinning wheel was comforting and comfortable. I began to relax from the long, fatiguing, and frightening struggle up the mountain. I almost drowsed off in this gentleness. Then I heard the sound of distant drums. The Old Ones were arriving! I knew those drumbeats so well—had heard them at funerals and celebrations. They marked tragedies, festivals, dangers, and triumphs in the Great Land.

"Arachne! Can I go out?"

"No." She had always been definite. "Not until the Old Ones have arrived and assembled."

So we waited while the drums continued.

After a while—just as I was beginning to relax into the hypnotic drum sounds—a great silence suddenly absorbed everything. Arachne lifted her spinning wheel and, beckoning me to follow, she flowed on her fragile, wispy feet into the night.

I came into a dramatic scene. From no apparent source a soft light—almost a silver light—illumined a great circular area of flat bare ground. At four points equidistant and opposite around the circle were the masked drummers, their dark bodies gleaming as they stood—each one behind a large drum. In the center of the circle stood the Old Ones—Grandmother, Dark Fire, Grandfather, and Owl. On the earth between the Old Ones and the masked drummers were the Guardians—Exi, Thaddeus, Grandan, and Arachne. The Old Ones and the Guardians and the masked drummers were as still as the luminous air, except for the hands of the drummers.

We who had come this difficult and dark way also stood very still. Zeke's face was alive with wonder—but he remembered to turn Domar's "eye" toward the scene. Waff, wonderfully enough, had removed himself from Thaddeus's pot and settled quietly on Scuro's back. Cat stood as if paralyzed, his eyes huge with what seemed like fear. I stroked him once and he quieted. I did not see Antic. He was probably perched somewhere to attend our arrival.

As for me, I was so deeply moved to see the beloved Old Ones and Guardians that I was trembling. And when Grandmother, soft and almost invisible in her strange robe, stepped away from the other Old Ones and came toward us, I could hardly keep from speaking. She moved slowly to where we stood. She turned her deep-set eyes in her wrinkled face from one to the other of us, slowly and lovingly.

"Children," she said, in her soft, rich voice. "Children, we are grateful for your coming—each and all of you—Maris, Zeke, Domar, Molasses, Waff, Scuro, Cat. Antic came from us. Thaddeus is our magician and a Guardian. We greet you. Grandfather will tell you our needs and problems. Then you will be fed and will have a place to rest a while." She returned to the Old Ones.

To a roll of drums Grandfather came to us. He also was as I remembered him—not big, but strong with a directness of gaze.

Then came Dark Fire, his robes drawn around him, his hidden face silent, as always.

Grandfather spoke. "Children, we Old Ones and Guardians are trying to solve a problem that is threatening the Great Land. Maris and Scuro will remember the past battles with Beasts and others. The Beasts who changed serve the Great Land faithfully, and live in the Land with us. Uno, Duo, Trio, Tusks, Twist—all these are loyal and helpful comrades. Quatro, who has always served Dark Fire, has vanished.

He paused and sighed deeply. "We have no doubts as to Quatro's loyalty. Therefore we fear something has happened to him—capture, imprisonment, injury, perhaps death." Again Grandfather paused—as if he could hardly believe what he was saying. "We have some reports that two renegade Beasts—Brawn and Potens—are gathering other Beasts together. Also there are rumors that Slithers has set out to rebuild the Kingdom of Worms—Worms are great dragonish crawling creatures now. The Great Land has always had a fear of them, but they have not been a threat. Now we fear they will join Brawn and Potens." He sighed again. "You see why we called you, children. Or do you?"

To my surprise, Zeke answered at once. "I think I do, sir. At least I have a hunch about it."

"Good. Please tell us." Grandfather looked intently at Zeke. "Tell us, Zeke."

Zeke stood before the Old Ones with confidence. I could not sense where it came from. "Grandfather," he said in a clear voice, "when we were each climbing this mountain in darkness alone I didn't know where I was or would be, but I got to thinking, in be-tween keeping my feet going up as Thaddeus told us to do—and I thought of what Antic said about the mists we could see that covered a mountain—and so in the dark I wondered if we were needed to go into that mist to find out what was happening there."

Silence held for a considerable period after Zeke stopped.

Then Grandfather said quietly, "Thank you, Zeke. Your ideas are very close to what we had thought. Actually, Owl has left to check the mist mountains. He does that often." He paused. "And Zeke, before we talk any further, I believe Domar and Molasses need to be with us full-size. Do you all agree?"

Zeke nodded, looked at us and saw our nods, and carefully placed tiny Domar on the ground. I could hear her voice squeak so I leaned down and explained what was going to happen.

Thaddeus was called by Grandfather. I found all the necessities in Thaddeus's pot, helped him prepare his magic, and with one wand, some colored earth, and a circle drawn around the tiny house soon we had everything ready. Thaddeus moved slowly to Domar. he put his salamander face very near to her. "Dear Domar, now we will hope that my magic can undo what has been done and return you to yourself. Are you ready?"

There was a tiny squeaked "Yes!"

With that, Thaddeus lighted a wand, grabbed his tail with his free forefoot, and went into a fiery spin. But this time the magic was so fast that Domar went from wee to her usual size almost instantly. It happened so all at once that Zeke was pushed over and Grandfather just stepped back in time.

I realized that both window and door were turned away from everyone. Zeke got up, and he and I moved her so that she could see all the assembled company.

"My goodness! What a lot of creatures—or people—or whatever or whoever you are! But you are all beautiful. Very beautiful!"

Grandfather stood before her door. "May I come in? I am Grandfather."

"Please do, Grandfather. It is not large—but I am honored."

He stepped in quietly and gently. From inside he asked, "And what is this in the corner, Domar?"

"Her name is Molasses."

There was a prolonged silence, then a whispering of voices, and finally Grandfather stepped out, smiling as I had rarely seen him smile, holding Molasses's shell with Molasses almost all outside it, her snail's foot on his hand. He showed Molasses to all the Old Ones in turn, and then spoke to the Guardians. Even Dark Fire emerged from his robes enough to look at her and to say, "Most unusual." After both Molasses and Domar had been warmly accepted by the present Old Ones, Grandmother said—her eyes filled with love—Now children, relax for awhile. Food will be brought, but meanwhile greet old friends and make new ones. Owl will return soon."

When the drummers and the Old Ones had gone, Scuro and I went wildly towards our familiar and beloved Guardian friends. Arachne the wondrous spider I had already greeted. Now I hugged her, and Scuro bounced happily around her. Then we rushed to Exi and Grandan, who were standing together—beloved black beetle and courageous red ant, each slightly crippled with age and battle scars.

"Maris, and Scuro. Maris, and Scuro." Exi's slow and familiar voice almost brought me to tears. All I could do was to embrace him and say his name over and over. And he said, "Dear comrades. How splendid to see you again, to have you part of our company. How excellent."

Grandan, the courageous old ant who had volunteered to risk his frail body for the sake of the Great Land, was not as easy to hug as Exi. But I laid my hand on him and said, "Oh Grandan, Grandan!" And he smiled as only an aged red ant can smile, and said, "Dear Maris and dear Scuro." We even greeted Thaddeus, for he too was a Guardian. And just after that there was a whoo-oosh in the darkness and Great Owl, the fourth of the Old Ones, alighted in our midst.

"Now this is a resounding reunion! Wh-o-o planned this party?" Great Owl was tremendously impressive in his big feathered body, with his great eyes seeming as if they could see right around the earth. "Some of our friends, no doubt." He looked intently at Domar. "You must be Domar. May I come in?"

"Please do. And you can meet Molasses inside."

Great Owl marched in, marched out carrying Molasses on his head, marched twice around Domar's outside so he could relate to door and window, went in again to return Molasses, then came out and stood before Domar's door. "I am pleased to know you, Domar—and Molasses—and I'm sure you will add to our company. You've got things we don't have, I'm certain. But now here comes the food and the etcetera's. Enjoy them!" And he whooshed off into the darkness again.

The food was carried in by three Beasts—Duo, Tusks, and Twist—each Beast with a sort of platform on his back—and on Duo's head was a large butterfly. For a moment I was puzzled by the butterfly, then I remembered what poor vision Beasts had and that we always guided them. And then I remembered Isia, and I ran to Duo, saying, "Duo, Tusks, Twist! How wonderful! And Isia, dear friend!"

"I'm not Isia," said the butterfly. "But I'm proud to be called Isia. He is a fine helper."

Meanwhile, Scuro was bouncing about in a fever-pitch of greetings. Duo was trying to greet us and keep the food from spilling. Zeke came to help and introduced himself to everyone. And finally we travelers sat down near Domar's door, introduced her all around, and began to eat.

We were a wonderful oddment of creatures—three Beasts, one large butterfly, four Guardians, and the eight of us. We all clumped together near Domar's door (Molasses sat on the door sill, her head poking out of her shell). We didn't talk much for awhile, and then Thaddeus moved to the midst of us, planted himself with his black pot beside him, and began.

"Friends, we all know why we are here, I'm sure. The Great Land needs us."

Unexpectedly, Zeke came in—almost rudely, but I didn't think he meant to be. "I'm not sure I *do* know why we're here. All of us except two of us—Cat and I—know this place and these others."

"You forgot Molasses and me." Domar's voice was not negative, but it was definite.

"I'm sorry." Zeke sounded uncertain as to whether he should go on—but he did. "I mean—well, I want to help all I can, but I'm not sure what I'm helping, that's all."

Exi stepped forward in all his aged black beetle calmness. "Your question is a good one, Zeke. But there is not time now for a long history. Maris must have told you something." Zeke nodded. "Very well, let me say a bit more. Because we cannot work together unless we all want to."

He looked at Zeke intently, cleared his throat, and went on. "The Great Land is what lives under and within all other lands. It is a sort of pattern of patterns. What happens here can alter what happens in other lands and countries and also in people."

I caught my breath at Exi's words because I'd never heard this, and yet somehow now I realized for the first time why it was so important to me—this Land.

"Do you understand, Zeke?" Exi waited.

"I'm—I'm not sure. Is it like—well, if I try to help kids that don't have as good a home as I have—maybe I start a pattern—sort of, for others?"

"That's part of it, Zeke. If the Great Land is disturbed and out of balance—as it is again now—it both affects other lands and is affected by them. That's all I know. The Old Ones know more, but they keep their secrets."

"Thank you, Exi, sir, for telling me. I guess I understand better why an earthquake dumped us here." He rubbed his head thoughtfully. "There's a lot I don't know yet—but I guess I'll find out as we go along."

"Very well," said Exi calmly. "May I request now that all of you who have just arrived come with one of us to places where you can rest—perhaps even sleep—until you are called. Maris, will you and Molasses go with Arachne? Cat and Scuro will follow Grandan. Domar will stay where she is in the center of protection. Waff is with Thaddeus. And Zeke will come with me."

As I carried Molasses into Arachne's tree hollow, very briefly I wondered why Owl had not returned. And then I fell asleep to the sound of spinning. I don't know how long I slept. I know I didn't dream. And I—along with all the others—was jolted into waking by a whoosh of wings loud enough to belong to a flock of geese over water. We landed on our feet—startled from our resting places, but ready to do battle—only to be faced by Owl and by a vigorous vulture almost as big as Owl and much fiercer looking.

"This," said Owl calmly, "is the eldest son of Da and Gada. His name is Dag."

Dag bowed his ugly vulture head. "I am pleased to meet all of you."

Dag then walked around with Owl, who introduced him to all he hadn't met—such as me and Zeke and Cat and Scuro and Waff and Domar and Molasses. When these formalities were finished, Owl said that Dag had something to tell us.

He stepped foward a bit shyly and awkwardly, but with much seriousness. "Well"—he settled his feathers again, "well, I am very interested in various sorts of glides in the air, of course—and I've been practicing from the top of Volcanic Mountain for quite a long time. I have to fly from our home—which is beyond and below this

Place of Them—in a huge detour to avoid that place that's always lost in a sort of fog."

He stopped awkwardly.

"Go on, Dag," said Owl. "Tell your story."

"Well—yesterday I decided I'd try to go into the fog. You know—sometimes a thing bothers you enough to want to try it—you get sort of mad until you do—so I took off from Volcanic Mountain—after my detour flight to get there. I soared as high as I ever have—there were great air currents—and when I was way above the mists I lowered my wings and dived. I wasn't sure I could pull out of the dive. But I did. Almost clipped that misty mountain. But didn't. What I saw for those seconds you wouldn't believe. I didn't—but I saw it!"

"Go on, Dag. Tell us." Owl was impatient.

"The whole mountain—or at least the top part of it—is covered with huge ugly holes with steamy stuff that stinks coming out of them. And in a few holes I zoomed close to I saw many ugly, wiggling, slimy-looking heads poking out. They were awful things!" Dag stopped abruptly. "That's all."

"Thank you, Dag. We'll doubtless call on you later. But you can go along now. Thanks again." Owl was always appreciative, and lifted a wing in farewell as Dag took the air. Then Owl turned his attention to us. "What do you think is going on within the mist? Let's have any ideas any of you have. I've got mine. but I want to hear yours."

I suddenly saw that during this exchange the other Guardians—and the Beasts—had also gathered with us.

"May I speak, Owl?" To my surprise it was Thaddeus.

"Please do, Thaddeus."

"It's only that—well, I didn't feel that all of the things that happened to us as we were coming in darkness up the mountain were done by the Old Ones. The darkness was—and our walking alone was. But I'm not sure that the wall we ran into was from Them—and I'm certain that the black abyss was not from Them."

Owl nodded. "I am as sure as you, Thaddeus. I am sure those things were evil."

"May I speak, Owl? Just briefly, please?" The three Beasts and their butterfly guide had joined us. It was Duo who spoke.

"Please do. Any of you."

Duo continued. "Well—you see we've been—well, we've been very unhappy about Quatro's disappearance. We've asked and questioned everyone we know—and some we don't know at all—and some we only know a little—and one item that we've learned from almost all of them is that there are quite a few cracks opening up—almost in all parts of the Great Land—opening for a few days, then closing again. All reports we've had are that foul-smelling gas and smoke came from the openings. One report described a crack that poisoned the earth around it for quite a distance. That's all I wanted to say. Except—and I know I speak for all of us—except that we Beasts are ready to go anywhere and do anything we can to help the Great Land, and to find Quatro."

Owl bowed to us all. "Now I believe it is best that you newcomers get some further rest—that is, all of you except myself and the Guardians, including you, Thaddeus. We need you with us."

They went away. Very soon all of us except Beasts were cozily packed into Domar, soundly asleep. The Beasts lay down just outside Domar's doorway.

CHAPTER 7

How long we all slept was impossible to guess, given the strange marking of time in the Great Land. It was long enough for me to dream of a fat, sharp-toothed dragonish creature with a struggling bird in its half-closed mouth. The bird resembled Antic and I woke myself crying out, "Help! Help! Antic!" That, of course wakened all my comrades.

"What's going on? Who's got into trouble?" Zeke sat up, his eyes wide with alarm, his face flushed. "What's happening?"

I reached out and touched him. "It was just a dream, Zeke. I'm sorry I wakened you."

He rubbed his head hard, as if he blamed it for disturbing him. Of course Scuro and Cat were on their feet, sniffing and staring about them. Then I felt Domar move under us. Only Molasses was absolutly mute and unmoving in her curled bed-house. I looked out at the resting Beasts and their butterfly guide. Their eyes were open, but no fear seemed to be in them. Their knowing was far older and deeper than ours.

Duo spoke softly as he came toward us. "Antic is all right, Maris. Whatever you dreamed is probably warning us to be aware, to stay alert for any learnings and any dangers. Dreams often tell us what to guard against."

How could any beast ever have turned evil, I thought, as I looked with love at these wonderful ugly creatures. Of course I had not forgotten that terrible stockade where Beasts had tried to destroy us in that earlier visit to the Great Land. Some had fled after they killed their own comrades. To keep myself open and loving I went to our three Beast friends. They had struggled up from their rest and were standing to greet me, their butterfly guide on Duo's back. I put my hands on them, stroking backs and rubbing ears, I was ashamed inside for any lapse of trust ever.

"What do you believe comes next, Maris?" Duo spoke softly. "We three cannot wait forever. We are concerned to find Quatro."

"I wish I knew what comes next, Duo. If he is in the Worm land, well, where is that, really? How can anyone get there? Except to drop into it, like Dag could have done, I guess."

Duo thought for a while, head cocked, shifting his weight back and forth from one foot to another—something I recalled from the past as a Beast trait, epecially when thinking was necessary. I was again touched—as I had been often in my previous encounters with Beasts—by their fierce ugliness and how, nonetheless, I could push through that and love them. Their hair was coarse and bristly and ragged, their feet were big and had long, ugly, sharp claws, their tails were long, thin, with a sparse tuft at the end, their muzzles were large and almost pig-like, with two curled tusk-like teeth and several smaller ones. Yet for all that the ones I knew—those who had changed and had chosen to serve the Old Ones—these had eyes of suffering and of love.

"Maris," said Duo, "I believe there is a way into the land where the Worms are. Do you remember where the great vultures Da and Gada live? Sort of on the back side of this mountain, halfway down, sort of. Well, below their house—Da and Gada, I mean—below their house is an opening—partly caved in—lots of weeds and vines over it—and once I stumbled into it—and I called—and Da came and pulled me out and said, 'Don't go in there! Bad things live there—creepy ones.' And he sent me on my way, but I'll bet it leads to Worm country."

Duo and I looked at each other as two conspirators, and we said nothing. I was thinking how I loved Da and Gada, and that I must get around to visiting them very soon. I felt certain that Duo was thinking the same thing. Neither of us spoke. Soon we were all fully awake and ready to do whatever was needed to be done in order to start the search for Quatro. We must find him as a part of unearthing what was harming the Great Land and what we could do about it. We had just begun to discuss possibilities when Owl arrived, sailing into a central place near Domar.

"The others are coming along," he announced quietly, settling his elegant feathers. "Wait until we are all together."

Very shortly they arrived—Arachne and her spider's spinning wheel, the old ant Grandan in all his modesty, Exi in beetle black, and at the end of the procession Thaddeus, his pot on his head with Waff sitting on top. Some vitally important action was obviously needed and so we immediately formed a circle. Owl went to the center of the circle, not because he was in any sense proud, but because he knew he was one of the Old Ones and spoke for Them.

"We, the Old Ones, with the help of the Guardians, have been discussing—as I suspect you have also been discussing—the matter of Quatro and of the Worms. The Old Ones feel that something must be done before the Worms become too powerful to be subdued. We have talked with Da and Gada and Dag. Antic and Waff have been sent on a small tour—being relatively small themselves—to see what they can learn from small places and persons. Dag is going to try another dive from the Volcanic Mountain to see what he can see. We cannot have any real facts for a while. Our suggestion is that we all ponder these matters, that we do not wander too far, and that we meet again together here at this place in a day or so—or when the drums of the Old Ones sound in the central square. They can be heard from almost anywhere in the Great Land. So go carefully, children—very carefully—and remember the danger."

With a whoosh of wings Owl was airborne and out of sight. We said goodbye to Exi and Grandan and Arachne—all of whom had to return to the Old Ones. After they had gone the little company of Beasts and us drew closer together. Zeke's face was excited. Scuro and Cat crowded in close, and I knew that the Beasts were eager to explore. In my deepest self I knew we should not try to do anything. I knew also that we would, because somehow a friend's life was involved.

"Let's all get inside Domar if we can," I suggested.

We almost could. Tusks stayed at the door, his head poked inside. The rest of us all made it, although it was a tight fit and we were literally nose to nose. We had explained it all to Domar, and she was delighted to have an increasing family. Molasses had wakened and emerged from her shell, and I was holding her and her rock in my hand so that she could see everyone.

"Well," said Duo, "I never anticipated such a company. Nor did I expect that we would be plotting something that we should not do. yet that is what we are going to do." He looked around at all of us, waiting to see if anyone would say we shouldn't do it. No

one spoke. "Very well. I guess we are all wanting to try to find Quatro. Am I right?" Everyone nodded. I had halfway expected Zeke to make one of his "I wonder" statements, as if he knew more than he really did. But he did not speak.

"Very well." Duo continued. "It seems to me that we need to explore on the other side of this mountain. We could do it in several ways—by going to Da and Gada's place, or by going around through the desert hills to the Volcanic Mountain, or by traveling down the farthest slopes of this Mountain of Them towards what was once the Beast Kingdom. Maris will remember that. And Scuro also. What ideas do any of you have?"

I kept hearing Owl's words about going carefully, and wondered if we could and should take matters in our not very strong hands. Somehow it did feel right that we should at least explore. Maybe we could get information that the others could not get because we were less important.

"Very well." Duo spoke, then looked around at this crowded and strange company. "Or is it? Very well, I mean. A dog, a cat, three Beasts, a girl, a boy, and a snail. It doesn't sound very impressive, does it?"

"I'm not so sure." Zeke spoke up boldly. I hoped he wouldn't say one of his awkward things. He didn't. "I wonder if maybe we need to be in twos or threes, each little group doing a different route. Or something like that."

"That sounds like a good idea, Zeke." Duo looked around at us all. "Perhaps one group could go to Da and Gada, another to the Volcanic Mountain, and a third toward the old Beast Kingdom."

"But there's only eight of us, counting Molasses," said Zeke. "If we eliminated one route, there would be four of us to two routes."

"You may be right, Zeke." Duo pondered for a brief time of silence. Then he said, "I think that is best. I believe that to try to go to the big mountain with the deep hole is the least productive and the most difficult. So one group will go to Da and Gada, and the others to the old Beast Kingdom. Because we Beasts know the old Beast Kingdom best—and because we are Beasts—I believe we should explore that direction. Molasses, I am certain, needs to stay with Domar." He faced Domar's door. "You do understand, Domar?"

"Of course. I will be here as a refuge for my family at any time. It will be comfortable to have Molasses with me."

Duo turned to me. "Maris, can you find your way to Da and Gada?"

"I think I could. Maybe. Scuro is the best guide. And Cat will help."

Duo paused and looked around at the company. "My, my! We are taking on a big task, are we not? But then if we don't, we won't—if you follow me. So off you go, you three. Oh, I almost forgot! I told Arachne the possibilities and probabilities. She scolded a bit—as she does—but she also said she would send Waff and Antic to us with spiderweb suits to protect us. So again, off you go!"

There was nothing for it but to go. Scuro and Cat took the lead, with me third and Zeke as rear guard. As we went downslope on a faint path Scuro had picked up, I turned and looked back and waved. But the three Beasts were moving obliquely across and around the other slope and soon dropped from sight. Suddenly, I felt how very alone we were and how very defenseless. I guess the feeling was mutual, because Zeke speeded up so he was right behind me. Cat and Scuro slowed their pace until we were together—single file, but we could speak to each other if we needed to.

The further we went downhill the rockier it got. Soon we were carefully picking our way among boulders in a confusing wasteland. Obviously, Scuro and Cat did not feel as I did. Scuro's nose was his faithful and trusted guide and he kept it close to the ground as he wove left and right and left among the rocks and the few starved-looking trees. Cat prowled along behind Scuro, from time to time detouring to explore a clump of bushes or a particularly ugly rock pile. Zeke and I stumbled awkwardly and they—friends as they were—looked back from time to time to be certain we were coming.

"Watch out!" Scuro shouted suddenly.

I looked up from the rocks at my feet to see Scuro on his haunches, braking his front feet to keep from sliding over an edge where the slope seemed to drop away into nothing. He managed to stop himself, sprawled on his belly.

"Lie still, Scuro!" Zeke shouted. "We'll get you! Maris! Cat! Stop where you are!"

Zeke walked slowly and very cautiously past me. "Maris, let me have your jacket." I gave it to him at once, not asking why. He took hold of one sleeve, crawled to where he could toss the other sleeve toward Scuro. A couple of tries and Scuro grabbed the sleeves in his teeth. Zeke began to pull on his end and slowly Scuro came crawling upslope to where we were. As he reached us he let go of the sleeve and just lay sprawled for a minute. "Thanks Zeke. Hope we haven't ruined your jacket, Maris—but it sure saved me! Wow, what a drop that would have been!"

He started to rise.

"Don't do it, Zeke! Let Cat creep over and describe it."

"Thanks, Scuro," said Cat. "I'll take my nine lives carefully." And he crept, as only cats can, first-foot-toes-heel, second-foot-toes-heel, soundlessly rolling on soft pads, foot following foot. Just before the steep part Cat put his entire body on the ground and sort of undulated forward, snake-like. He stopped and slowly put his head over the rise and after a brief time slowly pulled his head up, turned around, and snaked himself up to where we were.

"Well, what did you see?" "Tell us, Cat." "Can we go forward?" "What's there?" We all spoke at once.

"Hold it," said Cat to our clamor. "I'll tell you what I saw—but give me time. My breath is just getting home—and my purr may be on a long vacation. So give me time."

He stretched himself out, rubbed his head on the ground, rolled over twice, then sat up. "Now I can talk. What you partly saw, Scuro, was enough to scare anyone. The way we were headed was a very sharp drop, for sure, with a lot of rocks below. There is another way down—I'll lead you there—but do you really know what you're getting into?"

"You're going, too, Cat! Remember?"

"Of course I am, Scuro. That's why I'm telling you where we're going. It's steep. It's rocky. It's a long way. And it leads us in-to a whole bunch of bare mounds—ugly, and monster-like—and there's smoke or steam coming out of some of them. It's awful, ugly."

"Thanks, Cat, for preparing us." Zeke reached over and rubbed Cat's head and ears. "Can you lead us to that path down?

Or do you need more rest?"

"I'm OK. Sure, I can lead."

We strung ourselves out behind Cat—Scuro, then me, and Zeke at the end. Just as we got started there was a buzzing sound behind us, and we whirled around to see Waff zooming in over our heads to land just in front of Cat.

"It izz good to zee you all. Arachne gave me zpider web thingzz for each of you—and told me to join you. Mezzage from Them." He lifted his wings and buzzed a few inches above the ground, letting four tiny bundles drop. "One for each. Put them on right away, Arachne told me. Put them on right away. I'm wearing mine and it doezz not hamper my flying at all."

Soon we each had the incredible spiderweb suits on—each suit adapting itself to its wearer—cat, dog, human. With Waff added to the company we set forth again. Waff and Cat went first—Waff because of being airborne and Cat because of nine lives and because of having seen where the path led down. We zigzagged across the slope we were on—retracing some of our way in order to get on the downward path. As we came to it Cat said, "Be prepared." And Waff added, "And keep your eyezz on your feet."

As I came to the path I gasped at what I saw. To the right I could see a steep and narrow zigzag stitching itself across a raw stone mountain downward. No green was visible anywhere. The rock was wrinkled and fissured and bare. In the very far distance I could see faint outlines of another mountain. I thought I knew that the Place of Them was behind and above us. But it could not be seen. Somewhere, also on the right, was the Volcanic Mountain and also the Mountain of Mists, which was never really see-able.

And then I looked straight down and caught my breath in fear. Below us, where the path seemed to flatten out a bit—that is, what bits of path I could see—there I saw smoke in puffs and trickles coming from earth cracks—and I knew it was what Dag had seen and what my Beast friends had described. How could we cope with such fierce and cruel creatures? But we had to. If we were to be any help to Them and the Great Land we must find ways to deal with the evil power. And if the Great Land, as Exi said, did live under and within all other Lands—a pattern of patterns—then we needed to help the pattern change so that earth affairs would change also.

Or vice versa. In any event a large responsibility was upon us. Or we had taken it upon us, rightly or wrongly.

The cracks where the smoke came from, I began to see, were far down and far right—which had to be beyond the nest of Da and Gada. I said to Scuro, "I think we'll see our vulture friends before we see Worms." Scuro glanced around at me. "Hope you're right. Think you are. Everything's further than it looks in this crazy air anyway."

After a tiring downhill path, with all of us trudging along, incompetent and confused wayfarers, we came to a stretch of flat going. Waff buzzed ahead, with Cat close behind. Scuro slowed so Zeke and I could walk with him.

"Nice to be together for a bit, isn't it?" he said, taking a deep breath. "Do you think we're doing what we need to do?"

For a moment no one replied. Then Zeke said, "Yes, Scuro. What else is necessary?"

"Rest," Scuro said. "Can't drive myself like a dog even if I am one." And he sat down. Cat looked around, saw Scuro sitting, and immediately lay down on the path. I also stretched out and realized how tense I had been. "Waff," I called. "We're resting." And Waff promptly settled on a rock. Zeke came up to us and stood looking at us. "Everyone getting lazy? Let's get going."

Unexpectedly, Waff rose from his resting place and buzzed before Zeke. "Dear friend, why do you alwayz command? Or queztion? We are friendz, comradez zharing a difficult journey and trying to make bezzt choicez. Why do you not zpeak gently?"

Zeke was taken by surprise, it seemed to me. And he answered, "I guess I never learned how." He stood before us awkwardly. I had not seen this Zeke before. I realized that I had been aware of how harsh his father was sometimes. My door of caring all at once opened wide to him. "I'll help you, Zeke. We all will. Come and sit with us." I held out my hand to him. Awkwardly, he settled on the ground nearby and we all rested. When we were ready, Waff said, "Zhall we move on?" Maybe Zeke and Zcuro can change placez for a while."

I hoped that this action would help Zeke. It did—almost at once—when Zeke said tentatively, "Anyone gets tired, just say so and we'll stop. Waff and Cat, you're the leaders and you let us know." It was an awkward statement—but Zeke's face said more than his words. There was no defensiveness or cockiness that I could see. I walked behind him in peace.

For a brief time we stayed on the level. All at once everything changed, however, when Waff suddenly came to us saying, "We are almozt at Da and Gada'z home. One of them iz there." Soon we were standing on the crest of a small hill. Only a short way downslope was a huge, untidy nest—not really a nest at all, but a natural hollow in the rocky ground. In it—and on it—sat three huge, black, ugly vultures.

"Maris!" called the biggest one. "Maris! Welcome! Come and bring your friends! Welcome!"

I rushed down the brief hill to greet Da and Gada. It didn't matter that their heads were naked or that their voices were harsh or that they had ugly beaks. They were old friends. They had sacrificed much in struggling to save the Great Land the last time I had been here. During that period Dag had been only a large egg carefully tended. I was about ready to climb into their home when I remembered that they objected to that. So I called their names.

"Maris! It is Maris! And Scuro! Dag did not tell us who had come to the Great Land. How joyful to see you again."

In a few minutes we were surrounded by feathers and wings and I was introducing Cat and Zeke to these ugly and wonderful birds. Scuro rubbed his nose against their bodies in greeting. Zeke seemed somewhat awed by them—they were impressive with their bulky bodies and naked heads—but I could see that he liked them, because he gave a bow and said, "I am very glad to make your acquaintance."

Cat was a bit disconcerted—as any normal cat, I guess, would be when meeting two large birds almost as big as I was—but he carried it off well, bowing his head briefly from a safe distance.

"Come and sit down with us," Gada said, stepping from the rocky nest. "There is probably much to discuss."

We formed a circle on a relatively flat place near their nest and told them briefly how we'd come to the Great Land and how we were concerned over the increase of Worms and the disappearance of Quatro and that we obviously were needed and were wanting to help. They asked if others were helping also and we said they were. They did not ask if the Guardians and the Old Ones had sent us here, nor did we volunteer the truth—a serious omission that almost lost us some lives.

"Well," said Gada finally, "we need to do some cruising for our sake and for the Land's sake. Whatever you do, be careful. Worm traps are deadly, so watch out for them. They can suck you right in and down. I saw a small bird acquaintance of mine go that way."

A few flaps of their wide wings launched them and soon they were out of sight beyond the mountains.

"They're really something," said Zeke, watching them disappear. "Wish I could do that!"

"Well, you can't. So let's get moving." Scuro could be definite when he wanted to be. "I see some smoke coming from the ground down the hill!" And he took off at a fast lope.

"Scuro! Scuro! Come back!" I called. Either he didn't hear me or didn't want to hear me, because he kept on going. Zeke and I, followed by Cat, started after him. we could see the smoke coming in puffs from the raw and rocky earth. We could see Scuro. Then all at once we couldn't see him. And the smoke stopped.

"Scuro!" I screamed. "Scuro! Scuro!" But he was not there, was not anywhere on this rocky, barren, grim-looking slope of mountain. There was no vegetation. There was no smoke. There were no creatures except us. But I kept wildly running until Zeke and Cat barred my way and made me stop.

"He's gone! The Worms have killed him! He's gone!" I stumbled and fell and lay on the ground spent and terrified.

"Maris. Maris." Zeke began rubbing my hands. "Maris, we'll look for him. Maybe it wasn't Worms. Maybe he went into a hole by accident. Cat's hunting for him. Maris!"

I looked into Zeke's face. It was as distressed as I felt. "Oh Zeke! Scuro's gone! He's gone!" And I began to sob, but I stopped when I realized that hunting for Scuro was crucial and that I was needed in the hunt. So I sat up and wiped my face on my jacket.

"Good girl," Zeke said. "Scuro has as many lives as a cat."

"We have lots," said Cat. "Let's start looking."

We quickly divided into three sections the area we felt he had to be in. I was to take the nearest section, Cat was to search the area nearest the vulture house, and Zeke would take the farthest. With almost no further word we got to work. I found a small hole in the harsh earth of my sector—and I felt that my sector was nearest to where Scuro had disappeared. I went around it and around it in widening and then narrowing circles, examining every nook and twig and crevice twice and three times.

Suddenly, I caught a very faint whiff of smoke coming from my left. I spun around. There was a tiny bit of smoke dissolving in the air near a small crack. I rushed to it, lay on my stomach to see if I could see anything, was excited to find a strong smoke smell. I seemed to be peering into darkness. Then all things were blotted out.

CHAPTER 8

I felt I was struggling in thick darkness for endless and soundless hours, trying to get free from something which I could not describe. I stopped struggling. I felt I was not getting anywhere in this black silence. I knew I was unhurt because I could move all parts of myself without pain. I could not move any part of me more than a few inches, however. I seemed, from a certain inside place, quite calm, but from a deeper place I was terrified. Not only for myself but for Scuro and my other comrades. Were they alive? Injured? Dead? Perhaps my struggling was in a nightmare, and if I could waken I might be free.

So I took a deep breath and began to push my arms sidewise. Surprisingly, the determined pushing began to give me room to move. Wherever I was, it was darkness, but it was slowly expanded into a space. Suddenly, I knew I had to shout! Of course! How else would Scuro—if he was here—or any of my other friends—if they were seeking me—how else would they know where to search?

For reasons mysterious I shouted, "SHOUT! SHOUT! SHOUT!" endlessly, it seemed to me. I was just deciding it was all useless and hopeless when, after a last impassioned "SHOUT!" a strange voice said, "Creep, you've played enough! Take your other toys and go away! Now!"

At this command, I was rolled over and over in the darkness. Suddenly the dark was gone. I was on my side on a foul-smelling earthen floor watching a Scuro-sized worm crawling away from me and dragging a long black cloth out of an opening to somewhere else.

"Gl-n-n-k-s-p-t-z!" This sound come loud and terrible from behind me. I struggled to my feet and looked around. I was faced with the terror of an adult Worm as big as a Beast—not as high from the floor, but longer—with its huge fanged mouth wide open, giving forth harsh and awful sounds.

"Gl-n-nk-s-p-t-z!" Its voice was even louder this time. It spat the sounds out as if it had tasted some spoiled or poisoned food. By this time the long black cloth had vanished. The Worm turned toward me. I took a step backward. The Worm moved like a wave, coming closer.

"You should have been hurt—peering into our smoke hole. So should that furry black creature. It only banged its nose."

"Is it here?"

"I don't know and I don't care. It could have been thrown out, for all I know. Or put to work." The Worm examined me carefully with its cold reptilian eyes. "On the other hand, now, I'm sure you could be helpful to us—both you and your creature. Better helpful than dead, eh?"

Slowly, I realized that this monstrous creature was trying to flatter me into giving it information the Worms wanted. The Worms, I had been told, were cruel, fierce, aggressive, and—as I had heard and was now seeing for myself—not very bright. So, troubled as I was and filled with worry for Scuro and my other comrades, I decided to see if I could outwit these enemies.

"Well," I said in my pleasing-adults voice, "I've heard about the Worm Kingdom a lot, some bad things but lots of good things. Like how up and coming—a phrase my ancestors used for those beings who got things done—how up and coming the Worms are. Always busy. Always finding new resources and new beings to help them. So we came—me, my pets, and a friend—to try to visit some Worms."

"So why did you both peek in and fall in—you and your dog creature? Why not be polite and ask if you could come in?"

"We tried, sir—or madam—but we could not find any doors or windows or anything that meant a house, and so when we saw smoke—like from a chimney, you know—we peeked in—and here I am, and, I assume from your kind words, my creature is somewhere around."

The Worm bared its fanged mouth in what I hoped was a pleased expression. I had never been good at this sort of lying flattery and I was feeling more and more uneasy.

But it made a face that was supposed to be a smile, I was sure, because it said, "My name is Squirm. I am related to Slithers, our ruler. I regret that the small one—Creep—had you rolled in its blanket. Meant no harm. Just playful."

I smiled meekly, although inside I was angry and upset and afraid. So I did not risk speaking.

"Now," said Squirm, "I will take you to your creature. It is in another place." And the Worm turned and undulated toward the door through which Creep had gone. "Come along now," it said.

I followed its unexpectedly fast pace as well as I could. I was handicapped by the uneven floor—over whose roughness Squirm flowed like water. I was also struggling against the foul smells that made me want to stop breathing. But I hung on and managed to keep up.

Suddenly, Squirm stopped before a smooth rock in the wall, touched a smaller rock next to it, and a door of rock swung slowly open. "Your creature is in there," he said. And before I could say anything his monstrous head hit the middle of my back and I was shoved roughly into darkness and the opening was closed.

I had not outwitted him! He had outwitted me! I was furious. I began pounding on the walls and shouting.

"Maris, stop it. This won't get us anywhere. Calm down." And a loved dog nose touched my hand.

"Scuro! Scuro! It's you! Oh, Scuro, are you all right? Are you hurt? Scuro!"

"Now Maris, don't get hysterical. I'm OK. A small bump on my nose is all. Are you hurt?"

"No. I'm just mad as anything! He fooled me! I thought I was smart, and it was Squirm that was smart! I'm really mad!"

"Feelings don't solve problems, dear Maris. Got to think. Keep cool-headed. Plot and plan, that's what we've got to do. Plot and plan." Animals—particularly dogs—are usually smarter than people, so I went along with Scuro's reasoning although I was skeptical about what we could do in this dark place. But Scuro obviously had a plan.

"I've explored this room or cave or whatever it is at least fifteen times. My nose is getting raw. But I won't weigh my idea until you check it too. It's not very big. But do it carefully. And watch your head because this place has got a low ceiling."

"All right, Scuro. I'll try it. You get me started."

So with my hand on his head I was guided to where I had been shoved in. "Now start to your right and work the walls. Your hands are things I don't have. So use them. I'll stay here so you'll know when you come around." It was a long, tiring examination to explore this prison. It wasn't large and it wasn't high (as I soon learned after bumping my head twice). Scuro stayed very still. He spoke to me softly from time to time so I knew where I was and how far I had yet to go. At last I came the full round, bumping into Scuro.

"Well, that's that," I said wearily.

"Find anything, Maris?"

"No. No cracks. No holes. No openings."

"Me the same. I'm sure my nose would have picked up any opening."

"So what do we do now?"

"Well—my hunch is to explore the ceiling. You can reach it with your hands, I'm sure. I'll go along so my nose can help. If we start at the wall side and work our way in spirals to the center, I hope you can touch everything."

"What's this all going to prove, Scuro? Suppose we do find a crack or a hole. We can't go through it."

"That's true. But in some way maybe we can get a message out. Who knows? Funny things do happen in the Great Land, Maris. Strange and helpful things, remember."

I did remember. And I would do this. "You guide me in the spiraling. Dogs are much better at such things. Let's go." So we began. Scuro walked on my left said, touching me gently. His keen sense of smell and of direction were our guides. He nudged me from time to time to move left or right so as not to leave out any bit of ceiling. For a very long period everything was the same. Then suddenly my finger found a rough place—more than rough. It was as if it didn't belong.

"Wait." I whispered. "Wait. Let me explore it."

Scuro stopped, his body gently against my legs. I explored the roughness. It seemed quite large—at least two-and-a-half hand spans. And it felt too regular, too circular in shape, to be just another rock. I whispered as much to Scuro.

"Can you feel any definite rim, or anything to push or to pull, or anything?"

I went over it again very carefully, bit by bit, feeling, pulling, pressing, rubbing. Nothing happened. I was just about to give up when it moved. It was a very minute motion, so I kept touching and pressing until it moved again. This time I held my fingers where they were and kept experimenting until I was certain that, when I touched a raised spot and pushed on it ever so little, the whole piece moved very slightly. I described it to Scuro.

"Sounds possible," he said. "Wait before you try it. If it opens, it's got to open out, or it wouldn't stay in place. So push it very very gently. If it's a big enough hole you can lift me so I can see out and know what's out there—friends, or Worms, or nothing."

"Then what do we do?"

"How can we know until we see?"

"All right. Here we go." I went over the piece again very carefully. It was clear that when I pushed a certain place the whole piece moved. I put one hand flat against the whole, bracing my hand and arm to be ready to push. Very carefully then, with the forefinger of my other hand, I began to put pressure on the focal spot. I increased the pressure. I felt the whole piece move. A bit more pressure and all at once the cover came free and fell outward with a muffled "klonk." Light and air came in.

"Scuro! Quick! Let me boost you up!"

He was there at once. I put my arms round him as I had done so often in our lives and lifted him to the hole. Carefully, he put his head out and sniffed fully as only a dog can sniff. In a muted voice he said, "No one's in sight. I can get out and go for help. But you, Maris, you should go first!"

"No! You can go faster. I don't think it's large enough for me. Now go! Tell the others! Get help if you can!"

I shoved him up and out and he was gone. It was good to have fresh air—but what would I tell the Worms? How could I explain the opening? Well, I'd think of something—if any Worm came back. "Maris," I said, "Maris, you're tired and you need rest. Get some before the next thing happens." So I went to a corner far from the opening, lay down on the hard floor, and fell asleep.

I wakened when the door opened and more light came in. I jumped to my feet to face a huge Worm with a most evil and leering expression. "So here you are, all by yourself. How did the hole get open? And where is the black creature?" It stared at me with unblinking eyes as it moved toward me. I took a step away. It moved nearer and nearer until I was backed against the wall and its face was very near to my face.

"So you are one of the things from the other land, are you? You plan to take over our land, do you—you and your ridiculous band of nothings? You can't do it. You are weak and stupid. As are all those who try to rule the Great Land. We are the strong ones. Our great alliance of Beasts and Worms will soon be in command."

It stared at me until inside me I was screaming, but outside I kept silent and managed to stare back. Some voice within was saying, "Don't let it get you. Remember why you're here. Remember that the Great Land needs help." So I was able to be quiet and to keep my face toward the Worm. I felt it wanted me to turn away or fall apart and fiercely I resolved to do neither.

At last the Worm—not I—broke the silence. "Do you know who I am?"

"No, I do not."

"You will." The terrible face came nearer and nearer. "I am Slithers—the ruler of the this land. I will be the ruler of the Great Land eventually."

I could not reply. However, I was able to stare back without turning my eyes away. I was grateful that I had that much courage, at least.

"Why did you let your creature go? It will only be caught and eaten. And how did the hole get open?"

"You keep talking about a creature. What do you mean? Since I was pushed in here I've seen no one. And I found the loose rock—or whatever it was—and pushed it out because I wanted light and fresh air."

I glared at Slithers because I hated him. I guess that I also lied because I hated him. And I held my ground better than I would have supposed. I really think that he believed me—at least he half-believed me—because he looked at me in some annoyance, I'm sure, then turned away and undulated to the door. His final statement was, "That opening will be closed immediately and made secure." The door slammed after him and, from the sounds, was being securely fastened. Soon the upper opening was closed.

During the next period of time I was in a black and timeless silence. I didn't give in to tears. I had learned from past situations in previous journeys in the Great Land that to fall apart in fear or anxiety was to lose. Always. If there was some way to keep active, to plan, to try to escape, you could keep your balance. So I began to explore every inch of my prison room—the dank and smelly floor, the walls, the ceiling, the locked door. I went over the floor on my knees—inch by inch. It was smelly, rough, but obviously of a solid clay-rock. As were the walls. I found several places where rocks were embedded in the clay, and in each such place I tried to pry the rock loose. The first few rocks—when worked free by much effort—revealed to my fingers only more clay. Then I found a longer stone. After a long and tedious working at the task suddenly the stone came free. As I lifted it out of its hole I felt a slight rush of cleaner air. I put the stone down and plunged hand and arm into the rock hole.

I could feel sides—but no end. The air seemed cool and fresh. Why couldn't it be a larger hole, so I could crawl through? But it wasn't. Could anyone be in there? Another prisoner? Probably it was some sort of tunnel for ventilation—although that didn't fit, because it was clear that Worms do not like fresh air. I kept exploring the tunnel with my hands. It was large enough to let my arm stretch to its full length, I decided, so I pushed my hand just as far as I could.

Suddenly, my fingertips touched a soft furry something. I withdrew my hand and whispered into the tunnel, "I won't hurt you," and then put my arm and hand back, letting my hand be open with palm upward. Some slight and soft something climbed in. Slowly and gently I pulled my arm back into the dark cell.

"My, my, I'm glad you came along!" The voice was small, soft, friendly. "I was making a new tunnel to my house—the old one having been invaded—and my new tunnel ended at the wrong place. I'm not very good at directions, I guess. And who are you, please? It's too dark in here to see you. Except you're big."

"And you are very little. I am Maris. And who are you?"

"I am a very small mouse—smallest in my family—and I've been working at my first—my very first—nest. And my name is IstHer—because my grandmother, whenever I did anything bad while she was tending me, always said, 'Well, it's isther!' So that's who I am."

I was rescued from much of my fear and anxiety and lostness by IstHer's presence. Of course I was distressed and concerned when I wondered if Scuro had escaped and found our comrades, and if they had avoided the Worms. I also wondered if they had tried to find me, or had been caught, or injured.

So I sat down with IstHer and told her what was happening, and said that if I suddenly popped her into my pocket it was to deceive the Worms and that I was sure—I wasn't sure at all—that my friends would rescue us sometime soon.

There was no way of telling time in this dark place. Nor was there food we could eat. And for me there was no place to rest. IstHer could rest and sleep in her nest, in my hand, in my pocket. Neither of us was willing just to give up and give in. We worked out several possibilities, none of which had any merit. And then between us we came up with a plot.

I would bang on the doorplace—loudly, continuously, until a Worm came in. Then IstHer would rush over—secretly—climb on-to the Worm and start biting its body. Because all the ordinary worms I knew reacted to touch by thrashing about, I hoped these Worms would do likewise and would therefore be easy to confuse and to escape from. I knew it might be dangerous for IstHer as well as for me. I asked myself if I had the right to risk her life for the Great Land. I did not know the answer. I said this to her and her answer was, "Let's try it."

We had to act soon. I was weak from hunger and fear and worry and knew that unless I acted I—perhaps we—were lost. Having no idea whether it was day or night, IstHer and I decided we'd put our plan into action as soon as we counted to one hundred.

I could hear her tiny voice following mine: ". . . ninety-five—ninety-six—ninety-seven—ninety-eight—ninety-nine—ONE HUN-DRED!"—and I rushed to the door, carrying IstHer and putting her down close to the wall beside the door, and then I started to bang on the door, and kick it and shout. Very quickly the door was flung open and a large, ugly Worm entered. It was angrily snapping its teeth and glaring at us from little eyes which, I was convinced, did not have good vision. It was not Slithers because it didn't boast. It only said in a loud voice, "Stop this noise!"

I went on shouting whatever came—such as "SHOUT!" and "BULLY!" and "I'M HUNGRY!" —while IstHer was climbing up the Worm's rear and was digging her sharp little teeth into its body and then scurrying out of sight into another part of the Worm and biting again and hiding again.

To my amazement—because I had expected all the huge Worms to be aggressive and cruel bullies—this one was a coward. I'm sure our combined shouting and biting hadn't gone on for more than five minutes when it was evident that the Worm was frightened and wanted to run.

"Get off, IstHer, get off! Follow me!" I shouted it loud and fast, hoping the Worm would react to the shouting rather than the content. IstHer jumped to the ground. I gave the Worm a sharp kick and shouted "Get out! Go!"

As it squirmed itself off I put IstHer in a pocket and started along a dark corridor opposite to the direction the Worm had taken. This escape—if it was to be one—could not be rehearsed. We had to make it or not make it. I recalled as I ran that I had fallen *into* this place and that I had been taken *down* when I was moved to the second prison. So the way out, I hoped, was up. I ran along the corridor until I saw a side corridor. If it's up, I'll take it, I told myself. It wasn't. But the next one was up, and I took it. It got wider as it climbed, which was fortunate because suddenly I saw a Worm coming down it. I dropped down and lay flat against the wall on the corridor floor. I was certain that this was the end of us—but the Worm squirmed along over us and rippled on its way.

The corridor grew continually wider. It also was level now and had occasional openings overhead. Several more Worms came toward us, and each time I lay flat and they passed over us. It was scary to do, but each time it happened I was more certain that they were unaware, insensitive, and not very bright. My hopes for our being able to conquer them were growing, even if I was more irritated every time I was walked on.

Suddenly, I realized that there was light ahead. That could mean freedom. It could also mean walking into a whole gathering of Worms. I said as much to IstHer, taking her out of my pocket.

"Why don't you lie down against the wall again, and I can run fast and look out and run back fast and tell you."

"That's a good plan. But please be very careful, will you, IstHer? Please!"

"I will." And she scampered off down the corridor, so close to the sides that she quickly became invisible.

I lay along the wall-floor angle, as I had before. As before, a Worm came along and passed over me as if I weren't there. And very soon IstHer was back, scampering up to my ear and saying, "Now! Nobody is around. The outside is empty! Hurry!"

Grabbing IstHer and pocketing her, I ran at my top speed (which wasn't bad), reached the opening, saw in a quick glance that no creature was in sight and that a path seemed to go uphill towards a mountain or mountains. I didn't stop to decide whether I should follow the path or whether the mountains were familiar. I just ran as fast as I could possibly run—away from the Worms.

When I was almost completely winded and my heart was pounding like a jackhammer, I saw ahead of me a very large rock beside a ragged tree. I ducked behind it and dropped to a sandy space next to the rock. I was totally exhausted. I lay flat for a time, slowly getting my breathing in order, when I heard a tiny squeak and a voice saying, "Please! I'm being squashed! Please!"

"IstHer! Poor little one! I forgot!"

I apologized as I extracted her from my pocket and put her on my outstretched arm. She sat quite still and washed herself carefully from the end of her pink tail to the end of her tiny nose. "Are you all right, little mouse IstHer? Did I hurt you?"

"Not much," said the small voice. "After a bit more grooming. I guess I'm so little that I squish without being squashed. So don't fret, Maris. I am fine. So now what do we do?"

I was not at all clear as to what should be done. I was very sure that Zeke and the others were planning some rescue attempt. Had they called on any of the Guardians? If so, who was told? Or had some of my comrades fallen into Worm prisons?

And at that moment a huge shadow crossed over us. I fell flat, put IstHer in my pocket, and curled up against the tree in terror.

CHAPTER 9

I closed my eyes and held my breath, waiting for whatever evil thing was descending to destroy us. I was sorry that I had gotten little IstHer involved in this bad struggle. She was such an innocent. Why didn't the terror just grab us and be done with it!

"Maris! Maris, are you alive? Are you wounded? Maris!"

I opened my eyes. Standing over me was Dag, his ugly vulture face close to mine. "Now then, Maris, get on my back! The Guardians sent me to search as soon as Scuro made his way to the Place of Them. Get on! Now! We don't have much time!"

I did what he said. After a running start—Dag was not much bigger than I, but stronger—we were airborne. I hung onto his naked neck as his great wings forced his body and its unusual load away from the ground. I risked one downward look to see what we left behind. I saw raw rocky hillocks and bits of dirty smoke dribbling from Worm holes. As Dag climbed higher I could see behind us the ugly rawness of Volcanic Mountain, and ahead of us the Place of Them. Between these two heights somewhere—or at least somewhere nearer the Mountain of Mist and the Mountain of Them—would be the vulture's home. At this point I closed my eyes just so I could realize that maybe all of us could be free and safe. Whatever was still ahead we would face together.

To my surprise Dag sailed over his home and onward and, before I was prepared, he came in for a landing on the Mountain of Them—not at the central Place of Them, but at the place below where the Guardians gathered. I stumbled from Dag's back to be greeted by Scuro and Zeke and Cat and friendly Beasts. It was a happiness to know that no one had been hurt or lost. But before we could talk about anything, there was a great whoosh of wings and Owl stood before us.

We fell silent.

"Children, will you please follow me," said Owl.

We followed him in silence to Domar, where we all grouped before her door. We were a subdued company.

"I am sure you all realize that you went much too far in your explorations. All of you," said Owl. "The Beasts were somewhat more moderate and did not get into trouble, but had to be called back. Fortunately, no one was lost, injured, or killed." He paused, peering at each of us individually. I could not speak for anyone else, but I personally felt very badly.

"Owl," I said, "I am really sorry that I was cause for worry—and danger—for any of my friends and helpers. There are no excuses."

He looked at me with his great round eyes, but I did not let myself turn my eyes away. "Maris, thank you for your honesty. And before we proceed, may I ask what you have in your pocket? It moves." Of course Owl would notice! So I reached in, lifted IstHer out, and held her on my open hand.

"Don't be afraid of me," said Owl to IstHer in his kindest voice. "You are safe with us. Now, Maris, tell me your story. I heard Scuro's the instant he reached us. He had a very narrow escape from some Worms before he reached us. He will tell you about it later, I'm sure."

So I told him, very carefully, everything I did, every move I made, every encounter I had, my feelings about the Worms and their arrogance and their stupidity, about Slithers and his boastfulness, about those who crawled over us in the underground.

When I finished, Owl gazed at me long and pensively. "Despite your behavior, Maris—you and the others—I believe you have given us some helpful information that we can use in planning our campaign against the Worms. If we put your report together with our Beasts' learnings, and add to that the rumors we've picked up from other sources, plus Thaddeus and his magic knowledge, we do have quite a bit to go on. Tonight we will meet at the Place of Them and discuss all of this. For now, I believe you all need rest and quiet. Domar is ready for you." Lifting himself on his marvelous wings, Owl was quickly out of sight.

Soon we were stretched out on Domar's floor—me, Zeke, Scuro, Cat—and IstHer was curled up beside Molasses. They were whispering softly as I fell asleep.

I was wakened by Zeke's hand on my shoulder and his voice whispering, "I think I heard Owl arrive." Scuro and Cat were at once on their feet, and IstHer jumped to my shoulder, saying "Me too." The Beasts were already waiting near Owl. Once again I was impressed by their proud and almost regal manner, which affirmed their intention despite their ugliness. Maybe because of it. In any event they were wonderful.

Although I hadn't had enough rest and sleep, I felt better than when I stumbled from Dag's back. After we had all gathered near Domar's door, Owl stood very still, his eyes checking us all. Then he nodded. "You will please follow me to the Place of Them. In silence."

It seemed that we were going forever—I realized as we went that it always seemed so—but we followed after Owl as we were told to do. He was not made for walking but for silent, graceful soaring. Nonetheless he did what he told us to do. It was not long before we came out in the great plaza of the Old Ones. But it was silent this time. No drummers. No drums. Only the Old Ones and the Guardians were there, in a great semicircle facing us.

Dark Fire, Grandmother, Grandfather, and Owl took the middle of the semicircle. On one side of Them were Exi and Thaddeus and on the other side were Grandan and Arachne. I could feel the seriousness of this gathering. It was visible in the silence and in the expressions of all who were there. Including us. Dark Fire stepped forward, his hands palms up, held towards us. After a silent bow he began speaking, "My children—our children—we are approaching a crucial time. Together, all of us together." He paused as if to emphasize this. "No one of us, no small groups of us, can act to deal with the danger that threatens us. Each of us is necessary. All of us are necessary. All of us must know what the others are doing. The Worms—judging from information you have given—do not know what others are doing. They crawl over other beings and seem not to know they are doing so. The renegade Beasts are collaborating with the Worms, we have learned."

He paused, his gaze moving from one to the other of us as if he wanted us to know that he was speaking to each of us as well as to all of us. It was clear that Owl had learned from our group and from the Beasts' group all that had happened.

"So, my children, now we must begin to work together. What you have explored on your own—without telling us—has given us information we can use. However, it also puts some of you in terrible danger without our knowing. This must not happen again." He bowed to us, a sort of smile on his face. "The next hours we leave to the Guardians."

We all stood quiet and eager while the Old Ones departed from the great square. As soon as They were gone the rest of us gathered together—as if by some mysterious plan—on the downhill edge of the square, the edge nearest to the place of the Guardians. We were quite a company—Exi, Thaddeus, Arachne, Grandan, Zeke, me, Cat, Scuro, Duo, Tusks, Twist—and of course IstHer.

"Before we begin," said Cat unexpectedly, "I should think that Domar and Molasses ought to be in on this."

We all agreed, and walked down the little slope to the flat place where Domar was. Soon we were all together in a company, sitting or standing on the green where Domar could see and hear us. I had put Molasses in the doorway beside IstHer.

"Let's all tell what happened to us," said Thaddeus. "I mean all of you who had things happen to you. We've heard pieces of it. Now we want all of it. Why don't you start, Maris."

I described as accurately as possible, as I had for Owl, all my goings and comings in Wormland, including Scuro's escape and my finding IstHer. I tried to convey my experiences with impressions of the Worms.

Scuro continued the story, "Well, when Maris shoved me out of that hole I was scared. I landed in a sort of square—flat, smooth stones with big grooves in them. There were a few sticking-up rocks and I ducked behind one of those until I figured out which way to run. While I was hiding and deciding I saw several Worms come out of openings and slide along the grooves in the stones." He shook his head as if he was shaking them. "Ugh! They're awful! I couldn't follow them because they went into and out of their holes so fast—and anyway I wanted to get help as soon as I could—so finally not a Worm was in sight—maybe it was lunch time or something—and I dashed off uphill hoping it would lead me to Dag. Which finally it did. And Dag took messages to all concerned."

Exi asked, "Did you get any idea of the size of Wormland—or of the Worm population?"

"No sir, not really. There are lots of holes scattered around, and lots of Worm grooves—but it could be the same Worms going in and out and in and out. I don't know where that smelly smoke comes from, but I don't think it's from fires. They couldn't make fires. I think it's just their hot, dirty air that has to get out."

"Thank you, Scuro. Obviously you did not find Worms appealing as friends." Exi's words had a smile in them. "We know that Zeke and Cat—after Scuro and Maris had fallen into Worm rooms—started immediately back on the path they had walked to report what had happened. Gada brought news to us, and we asked Thaddeus to do some magic looking—which he did. Let him tell again what he saw."

In all his wonderfully absurd splendor—pot on head, his great tail going slowly back and forth as he moved to a central place—he was dear and unbelievable. He removed his black pot from his head and put it on the ground in front of him.

"Well now . . . let me see . . . where shall I begin . . . " and he closed his eyes and fell into silence. The silence went on and on.

Finally Exi said gently, "Thaddeus? Thaddeus? Dear Thaddeus! We are not mind readers. Thaddeus!!"

"My goodness, I must have gone wandering again. It's very exciting—wandering, I mean—because I'm never sure where I'll come out, you know."

"Thaddeus," said Exi, "please come back for now and speak to us. Than you can wander again."

"Very well, I will tell you." And it was a long and strange story, coming in bits and pieces, of what he saw in his magical gazing. Most of us knew him well enough to trust his truthfulness and his skill at in-seeing. He saw, first of all, that smoke came out of holes only when two or more Worms were in the same room. "They smell!" He shook his head. "And the smells join when Worms come together. Even they can't stand it, I guess."

He fell silent. Exi nudged him. "Come on, Thaddeus! We need your information!"

"Oh! I'm sorry. I am woolly sometimes, aren't I? Well—" And he launched into an incredible account of miles and miles of underground tunnels and rooms, some ventilated and some not, some for Worm gatherings and some for storage, he guessed. Although he hadn't seen them eating. "Maybe they eat each other! Who knows?" He paused, his eyes closed. Exi nudged him. "Oh, yes—I must report that I saw two—perhaps three—but for sure two—Beasts walking behind Worms. They—the Beasts, I mean—carried burdens on their backs. For the enemy Beasts or for the Worms, I suppose."

He fell silent, his eyes closed for quite a time.

At last Exi said gently, "Is there more, Thaddeus?"

"One more scene. I can hardly believe it myself, you know. That's why I haven't spoken it." He paused, closing his eyes again. "What I saw—or what I think I saw—or dreamed I saw—was a dark, small, ugly cave—at the back of one of the Worm prison rooms—and there was a Beast there, and a small white mare beside the Beast. They were starved-looking, but held their heads high as they stood very close together."

"Thaddeus, my friend," said Exi, "Was the Beast Quatro? Is that what you are saying?"

After a long pause Thaddeus sighed. "Yes, truly I believe it was."

"And the other?"

"I do not know. But she was lovely!"

Thaddeus lowered his awkward self to the ground with a thud and closed his eyes. I slid his black pot a little sideways so he could stretch out more. I also took the liberty of patting his head gently.

"Well, children," said Exi, "Suppose all of us should rest a while?"

We all agreed. We were very quiet. Even Domar did not ask to be told what was happening. Although I was sprawled on the ground comfortably, I was not sleepy. Against my closed eyes came the scene Thaddeus told us—Quatro and a small white mare. In a dark prison somewhere. I knew that of course we would try to do something about this. Even if we had to try it alone—which we wouldn't because the whole Great Land was involved. It could not be given over to Worms and renegade Beasts, this Great Land! And the words Exi had said—especially to Zeke when we were with the Old Ones and the Guardians—about the Great Land being a pattern of patterns, being what lives under and within all lands, these words meant that if anyplace was to be safe from enemies and darknesses that were evil then we had to make this Great Land safe and whole again.

I dozed and I dreamed that some tiny goblin-type creature was pulling my ear. I roused myself to hear IstHer squeaking "Maris! Maris! We're going to start somewhere, I think! Maris!"

As I got my inner and outer worlds into some sort of order I saw that a sizable company had gathered near Domar's "eye." Scuro, Zeke, Cat, Duo, Tusks, Twist, IstHer, and of all surprises Thaddeus. Before I could exclaim, down swooped Dag and settled beside Thaddeus, and I joined them. We were ten strange travelers, that was certain. When we clumped together to make plans I wondered if we could possibly do anything except fall over each other. We gathered around Thaddeus and his pot. He was the natural leader—as a Guardian and as a magician—who could get us out of difficult places better than anyone else I could think of.

"Now then," said Thaddeus, "I have orders—or perhaps instructions—or maybe both . . . " and he closed his eyes as if he had to decide. " . . . Anyway, here is what They advised—advised, not commanded. We are going to the far side of Volcanic Mountain. We will be an even dozen because Domar will be reduced to carrying size and she and Molasses will go along. We will need a place of protection and Domar will be that."

Then Thaddeus moved into action. It didn't take long for Domar to be reduced, with Molasses inside. Thaddeus was at his magical best and did not once ask for help. He was the leader and we needed to obey.

"Now," he said, "we must prepare to start. How many of you have spiderweb suits from Arachne?" He looked at us all. "So Duo, Tusks, and Twist do not. IstHer does not, but she will be in your pocket, Maris." He handed me three of the delicate, almost invisible web suits. "Please, Maris, will you and Zeke help Duo, Tusks, and Twist into these?"

I had never before seen Thaddeus in such a serious and authoritative role. He was carrying it very well, and I realized how he had altered since our first meeting. Zeke and I helped the three Beasts into their spiderweb suits. I hoped Thaddeus wasn't too annoyed with me and that I would have a moment somewhere to say how sorry I was.

"Well, are we all ready?" Thaddeus asked as he stood before us in great solemnity, his black pot on his head, some of his magical stuff in packs on his back, and some of it, I saw to my surprise, in packs on Duo's back.

We all answered, "Yes."

"All right, here's how we're going to do it." He looked us over carefully, one by one. "Duo, Tusks, and Twist, you will start out first. You are fast on your feet, good at being wily, and careful. You know the shortcut, I believe—because you explored it a few days ago. Is that correct?"

"Yes, sir, it is and we did. Sorry if we broke rules, Thaddeus." So the Beasts had tried some exploring also. I felt a bit less guilty for our disobedience. "Very well, off you go, friends. And please don't try to test new ideas until we all arrive at the same place." The three Beasts took off at what was a fast pace for them.

"But Thaddeus, how can they see well enough to go so fast?" I blurted out.

"You haven't heard of my invention, then. They are wearing invisible glasses that I made. It took me a long time to find out how but—oh dear, we haven't time for such stories! Come now, Maris. Dag will take you and IstHer to our meeting place. Then he'll take Zeke, then Scuro and Cat together—yes, together, and don't look so scared—then finally he will come back for me. Domar and Molasses will be with Zeke, of course. And the Beasts will get there just as soon as they can. So—off you go, Maris and IstHer. Quickly!"

I was less frightened to climb onto Dag's great back this time. And I almost forgot my fear when IstHer, in a wild, contagious excitement, climbed from my pocket and sat on my shoulder screaming with delight over everything. "Look, Maris! Look! Down there! See the smoke coming up!" And just as I thought I saw it— "Whee! Isn't this great! Oh, Dig, you are so strong!"

"Dag! My name is Dag, not Dig!"

"Dag, you are wonderful! Oh, whee-ee!"

Her excitement and fearless joy helped me to look out. I was able to see the smoking holes, the barren and sick earth around them, Volcanic Mountain in its dark and pockmarked somberness—and to recall some of the past events that had taken place in and around it. For a short time Volcanic Mountain disappeared and we flew blindly in a gray and eye-irritating haze. "It's the Barrier of Nothing. Remember it, Maris." Dag sounded relaxed, so I tried to be.

"Yes, I remember now. Do you know more about it?"

"Not yet. The Old Ones now feel quite certain that it's related to the Worms somehow. Not sure how, though. Anyway, time's about up. Hold on for a landing."

Dag circled and soared above Volcanic Mountain, in smooth glides coming nearer and nearer. I could see, as we went silently by, one or two features of the bare heights, features I felt were familiar—but I couldn't quite recall what had gone on there.

"All right. Be ready to get off quickly, as I must return for others."

He came onto a cup-shaped place part of the way up the mountain. All I could see as he braked to land was that nothing grew here. The entire hollow was of reddish brown earth—or rock—smooth as a bowl. I stumbled off Dag's back.

"Good flying!" I called. "Be careful!" But he was gone.

Suddenly, I was alone in a huge silence. Note quite alone, because IstHer erupted from my shoulder, touched my lower arm in a leap, and landed on the ground of the hollow. Within a few seconds she was sliding down one of the lava rocks—a shiny black one—landing on the bare earth, rushing back to try it again. I started to scold her for such frivolity—but thought, "Why do that? Let her enjoy herself before things really get difficult."

So I wandered and examined this place. It was large—as big as the plaza on the Mountain of Them. But this was hollowed out as if intentionally, similar to pictures I had seen in a book belonging to my grandfather, pictures of ancient theaters in Greece where the seats sloped down to the stage on all sides. Except this one was smooth-sided, empty. I looked upward and saw a kind of opening in the mountain where the sky showed through. Of course! I had seen that opening before—when the water was rising to trap Beasts! For a few moments I was pulled back into that frightful and frightening time when, over and over, it seemed we were lost. And yet we did not give up.

Immersed in that past time, I did not see Dag coming in. It was IstHer who alerted me. "Here they come! Here they come!" Dag braked fiercely, almost tipping but not. Zeke tumbled off Dag's back, stumbled momentarily, and in that moment Dag was airborne and headed back.

"I wish I could fly like that!" Zeke watched Dag bank and soar out of sight. "He's great, really. And he never boasts about himself.

Hardly says anything about anything." He watched the empty sky. Then he looked overhead and gasped. "What a weird and scary place this is! Why are we here?"

CHAPTER 10

Dag's arrival with Scuro and Cat was unforgettable. When the great bird circled as he dropped down into the opening, I could see two heads and four eyes and I thought I could even see dog and cat hair standing on end. Dag alighted as gently as he could. Scuro, who knew the great birds from the past, was not frightened, although I knew he would rather walk. He jumped out, wobbled a moment, shook himself, and came toward us.

Seeing the terror in Cat's eyes I went to Dag and lifted Cat in my arms so Dag could depart. Cat was trembling all over. "It's all right," I said as I stroked him. "I was scared the first time I rode Dag. You'll be fine as soon as you walk."

"Thanks, Maris. I'm sorry I got so wobbly. But being up so high—it's really scary. Dag is great—but up in the air—oh dear!"

I held him until he stopped trembling. "Now try your legs and you'll be all right." He did. And he was. He walked over to Zeke, who was sitting against a rock outcrop and gazing upward toward the opening. Cat rubbed against Zeke and Zeke made a lap for Cat to climb into and they both stared up in silence.

"Zeke. Zeke!" I had forgotten—as obviously he had—that Domar was inside his pocket and Molasses was inside Domar. "For goodness' sake let Domar and Molasses be with us and not in darkness, even if they are tiny until Thaddeus comes. Let them out."

"What a thing to forget! I'm sorry." Carefully he lifted the tiny house out of its hiding place. He set it down, its minute but glowing window-eye toward us. "Forgive me for forgetting, Domar," he whispered.

Her tiny voice piped back, "It's all right. I am here with my family and it is all right. Molasses is sleeping."

So for a time we all sat or stretched out, or moved about, or looked around, or closed our eyes. I felt like humming, so I did and Isther joined me with a shrill little hum of her own. It was very still in this strange mahogany hollow of stone.

"Maris," came the small voice of Domar. "Maris!"

I leaned down and put my ear next to her. "Yes!"

"Maris, you are troubled. Why? Can you say?"

So I whispered my concerns to the little listening house. When I finished I felt better. And even better than that when Domar said, "We will find Quatro. They are a part of us." She had a wonderful way of being very certain about outcomes.

At that moment of gentle assurance Dag and Thaddeus catapulted into us.

"Watch out below!" Dag screeched. "Scatter!" We did scatter toward the sides of the cavern, for Thaddeus's magic pot bounced and rang as it hit the cave floor, and wands and feathers and rocks and string and bits and pieces of unknown objects were flung in all directions.

Dag landed in the cave's center, looking totality worn out. And Thaddeus climbed awkwardly from Dag's back to the ground with his usual composure. "My goodness, what a welcome! Thank you, thank you!" Turning to Dag he said, "You have my total gratitude, my friend! All of it! I'm not easy to carry—and when my stuff is added it is impossible. But you made it all possible. Thank you."

Dag bowed his head. "Thaddeus, there is no being I would rather carry. Thank you for being you. If there are words from Them I will bring the message. Or other messengers will. Goodbye!" And he ascended and disappeared.

For a time we worked at gathering Thaddeus's magic stuff which was scattered through the cavern. I took his black pot to the center so we could put things away in it. He watched us for a time—and then he came and stood beside the heaped up pot. "And now, Maris, we must enlarge Domar. She—and we—must be ready when all the others come."

The Beasts that were coming on foot had a long and hard climb to do. And whether any of the Old Ones or any of the Guardians except Thaddeus would come was unlikely. So I helped Thaddeus in setting up his magic to enlarge Domar. Very soon she was her normal self, with her glowing door and window and Molasses in the doorway looking out. Domar, I realized, was comforting, loving, patient, honest, optimistic. That this great opening in Volcanic Mountain was a "fine brown room" to her was one of her motherly gifts of love and encouragement to us, her family. So why not go along with it, I thought, as I stepped into Domar. Very soon I was joined by Cat, Scuro, Zeke, IstHer. Molasses had climbed up the walk to the window, while Thaddeus rested his head on the doorstep with his body outside.

"How cozy this is, children." Domar's voice was joyful. "I wish I could feed you, but I cannot."

"Don't worry, Domar," said Thaddeus. "Before long the Beasts—*our* Beasts— will arrive, I am sure. And on Duo's back, in my magic packs, are collections of food so we can all eat. Let's rest a while until they come."

A gentle silence enfolded us. Even IstHer curled up beside Molasses and rested. Stillness cradled us all for a time unmeasured. I was watching Zeke's face when his eyes suddenly came open. "Did you hear something? I think the Beasts—our Beasts—are coming. Can you hear, Maris?"

Putting my finger on my lips to say be still, I listened. The silence in this awesome cave was total, I realized. I even diminished my breath until it was almost gone. And then I heard. It was a very, very soft "pat, pat, pat, pat" from somewhere. I arose slowly so as to make no sound. Zeke did likewise. We tiptoed out of Domar and stood in utter stillness by her door. The "pat, pat, pat, pat" sounds were coming closer. I kept looking downslope beyond the hollow place where we were. Then around a bend of the mountain came our three beasts, packs on their backs, trotting as if they had come only a short journey.

Joyfully we greeted them and led them to the place near Domar. We helped them out of their packs and let them rest after their long coming. They stretched out wearily. Tusks was the ugliest and the gentlest. After a while I sat down beside him and stroked his coarse hair and scratched behind his funny ears. He turned his head and gazed at me. "Thanks for that, Maris. It felt good outside and it makes me feel good inside."

"Was it a hard trip for all of you, Tusks? It must have been."

"Well—yes, I suppose it was — but those glasses that Thaddeus gave us! We could see things we never saw—ever—colors, shapes, mountains, and each other! We're not as ugly as I thought we were. At least we decided we had to stop hating ourselves and had to begin realizing that we were helpful creatures. Thaddeus is a great one, isn't he!"

"Yes, he is. So you three rest and we'll get the packs unpacked—or at least sort them out."

Zeke and I unpacked and stored everything inside Domar, taking care to separate out Thaddeus's magic food packs. We were all hungry, I was sure. I knew I was. And I hoped intensely that Thaddeus's magic food would adapt itself to our various needs and tastes. As we set out the magic food packs Zeke began to giggle.

"What's so funny, Zeke?" I asked.

"Are you reading the labels?"

"No."

"Do, and you'll be laughing, too."

So I did. And very soon I couldn't speak for giggles. The labels, in some strange script, said things like, "FOR MOUSES WHO ARE NOT IN HOUSES" and "KALE FOR SNAILS" and "CATS NEED FAT" and "DOGS NEED BOGS." Evidently either Thaddeus or some of his magic spells had a great sense of humor.

"Anyway," said Zeke, "Let's get everyone awake and put out the packages and eat, and we'll learn if the magic is accurate."

I went from one to another, wakening, touching, telling of the food packages, pointing them out. Most of the company went seriously to the packages labeled for them and began to open them and eat. All except IstHer and Molasses, who were together and overcome with giggles as each of them opened a package at the same moment.

"What is so funny, IstHer?" I asked.

"It's that—that everyone's package—everyone has the same thing, you see— and every package—probably—has in it the same things . . . She kept hesitating because of giggles. "Like there's yeast, and kale, and fat, and maybe berries from bogs, and curds, and outdoor air, and whatever helps vision. And we should all feel better for eating."

"And laughing," said Thaddeus. "Whoever makes my magic—and I don't know who it is but I have ideas—is a very wise being. And IstHer guessed that, because IstHer has a rare wisdom of laughter and joy in hard times. This is a hard time. So we need to eat richly of whatever we each decide our package is. And then we can plan. So eat and be filled. And laugh."

I had never heard Thaddeus so lucid, so definite, and so free. And we did what he said. When we had all finished, Thaddeus requested that we put all package wrappings in a hole he made in the stone floor with his magic wand. He said some words and went into one of his spins, and all package wrappings just vanished. Then he called us all together near Domar's flowing door, which shone more richly as darkness came over Volcanic Mountain and slowly the sky dimmed and vanished in the opening above us.

"So here we are—where the Old Ones—and the Guardians as well—agreed that we should be. They were to meet and discuss what we should—and could—do from here. We are further from the Great Land's goodness and almost on top of its badness." Thaddeus turned toward me. "You, Maris, still recall the terrors of battle floods in this area, and the death of brave Beasts and the flight of the Beasts who wanted to kill and rule, and the terrible desert beyond us."

I nodded my head, and my eyes clouded with tears for the loved Beasts who died in battle.

"Yes, it was sad. But slowly the good returned and the Great Land began to live again. Until some Beasts joined with the Worms. You know all this, but it is good to remember again so we are strong against the pushing darkness. And I propose we rest, as the dark comes, leaving Domar as our light." He bowed toward her. "I would guess that we all get a message from Them before too long. So rest, my children, rest. I will call you.

Soon all the company but Thaddeus and I were clumped together inside or close to Domar, resting and letting our strange food digest. Some were awake, their eyes focused on the great dark vault overhead, as Zeke was. Thaddeus and I sat outside Domar, I leaning against Domar and Thaddeus resting his head on his black pot. He spoke softly.

"I hope that very soon we will have some word from Them. All possible messengers and secret beings were sent out by Them to learn any and all possible facts about Worms, about enemy Beasts, about other enemies—and, above all, about Quatro and the white

mare. Whether Waff, or Antic, or another will be messengers from
Them, we must wait and know when the time comes. So now we
rest." I closed my eyes and relaxed as well as I could. Which wasn't
very relaxed.

Suddenly, Thaddeus raised his head and looked around
"Something—someone—" he turned his head back and forth and
back and forth. "Yes—someone is coming—" And almost before he
finished there was a flutter of wings and a buzz, and Waff and Antic were standing in Domar's eye.

"Be z-z-till," Waff whispered. "Let uz-z-z go into Domar if we
can, and talk z-zoftly."

We managed to do it—only just—with the three Beasts outside, their heads in the door. Thaddeus as Guardian was central.
Zeke and I, being tallest, stood against a side, the others distributed
themselves in the middle space from where they could see Waff and
Antic.

"Can you hear me?" Waff buzzed his wings and settled them.
"Lizzen carefully. Mezzage from Them izz: Wormzz are agitated
and afraid. The Old Onezz have been zending loud noizez, night
and day, down into Worm tunnelzz. There zeemzz to be a
retreat—or flight—from Worm tunnelzz near the zurface to the
older tunnelzz—deeper onezz—where they lived before—and
where Marizz, Zcuro, and otherz fought them and caught zzome of
them before with netz. Zzo, the Old Onezz believe that Marizz, and
Zcuro, and maybe Zeke and Izzther, and one of our Beazztz, can
go—very, very carefully—into the old tunnelz and report to the
Old Onezz, what the zituation izz. That izz the mezzage."

Thaddeus, as Guardian and leader, thanked Waff and said to
tell the Old Ones that the company would obey and do the very
best it could.

"Perhaps," he added, "perhaps either you or Antic could stay
with us and be our messenger if we should need to communicate
with the Place of Them."

"Antic will join your company. The Old Onezz thought of
that. Zzo do what you can, be careful, zzend any newzz azz zoon
azz you can."

With a soft buzz of wings Waff was gone and Antic was alone
in Domar's window. For a time no one moved or spoke. I
couldn't—and I guess Scuro and some of the others were also

stunned into silence at the prospect of having to find and enter those terrible Beast tunnels again. But if that was what we needed to do—well, then we would do it. And so why not be warm and welcoming to poor Antic, who continued to sit in Domar's window in silence.

"Welcome, Antic! Welcome!" I said. And all the others said "Welcome! Welcome!"

"Hello! Hello, hello, hello!" His voice was as loud as ever, and his clown colorings as wonderful. "I am proud to be your messenger. Thank you. Thank you!"

Reluctantly, I turned to Scuro. "Scuro, it looks like you and I—"

"And me too," piped IstHer.

"—and IstHer, and Zeke, and a Beast have been elected to be spies in the tunnels of the Worms. Scuro and I were in those tunnels once long ago and they are very, very dark and dangerous. That was where the good Beasts—like our friend here—became helpers of the Old Ones." I turned to Tusks. "Will you go with Scuro and Zeke and me, Tusks?"

His ugly face was shining with happiness. "Dear Maris, nothing would make me more joyful than to be a part of this task. I haven't been in the tunnels under these mountains for a long time. But I'm sure I can find ways to go. Yes! Yes!"

I laughed aloud. "What an assortment! A boy, a girl, a dog, a mouse, and a Beast! The only good thing is that each of us, because of these differences, brings various different skills and awarenesses. So—when do we start, Thaddeus? You are a Guardian."

He stood beside his black pot. "Well . . . " and for a time he gazed off into nothing.

"Thaddeus," I said finally, "Thaddeus, please be with us, dear sir."

"Did I leave you! I suppose I did. I guess you can depart when you are ready."

"How do we know when we're ready?"

"Well . . . I guess I'd better give you some magic first. Not much, but enough to protect yourselves. And also some sticky stuff to catch Worms—or bad Beasts. As soon as everything is ready, then you can start."

Thaddeus went into one of his magic moods—pulling everything from his black pot, putting things together, separating things, recombining, sorting, starting over again. At such times he seemed sort of half-witted, but, from experience, I knew that his goals were clear and his way of getting to them was excellent, eventually.

We watched and we waited. At one point Domar shook herself and asked, "Have some of my family gone? It is so quiet. Is there trouble, please?"

Thaddeus laughed, which he rarely did. "No trouble, dear Domar. It's only that magic takes time. As soon as I can know—or have decided—what steps are necessary—well, then I will announce them."

"I hear what you say, Thaddeus, and I trust."

After another piece of Thaddeus's time, there finally came a great belch of black smoke, and in the middle of the cave floor a huge barrel-like container appeared. It stood there impregnable, black, mysterious. Thaddeus went over to it. "Maris, come and help me." So I went. I put wands at four sides, I sprinkled powders from wands to the container and put other items from his pot as he asked for them.

He stepped back and surveyed the confused scene. "Very good. Very good. Now Maris—and all of you—stand very quiet. Whatever happens, don't move."

We stayed as he commanded and Thaddeus stood beside the black and silent container peering at it as if it was about to explode. Suddenly, he went into his magician's spin—faster and faster and faster—and then there was a brilliant but small explosion, and the container was gone. In its place was a shining silver basket, with a word on it, in large glowing letters: OPEN.

Thaddeus stepped forward. "Well, it worked. Now let us see what we have. Come and help." We all moved forward under Thaddeus's sureness. He asked us each to take whatever our hands touched as we reached into the open box. Everyone of us took something—except Domar, who said in her gentle way, "Just show me what you find and tell me what it is."

Soon every item in the box (which vanished as soon as the last thing was taken) was in the possession of one of us. We took time to open them and put them where all could see—most particularly Domar.

Thaddeus said he would call our names and then each in turn would discover what was there.

"Maris, you are first."

My bundle was bulky and seemed to have sharp somethings inside—and it was moderately heavy. It took quite a time to open it and when I finally got into it, at first it seemed like a bundle of unrelated junk, mechanical and beyond my understanding.

"Maris," said Zeke. "I know what it is. Can I help, if you know it is yours?"

"My boy," said Thaddeus, "Everything belongs to the whole company. So help her."

I handed the heavy bundle over, and Zeke stood with me while together we opened it. When it was all unwrapped it turned obt to be a sturdy folding cart, which could carry a lot of stuff but could also carry at least two beings, even of my size.

"What good will this be?" I asked.

"There's no better way to carry supplies—or one of you—or a captive enemy, perhaps—or some other weighty item you might find, etcetera." Thaddeus was so pleased at his magic cart that I had no alternative but to accept it.

IstHer's bundle held a net of spiderweb silk which, as Thaddeus explained, could be carried by a mouse but could capture a Worm or an enemy Beast. Zeke also had netting—much more than Isther—enough to hold several Beasts or Worms.

Zeke opened Tusks's bundle for him. It was larger than the others, bulkier but not too much for a Beast. It was a sort of folding tent which would, as Thaddeus showed us, open up to hold all of us—but it also, if turned inside out, became invisible if we needed to hide from enemies.

"So, children," said Thaddeus, "you must rest and be ready when I call you."

Chapter 11

I rested—but I was also restless. I wanted to get started on a journey I dreaded. And also I was eager to begin the search for Quatro. I was a confused journeyer—as I had been before—and I knew that, but I also knew that I was a dogged journeyer who had hung on in terrible situations. And when Thaddeus's voice broke into my musings I was ready to go.

When the tent was fastened on Zeke's back and the folded up cart on Tusk's back, and the netting on Scuro's back, and IsHer on my shoulder carrying her webbing on her back—Thaddeus stepped forward.

have prepared five guardian feathers—they are very special feathers from a very secret place—and I will hear and do what I can. Don't run away. Trust my magic. Most of the time it will work."

He gave us our feathers. Then he turned to the other two Beasts and Cat and bowed. Duo and Twist bowed to him. "I know," he said softly, "I know you would like to go with them. But there must be some of us here to be ready if the Old Ones call, or if help is needed by the others. Domar, brave as she is, needs part of her family with her. She will have Cat, Molasses, Thaddeus, and off and on, Twist."

"Thaddeus, sir," said Twist, "I—we—are happy to stay with you and Cat and Domar—to serve you in any way we can. We can guard. We can run errands. We can fight if necessary."

"Thank you. Domar, Molasses, Cat, I, and you two will make a good company." Thaddeus turned to us. "And you five—do please be very careful. Watch over one another. Be on guard. Trust no one—and I do dislike saying that—but trust no one unless you are very sure. Now—" he looked at us intensely "—do you know which way you are going?"

We looked at each other apologetically and then at Thaddeus. I felt I was the most responsible because I had been here before and because I was the leader. "Honestly, Thaddeus, I hadn't thought. I'm sorry. But first I must hug Cat."

He waited in silence. I stroked Cat and hugged him—also in silence. After a time an idea forced itself on me against my wishes. It seemed impossible and yet it also seemed irresistible. "Thaddeus, the thought that has come fiercely into my head is that we should climb up and out of this mountain, and beyond it we would find the Worms."

"And how would you get out?"

"Well—with your magic—and I remember that toward the top of this huge opening there was a path—narrow and dangerous—but I believe it led out and down into Beast places, and the place of Volcanos."

"And Worm places maybe," said Scuro unexpectedly.

"Yes, Scuro. And Worm places maybe. Thaddeus, do you think I'm crazy to have this idea?"

He closed his eyes for a few minutes. "No. Although I see no path at our level—but if you look up toward the opening you can just make out—or at least I can just make out—a shelf that slants up toward the hole."

We all stared upward. Finally, Zeke said he could make it out, and Tusks—with his new glasses—could see it, he thought. I saw it also. Scuro couldn't. IstHer could, she was sure.

"So how do we get up there?" Zeke raised the relevant question—as he often did.

"Well," said Thaddeus in his slow fashion, "Somehow, with someone's help, we'll have to get one of the climbing webs up there. Dear me, if only Arachne was with us. But she isn't. Or some other good climber."

"What about me?"

We all turned our faces to Domar's window. There sat Antic, looking a bit like a bird in its moulting season. "I may be little and unimportant and forgotten," he said sadly, "except when messages need to be taken, but I could—if anybody trusted me—I could fly up to the hole and fasten a climbing web . . . " and his voice trailed away.

"Oh, Antic!" Thaddeus used his father-oracle voice. "Antic, of course you are trusted! You are the messenger for the Guardians. And of course you can carry some webbing up there. You are the one to do it. We did not want to ask you because you had orders from Them. Thank you, Antic."

I felt that Thaddeus overdid his speech. But Antic was pleased, I could tell.

"Thank you, Thaddeus. I am happy to serve. I will need a helper, though—as I'm not Arachne—I'll need someone to tie the web to something. So I will ask if IstHer trusts me enough to ride on my back and to fasten the web securely."

I was amazed and delighted at Antic—and it was evident that Thaddeus was also. And so they went—IstHer straddling Antic, clutching the roll of incredibly fine and strong web-ladder and, as they took off, IstHer gave one more "Whee!"

We watched Antic with his passenger and freight circle as they rose in the enormous vault. For a few minutes I could see them clearly. Then they became a blurred speck etched against the sky hole. Then we couldn't see them.

"Are they all right, Thaddeus? Can you see them?"

"Be still," he said. "My magic needs silence. Do be still."

We all obeyed. I stroked Cat and tried to concentrate on them being safe and fastening the web. That was all I could do. No one spoke—not even Domar. We waited forever, it seemed to me. The great stone cave was silent. Nothing moved or changed. No one looked at anyone because we were all staring up into the emptiness.

"There they come!" It was Zeke who spotted them first. "You can just see them—they're drifting down—why so slow? Oh, I'll bet they're following the bottom of the web as it falls—yes, they are! Can you see them? Over there! Over there!"

"Zeke, my boy, a little quieter, please." Thaddeus was not angry. Just cautious. "All of us be quiet."

Before long we could see Antic with IstHer on his back, floating around in circles near the walls below the sky hole. Slowly they came. Then we could just make out the web as it floated down. The nearer that mouse, bird, and web came, the more it was like a great waltz. When IstHer came drifting past on Antic I waved. She waved down to us and up to where the delicate web was still unrolling. And then, before we knew it almost, the web was before us. Thaddeus put his pot on the web's end, and then all of us welcomed IstHer and Antic joyfully.

"It's very exciting up there!" IstHer was her usual self. "What you see—even with so little time—is space—and desert—and several pointed mountains with holes in the top—like this one—and far away a river. Oh it's exciting! And scary!"

"Why scary, IstHer?" asked Thaddeus.

"Well—because—because—it felt lost—and alone and empty, I guess."

As she spoke in her intense way I recalled that empty land that we had gone through when we were trying to stop the evil Beasts the last time. "You're right, IstHer. It is a lost and empty land—that is, probably empty of goodness. That's why we have to go there, I guess." I turned to Thaddeus. "Am I right, Thaddeus?"

"You are. I wish I could go with you five! But I'm more use here." He shook his salamander head. "Now then, let us get started. Stand before me, travelers."

We lined up in a row like schoolchildren—IstHer, me, Tusks, Scuro, Zeke—each of us carrying portions of gear. Thaddeus gazed at us like a father, and Domar's "eye" was toward us so she could see us.

Thaddeus, nearest Domar's "eye," smiled at us. "You are ready to go. After all are up, drop the net and I'll put your supplies in it. Tusk, you are the biggest. Let me see if you can climb a net."

"Well, I've never tried—and I'm a bit scared—but here goes!" He walked firmly to the delicate and almost invisible net, gazed at it a brief time, and then, with a sigh, put his large feet on it and began to pull his awkward body upward. It was moving to watch his courage and tenacity as he labored up the great stone wall. He was helping us all to risk ourselves. Slowly, he went up the rock face. When at last he reach the top, pulled himself out, and dropped the webbing, we all untightened our muscles and sighed with relief.

"Gosh, he's terrific!" exclaimed Zeke.

"He is," said Thaddeus. "Now you, my boy. Put the tent beside the cart. They will come up later." Zeke, as I had expected, clambered up the net with east as if he enjoyed it—which I felt he did.

As I walked to the net, Scuro stepped forward. "Maris, I don't have claws like Tusks has—or IstHer—or fingers like you have. I've *got* to be with you. But how?"

"My friend," said Thaddeus, "I understand. It would be the same with me. What we'll do is to classify you with the tent and the cart, and pull you up in my magical nets. So don't worry. Just wait."

"Thanks, Thaddeus. I'll wait."

I went to Cat and said, "Take care of Domar and Molasses." He rubbed me a "yes." I didn't really like the climb, but I took hold firmly, clenched my teeth, grabbed the web-net, and began to climb. I knew I must not look down or up but just go hand over hand—with feet following—until I got there. It seemed endless—that climb. I didn't look down—just kept my eyes on my hands and feet and the webbing. Then Zeke's hands grasped mine and pulled me onto the slanting rock shelf.

After Tusks and Zeke greeted me and let me rest a minute, I told them about Scuro. We knew Thaddeus would get it all organized, so we waited for some signal. The signal turned out to be IstHer suddenly popping over the edge into our company, saying, "Scuro's all wrapped in the web and we're to pull slowly—so he doesn't bounce and get sick or bruised. Thaddeus is helping from below with some magic. Pull right away. That's what Thaddeus said."

So we pulled—and to our surprise Scuro came up as light as IstHer would have been. "Wow! That was some trip! Give me a minute to get my weight back. Thaddeus said to count to sixty and I'd be normal again." We waited until he said, "OK. Now we drop the webbing and pull up our stuff." We did. Two more pullings and everything was with us, together with the webbing which now had to be rolled up. We stood looking at all our gear in some dismay. Down in the big cave it seemed little. Here it loomed large and unmanageable.

"Do we really need all this?" Zeke asked. "We can handle the webbing all right. But the other stuff will be awkward, won't it?"

"It does look like a lot, doesn't it," I said.

Suddenly Scuro spoke. "Oh, I forgot! In my dizzying trip up I forgot! Thaddeus put a magic package inside the tent. There are four magic prayersticks, he said, and several packages of black powder. He said Maris would know how to use them to make things get small and then large again—only when it was necessary, he said. Also he said that a large tent and a proper cart would frighten Worms and Beasts, he was sure."

"Are you saying, Scuro, that for traveling out of here and down into desert or wilderness or whatever, we can make our gear small? And then enlarge when needed?"

"Of course, Maris. So let's get ready to go."

The rock ledge was not large, but we all were there, and I could see there was room for magic. Surprisingly, I did remember the sequences Thaddeus had taught me, and with only one or two mistakes and retries I managed to reduce the tent and the cart to small enough sizes to pack them on Tusks comfortably, along with the webbing.

"So how do we go now, Maris?" Zeke asked. "You and Tusks only, I guess, have been here. Maybe Scuro?"

Tusks and I looked at each other. "I'm not sure," I said. "But—yes—I remember the mountain with no top and how hard it was to face it—and cruel Beasts—and Grey Worms—I guess this is like that.'"

Scuro said, "I don't remember it. Maybe I was chasing Beasts."

"I believe that if we can get out of here—at the top—we'll be near the volcanic craters. But it looks very, very difficult. So let's start and see if we can make it."

It was a rough slope, fairly steep, slanting toward the sky hole, which seemed an endless distance away. After only a short while every one of us—excepting IstHer—was exhausted. And also we seemed not to be getting anywhere.

At last Zeke stopped. "We've got to rest. All of us. We don't seem to be climbing at all. Or hardly climbing. As I look up, the hole seems miles away."

We all stretched out to get our breath. All except IstHer, who wandered about happily poking into cracks and crevices in the rock, and as I was watching her she disappeared. I got to my feet and was about to call her when she reappeared and scampered over to us and said, "I just met a friend, really a cousin, he says. Because he's a bat. He knows Ears, he says. He'll show us a shortcut, he says. Come and follow me. Come on, it's not far. Come on! It's safe!" And she vanished. I followed, putting a hand out to touch the rock side. I could hear mutters and scratches behind me, so I knew my comrades were following. Soon we came into a wide and dimly lit place—really a huge rock fissure open to the sky by way of a small round opening above. In the dim light I could make out movements on the walls. Of course! Bats! A bat chamber! And before I could say anything IstHer leaped to my right shoulder and something also landed on my left shoulder.

"Meet Twilight," said IstHer. "He's a cousin of Ears. He will lead us out."

Having had a close friendship with Ears, I was delighted to see the odd little bat face looking at me from my left. "I'm happy to meet you, Maris," it said squeakily. "And all Ear's friends. And we all hate the Worms. And we will help where we can. And I will lead you out into a safe place for a camp after you met Big Bat."

"Thank you! Thank you, Twilight. Lead us wherever. We trust you, and we would be honored to meet Big Bat."

We went carefully through the large bat chamber. The walls were rippling with bats. Obviously night had not yet come outside. Suddenly, Twilight spoke from my shoulder. "Stop please. Big Bat is here to greet you."

"Where, please?"

"Turn and look to your right."

I stopped and looked past IstHer, and on the cave wall just beyond my shoulder was an albino bat, about half again as big as Ears or Twilight. I moved nearer, peering into his droll, clown-like face. I remembered Thaddeus's instruction of long ago: "Maris, when you meet a new inhabitant of the Great Land, curtsy." So I curtsied to Big Bat, then leaned toward him and whispered, "I am very honored to meet you, sir."

"We are also honored to have all of you, Ears's friends, in our cave briefly. Because we also believe the Worms must be encountered and changed, we are giving you all the help we can. We will tell you what we know, and also some of our ideas."

So we were guided into a large vaulted side chamber with a high ceiling and a sky hole through which a few bats came and went busily. In the center was a large round rock on which Big Bat rested, head down, peering at us. He was surrounded by eight smaller bats—a sort of honor guard, I decided.

"Maris and company—all of you together—we will tell you what we know as night wanderers and we will work with you where we can. Can everyone hear?" We all nodded, and the walls rippled with nodding bats. "All right. Let me be brief. We have learned in our night wanderings that on the back side of this volcanic upthrust, there are several smaller ancient volcanic mountains—with no tops—along the edge of the barren desert wilderness. Ears told me that some of you had been there some time in the past. Anyway, several of those dead volcanoes have been taken over by Worms. And now Beasts are using the Worms as slaves to dig out and enlarge the underneath caverns. It is clear to us, as we explore this area at night, that the Beasts—present company excepted—are trying to build an empire from which they will rule the Great Land. The courage of you, Maris, and your comrades past and present, saved the Great Land before. And now, it seems to us, you have again been summoned. And we Bats are here to serve you."

I was deeply touched by Big Bat's courtesy and concern. Such little darklings bats were. I loved them all. "We thank you. We are more than pleased to be able to work with you, and to work for you. Tell us what you believe is the best way we can help."

The rock chamber grew very silent. I turned to our Beast. "Tusks, you know more of this than I do. What is your opinion?"

He remained silent for a brief thought-time. Then he began to speak in a soft but sure voice. "Big Bat, all of us Beasts who care for the Great Land—and there are very many of us—are convinced that if we could do something to the Worms, like if we could pen them up and train them to do useful things—they are not bright, but could be taught—if we could separate them from the negative, destructive Beasts, well, maybe the negative Beasts could be educated. As I and my Beast friends were educated in the past."

"Tusks," said Bat, "You have helped me—and all of us here—to see somewhat more clearly. The question now is, how to proceed. How can we help all of you to turn power into a shared peace for the Great Land? Can you tell us?"

I fancied I could hear the heartbeat of silence. And then of all things to break that silence was the high small voice of IstHer—coming from my shoulder into the bat chamber like a bell rung under the sea. "It is lovely as nightfall and golden as day—what we must gather in the dark, what we must save and heal, what we must fling into the light—not power but our caring—neither rage nor laughter but a golden river of peace—" Her voice stopped suddenly.

I reached to touch her tiny body, and folded my fingers gently around her. I could feel her paws trembling. And I whispered, "Little IstHer, you are our voice."

After a rich stillness—as if each of us in this charged rock room was bringing an individual self to solve the matters at hand—Big Bat spoke.

"It is clear that the small is weightier than the large, that the stillness is richer than the loud, that the question is more accurate than the reply, and that caring is stronger than hate. In the face of the angry Beasts we are small, still, questioning, and caring. These must be our weapons. I request that someone—perhaps more than one someone—will memorize the words that IstHer spoke. Can IstHer repeat it for us?"

I whispered and asked her. She was no longer trembling, and she nodded an eager "yes." Her small voice was more bell-like than before, and fuller, as she sent the words into the dusk of the chamber: "It is lovely as nightfall and golden as day—what we must gather in the dark, what we must save and heal, what we must fling into the light—not power but our caring—neither rage nor laughter but a golden river of peace."

After a long space of silence Big Bat said, "Our recorder bat has written this down. It will be carved into stone *outside* our cave so that all creatures who pass this way will see it. But now our travelers must be sent on their journey."

So we followed in and out of the convolutions of the bat cave until we reached a narrow fissure going in a downhill slant—not too steep, but definitely descending. "This is narrow, I know," said Big Bat. "But it is safe, will bring you out at a place where you can see, probably—unless the Worms are at their smoke screens—some of Volcanic Mountain behind you, and the Place of Them, unless the mists are heavy. There is some desert and some wilderness. And may I suggest that you make your place inside this narrow fissure with your tent—and whatever else you have. You can go in and out, and yet you are hidden. And we can watch over you. So go as well as you can on IstHer's golden river of peace. Goodbye."

He was gone. We were alone, totally alone, going carefully over the stony ground downhill. It was rough. The walls were very high. I stumbled from time to time and I could hear Zeke stumble. Scuro and Isther were soft-footed and Tusks's feet were clawed but almost soundless. For some long time we proceeded so—gently and carefully. Suddenly, IstHer, who had been trotting ahead of the procession of us, rushed back. "We're at the bottom! We're at the bottom! Come and see."

We did. And standing wordlessly, at the opening of our narrow canyon we saw the top of the Place of Them, the misted mountain, the desert lands, and the cones of two volcanic mountains. And also plumes of grey smoke rising from the ground.

Chapter 12

Light was pushing back the night and displaying the stark bareness of this corner of the Great Land. It was wonderful to see in the distance the heights where the Old Ones and the Guardians were. It was equally terrible to see dirty smoke coming from innumerable volcanic craters, and also to realize that somewhere in the wilderness of craters and sand and power-lusting Beasts and stupid Worms were Quatro and his lady. How could we ever find them? And if we did, how could we free them?

Zeke spoke into the silence. "It's scary, really scary. So what can we do, Maris? But there must be ways of getting at both Beasts and their slaves."

"Tusks, what creative ideas do you have?" I asked. "Tell us what you think would be ways to get to them." He brought his left rear foot up to his frayed left ear. "Well," he said, scratching awkwardly. "Well, I'd guess that—well, Worms are easier to change than Beasts. And if we can change some Worms over to our side—maybe by being nice and kind to them—we could use them as helpers. They're being pushed around so much by the enemy Beasts that I should think they'd be ready to revolt. Of course it will take come convincing."

"How should we get started?" Zeke asked. "What are your ideas, Tusks or Maris or Scuro? All of you have been here before."

"I have been trying to plan how we can convince a Worm to go with us," Tusks said. "They're so used to being pushed around, flattered and pushed around—flattery rewards push and push is payment for flattery, it seems to me. Now—if we could not flatter and not push, but just ask for something and say "thanks a lot" if something is done—maybe then the poor Worms would have a different feeling about themselves. Maybe they would become honest and helpful."

"Tusks," said Zeke, "that is a real good idea. Maris, I think Tusks is right—except that first we'll have to be sure to find Worms who have not been so very harshly taught that they're afraid to trust anyone."

"Right," Tusks replied. "But there are ways to tell if you're trusted by a Beast—especially if you're a Beast yourself."

"What ways?"

"Well, if the Beast—let's say me—if I meet someone I don't know, and I have a sense that someone is afraid of me—not because of me but because of others like me—well, then, I try to be very honest and say who I am and that I am not mean and I don't intend to boss the someone, or hurt it, or insult it, and that I only want to be a friend."

"Would it trust you, Tusks?"

"Well—sometimes it does, and it might again if I was really honest and if I said what was true. It's happened. Could happen again, I guess."

"And what about us non-Beasts? Could I get them to trust me? Could Zeke? Or Scuro? Or IstHer?"

"I can't say. You or Zeke might have a harder time because you are so far from Worm-ness. Scuro is closer to Beasts, and IstHer is so—so well, so—whatever it is she is—that she might charm them."

"So perhaps Scuro and IstHer would be best? Is that what you're saying?"

"I'm not sure. Perhaps Scuro and I—walking along together—with IstHer riding on one of us—and, with Thaddeus's glasses on, I can know what's happening all the time—anyway, it feels exciting. And possible."

"It still feels a bit vague to me, Tusks. If you were going out alone into this deserty land to catch Worms, what would you do? Describe it."

He scratched his right ear with a rear foot. "Well—I guess first I'd walk to where smoke was coming out of the smaller volcano—like over there—" and he pointed to a little crater several hundred feet away "—and I guess I'd go to the opening and I'd say, well, something like, 'I'm a Beast looking for a decent Worm.' And I'd smile and say, 'I will pay well, and I am kind'—and then I would wait and see what the Worm would say to me. And if it said, 'No,

I'm working for a Beast already,' I'd say I'd be a better Beast. It might hear or it might not."

We stood silent for a time, peering out from our narrow bat canyon, watching the dribbles of dirty smoke coming out of the small volcanic cone.

"Well," said Scuro at last, "I say we should try it—Tusks and IstHer and me."

"I'm ready!" said IstHer. "It sounds exciting! Who shall I ride on?"

"Try me first, IstHer," said Scuro, "because Tusks is our leader and has to say and do the proper things. And we'll be followers. And you can hide in my hair—and you couldn't in Tusks' hair."

Like an enormous flea IstHer landed on Scuro's back at his wooliest spot near his shoulders and buried herself there, her pert pointed little head peering out from behind one of his ears. "Let's go!" she squeaked. "I am ready! Whee!" She sounded like a little idiot—but she was to be trusted as a remarkable being.

"Shall we go?" Tusks asked us.

I looked at Zeke and he looked at me, both of us, I guess, hoping that the other would decide. So at the same moment we said, "Yes, I guess so." Tusks, Scuro, and IstHer were about to depart when Zeke said, "We'll go back and get our tent and stuff set up. And get Thaddeus's magic in order so as to be ready for anything. And, do each of you have Thaddeus's magic feathers?" They nodded.

Soon they were walking calmly out into the desert toward a small, smoking, volcanic cave. I longed to stay and watch, but I knew better. From past experience I learned that it was wiser to move in a creative direction and to act rather than watch and wait. So we reluctantly but firmly went back into the narrow-walled canyon. With the help of Thaddeus's magic I did make it work so as to enlarge our tent and we got inside it. With some other magic I arranged for some food—poor stuff, but we munched it all anyway.

Zeke and I hadn't been alone together since we had so precipitously been dropped into the Great Land. So we sat near each other and nibbled at the magic food. It appeased our hunger but did not satisfy the deeper places.

"Are you worried for our comrades, Zeke?"

"I'm trying not to be. Are you?"

"Sort of like you, I guess. I'm not. I am. I wish I knew where they are. I wish I was with them. Should we try to call Thaddeus?"

"Not yet. Let's wait a while longer. When it gets darker—" I looked up, and the slit of sky above the narrow gorge was still a bright silver. "—when it gets darker I'll bet our bat friends will go out and bring us some information. Let's try to rest a while so as to be ready."

We both stretched full length in our tent in a position where we could see out the door flap. I dozed off although I was sure I wouldn't, and was wakened by Zeke shaking me and saying, "Twilight is here, Maris. Twilight is here with words from Ears and Scuro and IstHer. It is dark now."

I sat up quickly. "Are they all right? Our comrades, I mean? Are they? Are they?"

Zeke patted my hand. "Take it easy, Maris. Wake up and listen to Twilight."

Zeke and I sat close together with Twilight clinging to Zeke's knee as he talked.

"I have several things to tell you. First, Ears brought a message from Them saying that They are watching all Beast movements—as well as knowing what we are doing here—and They believe the Beasts are more aggressive than ever, but also more disorganized. They said not to risk too much. Perhaps Arachne will come to join you here. Second, as best as we can tell, your friends Tusks, Scuro, and Isther have moved into a small crater and have hired the resident Worm to work for them. So far it seems to be safe. The Worm is young and is open to new ideas. A little brighter than most Worms. So your comrades are all right. Third, they said that there is another small crater nearby—and as of now no being is in it—so maybe you two could sneak out and get in it."

"What do we do with our tent and cart?" I asked.

Twilight said, "Leave it. We will guard it—even move into it while you are away. We will care for Arachne if she comes. And all bats have chosen to join forces with all defenders of the Great Land. So know that in all dark hours we will bring our force to aid you."

"How can we—two human beings—get to the crater? We can't see at night. We don't look like Beasts or dogs or mice or Worms."

"We bats are here to guide you. I—Twilight—and a bat comrade, Squeek—we will sit on your shoulders and lead you. Are you ready?" After a bit of fumbling for our jackets and our magic feathers from Thaddeus, we walked out into the darkness.

Our guides whispered instructions in their squeaky voices. Zeke and I stumbled along in the night over the uneven ground of the narrow canyon. It was a relief to emerge into the wider wilderness land because under the wider sky there was a sense of space above and beyond us. I could see the black outline of the Mountain of Them against the less-black sky. I could also see a dim flicker from a distant crater, evidently occupied.

"Look, Zeke! Do you see that light?"

"Yes. What is it? I mean—where and what is it?

"I believe it is where your friends are," said my Bat guide. "They must be busy at beast education. I'll go over and see. You two stay here with Squeek. I will return quickly." And he was gone.

I touched Zeke's arm for reassurance. He patted my hand, saying, "It's all right, Maris. I'm here and Squeek is here. Let's relax and wait."

It seemed a very long time. I knew it always seemed long in the dark—and knew also that it was never what it seemed. But knowing and feeling are not the same. I had learned that during my first visit to the Great Land. So I tried to relax and wait. It became longer and longer, and more and more uneasy, and I was just about to move when Twilight was on my shoulder saying, "They want you to come. No time for questions. Come!"

Stumbling and somewhat frightened by Twilight's urgency, we followed his direction. He was careful and very calm, but he made us go as fast as we could over the uneven ground. As we neared the crater with the light coming from its top, Twilight and Squeek said to stop.

"Now," said Twilight. "Now you go through a sort of tunnel—right beside you in the ground and it's not long—and you crawl a bit and come up into the place where your friends are—and their Worm. So right by your feet is the tunnel. Off you go. And we will keep in close communication."

Zeke and I knelt on the ground and felt over it and we found the tunnel almost simultaneously. "Let me go first, Maris. I'll enlarge if it's needed. And also watch for problems and dangers."

"Thank you, Zeke. But I've been in many tight places in the Great Land, and I can make my way."

"I know it. But can't you let me? Please?"

So I let him. I held onto the bottom of his jacket as we crawled through the tunnel. I wondered if our comrades had crawled in this way. It was difficult to imagine Tusks going in. Scuro—yes. IstHer—of course. I felt a deep fear rising in me. Zeke must have sensed it because he stopped and whispered, "We're OK. I see light ahead. It's a tight squeeze but we'll make it. I'll go in and pull you through."

I let go of him unwillingly. He disappeared, and in just a brief moment I saw a hole with light coming through. And then Zeke's hands were there to grasp my hands, and he pulled me through the hole. I was soon sitting on an earthen floor, in a good-sized earthen room with a small fire burning in the middle of the floor. Beside the fire—or, more accurately, around the fire—were a smallish Worm, with IstHer stretched out comfortably on its back, Tusks—who winked at me and said "Good evening, my friends, we were hoping for a visit" —and Scuro, who put his nose in my hand and said, "We're glad you came."

It was a strange circle of creatures in the glow of a small fire whose smoke went straight up and out a small crater. Probably one of the ones we'd seen. I bowed to the Worm—as I knew Tusks wanted to have a good relationship with it. He introduced us.

"This is Annel. He says that was an ancient name in his family history. Annel, this is Maris," and Tusks bowed to me, "and this is Zeke," and he bowed again.

"I am glad to meet you, Annel. Very glad." I said.

"And I also," said Zeke, bowing.

IstHer broke the politeness and formality by a giggle from her place on Annel's back. "He's really nice and comfortable to be with, and exciting when he ripples. Please ripple, Annel."

And he did indeed ripple, sending waves along his body from head to tail, with IstHer giggling happily as she rose and fell. "That is enough now." Tusks sounded firm and both IstHer and Annel stopped playing. IstHer came and greeted us soberly. Then Annel lifted his front end and bowed to us.

Tusks winked at us. "They are already becoming good friends. She is teaching Annel how to do things like cleaning a room, like keeping a fire, like being friendly. Annel is learning well. His parents abandoned him and went away. Now, Annel and IstHer, it is time for you to go to the big room and do your learning."

IstHer climbed on Annel. Annel rippled away into another hole on the other side of the room.

Zeke and I hugged Tusks and Scuro in a rich reunion, all of us talking at once until one of us—I don't know who it was—maybe me—said. "Let's each group tell what has happened." Zeke and I told together of the bats and their helpfulness and the tent in readiness, and the report of the Old Ones from the Place of Them. Tusks was excited by the possibility that Arachne might join us.

"Now, Tusks and Scuro, we need to hear from you." I could have let Zeke ask—but I felt I'd been at all this longer than he had.

"We have a good comrade in the young Worm, Annel." Tusks said. "He is intelligent and does not like what most of the older Worms are doing in joining forces with the evil Beasts. He and some of the younger Worms are working against the Beast-Worm alliance. We are soon to meet with some of the younger Worms in a secret place. They have copied IstHer's words from the stone plaque outside the Bat's Cave. We didn't know it had been put up until some young Worm memorized it and wrote it down, for their secret meeting place."

"When can we meet with them?" Zeke asked.

"I would guess it would be soon, from Annel's urgent excitement," said Tusks. And at that very moment Annel and IstHer came in through the hole through which they had excited. Both of them seemed tired but pleased with the world.

"How is the learning?" Tusks asked.

"Good." IstHer replied. "Annel is very smart and learns fast. Annel knows more and more words from the language of the Great Land. Annel says Worm words are very old and very limited and very awkward."

Annel lay stretched out, head lifted high—as high as Scuro's back. "Almost I say IstHer's words. Not know yet meanings. Nice. Can read many. Many. She good to teach. This night we meet others. Like me. See where can help. Will come back." And he undulated silently out the hole through which he had come.

When we were alone Tusks asked us to listen carefully to his proposal for next steps. "I'm not making decisions for anyone. Each of us must give opinions individually and freely. But we need to gather some ideas and make some plans or we will not be any help to the Great Land. The Old Ones and the Guardians are ready—but we must also be ready. What thoughts have you had, Maris and Zeke? Tell us as briefly as you can." I suddenly felt unhelpful. We hadn't talked plans. The only ones had to do with the bats, their caring for our tent and cart, and of course their watching over us, their bringing messages. I realized that we needed them more with us.

"Now I know something, Tusks. I believe we need a closer relationship with our bat friends. With Ears bringing word to the bats from the Place of Them, I think we should have at least one bat with out company all the time."

"I agree," replied Tusks. "How can we ask for one?"

"Let me go back out through the tunnel," said Zeke. "If a bat is near, I'll bet it will see me and come to me. They said they'd keep in touch. Is it all right if I go, Tusks? I'll be careful."

"Go, Zeke—but do it cautiously. If a bat friend comes bring it in, please."

"Yes, Tusks. I'll do all you say."

When Zeke entered the tunnel we all became silent and uneasy. Before we expected it we heard Zeke's voice. "Here we come, Squeek and I." And Zeke emerged with Squeek riding on his shoulder.

"He was fluttering around outside to see if he could be able to locate us. All the bats wanted to know. And to help where they could."

Squeek was introduced to everyone whether he knew them or not, and in the midst of the excitement Annel came in from his tunnel. Worm and Bat were startled but were friendly. Squeek said he had things to say. Annel said he did also. We laughed, and Tusks said, "Let's sit in a circle and hear from each one—Squeek first because he is the guest."

So Squeek sat on Zeke's shoulder and told us what he knew. "First, the messages from the Place of Them by way of Ears are that Arachne is being brought to your tent in the canyon, and that all of your Beast comrades are en route to meet you in the canyon. Second, the enemy Beasts are gathering—very slowly—in the old Beast Stockade across the river from this part of the Great Land."

"I remember that," Scuro remarked. "Dimly."

I remembered it also, with a shudder of fear. "What a monstrous place! It belonged to evil Beasts then, and so they're taking it again! It's terrible!"

"And what is your message, Annel? Please tell us so we can decide what must be done."

"Yes, Tusks sir." Annel spoke slowly. "Worm friends say work with us. Scared. Want to. Want to see what is. Willing."

"Good, Annel. We will meet very soon. Please wait."

"Yes, Tusks. Will wait. Thank you." He curled up. IstHer settled on his relaxed body and said, "They're ready to join us—Annel's friends, I mean. They're great."

"Yes, I hear you, IstHer." Tusks sounded authoritative in a good sense. He turned to Squeek. "Can you tell us how Arachne is being brought? And when she might arrive?"

"Yes sir. I can tell you. You may not believe it. She is being brought riding in one of her own webs which is being carried by six strong bats. Ears is one of them. I don't know which others. I wouldn't be surprised if Big Bat was one of them because he is deeply concerned to save our Great Land."

"Well, well, I like that picture very much! Really I do! Arachne bouncing about in her own web with six bats in the dark of night! I wish I could see it! Oh my, how I wish I could!" And he chuckled deep down in his warm Beast self. "Now then, let's make room for Arachne's arrival. Zeke, Scuro, each of you take a tunnel and be sure it is clean and ready. Maris, can you do anything to make this room neater—even larger? It needs a feminine touch. And you, Squeek, will you be the outside watcher to let us know when Arachne arrives?"

We all got to work as best we could. There really was not much that could be done when inside a small crater But we did wipe away big spots of dust, and removed rocks. Actually, as I looked around it wasn't too bad. It was large enough. The sloping walls were russet-colored and warm. There were no chairs—but nobody had people chairs in the Great Land. We left the tunnel entrances clear and placed ourselves around the walls so the room actually seemed enlarged. And I recalled how, in my first time in the Great Land, I had fallen into Arachne's delicate and gentle room and had met the plump black spider, surrounded by yards of exquisite silken cloth, seated at a snow white wheel, spinning. She was forthright, honest, brusque, loving. She had become a Guardian in the Place of Them. And now she was being flown through the night by bats, once more to give herself to the Great Land's needs!

Suddenly, Squeek flew in. "She's coming! Make room!" And he flew out again. We all stood against the walls and back from the openings. Silence was present. Then we could hear rustles and squeaks, and at last Ears and another bat came through the tunnel into the firelit room, pushing and pulling in the roll of webbing to the middle of the room. IstHer was wiggling with excitement.

Arachne came from the tunnel with two of her feet brushing the dust off her gleaming black body. "Well, there are friends here! Maris. Scuro. Tusks. Ears. And others I do not know yet—but I will." I could not keep myself from her. But I made myself go to embrace her. "Oh, Arachne! How wonderful!"

"Now, now, Maris. Don't be sentimental!" She patted me with two of her feet-hands. "We've lots to do, my dear! Lots to do!"

Chapter 13

"Lots to do" from Arachne meant much more than it meant from anyone I ever knew. It meant that she had read IstHer's words carved in stone outside the Bat Cave, and she had to meet IstHer right away. It meant that she had to examine every inch of her incredible webbing to be sure it would hold heavy weights of ensnared enemies. It meant that she wanted Tusks and Big Bat—she had met them en route although Tusks wasn't one of the bearers—to get together and work out new and better ways to defeat the Beast-Worm alliance. She wanted a map drawn so she could see what places could be traps for enemy Worms and Beasts and how her webbing could be used.

On the other hand she was always relaxed, even under extreme pressures. She took time to talk with IstHer, asking how she liked Annel, and why. She took time to talk with Tusks at length, after a map had been drawn on the dirt floor showing at least tentatively where were the worst groupings of negative Beasts with negative Worms. From this talk came the Great Plan.

The Great Plan involved all of us and came out something like this: If all the collected "facts" *were* facts, it seemed as if the Beast-Worm alliance was spreading, but more in some directions than in others. All evidence pointed to a Beast-Worm cooperation in the borderland of wilderness desert, where existed many craters— much larger and farther from the river and forests than where we were.

"Maris, do you remember the Barrier of Nothing from the last time you were here?"

"Yes! Of course! It is the edge of wasteland! We must be almost in it now. And—oh yes, our tunnels went from Beast Volcano to Underground Orchard. Does that tunnel still exist? And the orchard? And the Lake of Reeds? Do they, Arachne?"

She thought quietly. Then she spoke. "I cannot be sure what paths still exist—and if they do, in what condition they are. In the beginning all places were livable. There was not a Barrier of Nothing, no Beast Stockade, no evil Worms. There were no hatreds and jealousies. But at some period a large piece of anger was dropped into the Great Land from an unknown source. From then on there were more and more evils and hostile acts. The terrible Beast Stockade was the worst—as you remember well, Maris. Whether the underground orchard and the Lake of Reeds are still there and useful, I do not know. But we will find out. The River, I believe, still flows between the Place of Them and the wilder places—and where the Beast Stockade is."

For a time we sat in silence. I closed my eyes and could see only darkness. And then to my intense surprise I saw before me the carved wooden statue of Red, the gentle loving Ant who died defending the Great Land in that first visit. And I saw in my inner darkness the glowing Ant with his sword held high, and I said the unforgettable words of Red before he was killed, 'I'll do what I must." And I cried.

At last Arachne's voice brought me back. "Maris, dear Maris. We hear Red's words, 'I'll do what I must.' They are good ones for each of us to remember and to repeat many times. For Red, and for the Great Land. So, let us begin to lay our plans—if indeed we have any. Perhaps you, Tusks, are the one to begin."

Tusks bowed. "Thank you, Arachne. First, I want to remind us all that, according to Bat reports, our Beast comrades are on the way to join us. I presume Bat friends are helping and guiding them. Also, Annel wants us to meet with some of the younger Worms who want to change and to be on our side. From the young Worms we can learn much, I am certain. From our Beast friends we will have all the information we need. And our Bat comrades are loyal and hardworking. My suggestion is that while we await the others we could have Annel and his Worm comrades tell their concerns."

We all agreed and IstHer went to get them. Very soon in our small crater room there were five young Worms—each curled up, head on coils—five bright faces looking at us with their lidless eyes. IstHer sat beside them, her face turned to them. "Tell them, Annel—your new friends here, I mean—tell what you and your comrades want or hope for."

Annel cleared his throat, looked at us shyly, smiled at his Worm friends. "Well—your words not easy for me—Tusks, sir. I try. My friends not speak your words—are try learn. They want learn—and go same way. To help Great Land. Not hurt. You tell. We hear. We help."

Tusks bowed to the Worms. "Annel, I will tell you, and you tell your friends in their language—until they learn ours—how you can help. First of all, help us to understand why the older Worms want to join with the bad Beasts. Why do Worms want to be cruel and hurtful? Why do they want to destroy and kill? Ask your comrades. Then tell us." For a time we sat quietly, listening to the strange and rippling language of the young Worms. They obviously were concerned with the questions and were struggling with them. At last Annel turned to Tusks. "Sir, we say what know. Know older Worms paid by Beasts to be mean. Not understand why. Poor. No food. So say yes to Beasts. Not happy, but can eat now. Not happy. Annel happy. Friends like. Will help. Thank you, Tusks. Also others."

"Annel, we want you and your friends to be with us, to be a part of us. We need you. Tell big Worms we give more than evil Beasts give. Great Land will be happy to have you and big Worms. Let us—"

Tusks's words were cut short by a sound from outside. Silence filled the room—silence and fear. More sounds from outside. What enemy was there? What could we do in this crowded place? Something small fluttered in. It landed on my shoulder, and a familiar voice piped out, "Maris. It's Ears. I've guided Duo and Twist to you. How can they get in, please?"

The room came alive and excited. Tusks said, "First, Annel and friends, please go other room. We call you. And I'll go out and show them how a Beast can wiggle through a Worm tunnel."

I had wondered how Tusks got in, but never asked. Now I knew, seeing him tuck himself together, head down, his front feet close to his body and his hind feet trailing behind as he disappeared into the hole. He was a wonderful and lovable being, ugly and very dear. If there were enough like Tusks, the Great Land could be saved.

We could hear sounds outside but could not make out the content, except once Tusks's voice said, "Not that way! *Head* first, *not* feet first!" Then came a long period of grunts and snorts and other assorted sounds and finally Duo's head and body struggled through the opening, and as he got to his feet Twist's head and body came in. At the end came Tusks. "You see," he said as he climbed out, "I was right. You both fit."

After greeting old friends, Tusks called us to listen. "Arachne, as the most important person here from the Guardians of the Great Land, perhaps you would speak regarding what comes next. Please."

Arachne surveyed the small room holding three Beasts, herself, me, Scuro, Zeke, Ears and IstHer. "Should we have our young Worm friends here with us?"

"I believe it would be better to wait. At least until we in this company have some ideas, Arachne. Do you agree?"

She nodded. "So, as briefly as possible, let me tell what the Old Ones and the Guardians believe is best."

Silence came over us. We all knew, I was sure, that danger and perhaps battles and wounds and terror lay ahead for us all. Who would be where and under what circumstances we could not know. And again I heard my dear Ant friend Red, before his death, saying, "I'll do what I must."

"What the Old Ones advise—not command, because They do not have all the facts—what the Old Ones advise is that we begin by learning everything we can from whatever Worms we encounter—and, most important, that we go to the lands where the Beast Stockade is and learn all we can of what is happening there, and what could be done to stop it. They also advise that we ally ourselves with the Bats as some of the bravest and best and most loyal citizens of the Great Land. I saw their territory, their splendid canyon—and your great tent—" she nodded at Zeke and me—"and by the way brought some food for us—and also believe they will be very, very needed in many ways. So I propose—*not* command, because it must be all of us deciding—I propose that we prepare to leave as soon as we can—almost all of us—to make our secret way to the Beast Stockade."

There was a deep silence.

My silence was flooded with remembering the horror of the Beast Stockade when I was imprisoned there, tormented by the Beasts, forced to sing. And Jetsam. I wondered what happened to him. And wondered if the Beast Stockade was still such a terrible place. Unredeemed Beasts had tried before and failed, but apparently they were growing stronger again and intended to win this time.

"What are your reactions? Are you willing? Unwilling? Please, let us decide!" Arachne's voice was urgent.

Tusks said, "Arachne, we are slow. But forgive us for it. We hear the needs of the Great Land and we wish to do all we can. Do you all agree?"

A chorus of "yes!" filled the little room.

"Very well." Tusks was clearly taking charge with Arachne. A strange pair indeed, but marvelous. They stood side by side—the round black spider and the ugly disheveled Beast—each of them incredibly trustworthy and brave. We applauded. They bowed.

"Now, all of you. One question." Tusks was very serious. "Should we take Annel? His grammar isn't very good yet, but his heart and will are. Arachne feels we need someone to speak Worm language."

Everyone agreed, and we sent Isther to get Annel. He was shy, embarrassed, excited, and thanked us over and over. "Friends stay. Ready if want. Very ready, all them."

"Very ready, all them" were good words to describe our unbelievable company. When we finally were all outside the crater—in a silver half-light that could be either day coming or day going—we gathered near Tusks. Of all remarkable things, Arachne had seated herself on Tusks's back. Duo and Twist were near. Scuro and Zeke stood beside them with Annel, and IstHer on Annel's back.

Suddenly, Ears said, "I must go back to Them. But Twilight is nearby. Don't you want a messenger along?"

"Twilight," said Tusks, "Wherever you are, join us."

From somewhere he came to us and settled on Duo's back.

"I can carry Zeke or Maris also," Duo said. "The other can ride Twist."

Zeke got on Duo's back with Scuro standing beside them. Twilight moved to Duo's head. I got on Twist, calling IstHer to come with us—but she said she was on Annel. So we moved off into the strange half-light—in the proper direction, we hoped—ten assorted beings daring to trust that they could help to save the

Great Land. For a time we moved hesitantly and continuously in this place of barren ground spotted with craters, with Arachne and her food bundles on Tusks in the lead. We had been inside long enough to be somewhat confused as to whether the light was coming or going. But at least we could see. Twice, in the first period of travel, we made a detour around craters that were smoking. "Never sure," Annel said. "Maybe safe. Maybe not. Be wise."

It was land that was becoming more and more raw and naked and without growing things. Soon we were stumbling along in rocky, sandy ground, very ungreen and empty, and it was difficult going, hard to walk on and very hard for Annel. Then the sky lightened, and all at once Scuro said, "I smell water ahead." And he started off.

"Scuro!" Tusks's voice was commanding. "Scuro, come back!"

He did as he was told—and I was glad for that. Tusks was not too hard on him, but made it clear that no one was ever to rush ahead. Not ever. We were a company and we were to act like a company. Scuro apologized.

Nonetheless, as we made our way up a small hill with shrubs on top, I could smell water, and the Beasts were raising their muzzles and sniffing. As we crested we could see the river, its silver twisting in its sandy channel, and beyond it we could see green forest. Tusks and Arachne stopped. The rest of us halted behind them. It was, despite the dangers that were ahead for us, a beautiful sight. Green lowlands in the river valley, blue and silver water glistening in the light—and beyond the river were the dark forests within which the Beast Stockade lay.

"So much that is benign and lovely surrounds the dark evils," said Arachne in a voice soft and filled with sadness. "But, my children, that is over and over how it is. Each time the evil comes forth again—as if it had to do so—each time the beauty of goodness comes forth to push back the dark negations. Let us keep that in our hearts as we go. Tusks and I believe that we need to proceed as fast as we can to the river and its cool rushes. Before the day wears out."

We all stayed very still after Arachne spoke. It was as if the morning air held her words about "goodness" and the "dark negations." I saw—I know I saw (though no one else saw)—a golden bird and a black bird fly across the river valley.

"Shall we go?" Tusks asked. Arachne nodded. And we moved out, bunched together "like a school of fish," in Twist's words. It was a good way to go because we were close enough to talk to each other and to be sure everyone was in sight. On this side of the river there was not a great deal of cover. There were low grasses on hillocks, sandy circles where water had once been, and twice en route we found tiny pools.

At one such pool we stopped to rest. Arachne asked me to open the food bundles. They were very dull but also very filling—so we went on toward the river.

As we neared the water I was almost overcome with memories of that past time on this river on our funny Starflower raft on which we fled the terrors of the Beast Stockade. It was a difficult time then—getting away from the monstrous cruelties of the Beasts—but we did! Oh, how I hoped we could do it this time! Just before we reached the river Tusks and Arachne stopped in a small grove of trees. In the center of it was a very deep still pool. We all gathered around the water and stood in a complete circle—Tusks, Arachne, me, Twist, Duo, Zeke, Scuro, Twilight, IstHer, and Annel. Each of us was alone. Even little IstHer stood by herself.

Arachne spoke. "We are near the danger now. And we must meet it as we can. Our task, as you remember, is to learn what is going on in the Beast Stockade. Do you know the way, Maris, when we cross the river?"

I felt back into time to that first fear-filled entry. "I believe I can find it, Arachne. I remember a long rise of jungle, and at the bottom of it a barren valley where all growth was dead. And in the middle was the terrible stockade. If we find the rise—well, then we'll find the prison—or whatever it is now."

"How do we get across the river?" Tusks asked. "Any ideas, anyone?"

"Sure," Scuro said. "Swim. Find a narrow place and swim."

"Not everyone can swim, Scuro," said Zeke.

"No problem. Non-swimmers can ride on swimmers."

Zeke grinned. "He's right. There's at least five of us can swim, I'll bet. Me, Scuro, Duo, Twist, Tusks. And we can each carry someone."

"I swim," said Annel. "Can't carry anyone. Under water lots. I swim."

"I can swim, too. If it's not too far." I was scared, but I knew I could do it if I was near someone.

"Twilight can fly across. Right?" said Zeke.

"Of course," he piped.

So Arachne and our food packages would ride on Tusks, and IstHer on Duo. And Twist said I could hold onto his back if I needed to.

For quite a long period of time we made our way as carefully and as quietly as possible along the river—keeping in the tree cover and being silent. When we reached a narrow stretch we stopped. Hiding ourselves in the thick growth we rested and planned. Zeke—as a good and experienced swimmer—made his suggestions.

"I don't think the water's too fast here. And it's not too wide. May be cold though. So we must move fast. I'll go alongside each swimmer—to help if need to. Maybe our leaders, Arachne and Tusks, first. Then Maris. Then IstHer and Duo. Twilight can fly. Annel can swim. Scuro can swim. And Zeke—me. That's everyone. So let me swim it first, just to see how it goes."

He tied his ragged shirt around his waist, his shoes around his neck by the shoelaces, and walked into the water. It didn't take him long to go over and back. He emerged wet and grinning. "Not hard at all," as he pushed his hair back. "And not too cold. OK, Tusks and Arachne."

One by one, Zeke shepherded the pairs and singletons across. I went alongside Scuro—his furry body giving me a sense of safety. And Zeke came behind me. It really wasn't too cold, but it was good to climb out and lie for a few minutes on the earth. And good to stop shivering. No one seemed too cold or too afraid. IstHer was so excited and elated about crossing on Duo that she had to be quieted.

At last Tusks turned to me. "Do you know how we go now, Maris?"

No one in this group had been here, except me. And—of course—Arachne! Who had helped our escape! But she had come another way and did not know the land by day. I looked about, trying to see if I could find the long slant of hill from which I'd first seen this awful place we were seeking. As I lay on the ground, drying out and gathering strength for whatever came next, my eyes picked up a place with taller trees. Were there trees that tall in this

forest? No. There had not been such tall ones here. So—of course
That was the rising hill!

"Zeke! Come with me! And the rest of you wait! We will be
back very soon!" I leaped to my feet, Zeke after me, and we struggled our way to the hill's top. We stopped, stunned and terrified at
what we saw.

"It's awful! Terrible!" Zeke whispered.

And it was. Below us, in a great clearing, was the Beast
Stockade. It was crowded with Beasts and Worms. The smell was
unbelievable. The stockade was not a prison, obviously, as all
gates were open. But Beasts roared and Worms screeched, and
Beasts fought Beasts and Worms wrestled Worms, and Beasts and
Worms were in mock battles with each other and blood was on the
ground.

A bell sounded. The noise and battling stopped. A very loud
Beast voice said. "Time for rest! Eat some flesh! All Worms doing
well—except for 13 and 29. Beatings for them. More practice when
bell sounds again."

Zeke and I looked at each other. "Zeke, it's awful! How can we
do anything to them? How can we help the Great Land?"

"Let's not give up, Maris. It is awful, I agree. But we must do
what those—Guardians—those that I don't know—except Arachne
and Ears—what they want us to. So shall I go and get them?"

I nodded. I knew I needed to watch what was going on because
I was more familiar with the Beasts and had lived in this horrible
place.

"Go and bring them. Very silently. I'll watch."

Zeke left. I watched. Beasts beat Beasts and Beasts beat
Worms. Beasts obviously were training Beasts and Worms to be
strong and brutal—and if they were strong and brutal they were
rewarded with food (and flattery, which was obvious). It was
unbelievable and horrible to watch. If they were not strong and
brutal they were kicked and beaten and finally carried off like
discarded rags.

Just as I saw my comrades coming up the rise, one of the Beasts
in the Stockade had done something wrong and was literally being
beaten to a pulp. It let out three tremendous screams before it collapsed and was dragged away.

I covered my face with my hands and dropped to the ground,
flooded with tears.

CHAPTER 14

The terrible brutality had stopped and the Beasts had moved away momentarily when my comrades came to where I was. I had been able to get myself quieted and in hand by that time and whispered to them what I had seen.

"I believe we should find a place more hidden than this hilltop," Tusks said.

"Yes," Arachne replied. "And immediately."

"Where?" said Zeke. "It all feels exposed wherever I look."

Isther spoke up. "Annel saw a Wormhole off in the woods as we came up. He said it looked big—and he could tell it had been abandoned." She turned to him. "Could we use it, Annel?"

He pondered. "I say yes—maybe. I see first. Yes?"

Tusks heard the question. "Yes, Annel. If you say you go softly. Yes?"

Annel understood. "Yes. I go—soft. Yes. Now?"

Tusks nodded. "We wait." As IstHer scampered toward Annel, Tusks said, "No, IstHer. He must go alone."

She stopped and came back, her little mouse face very solemn, her eyes blurred with tears. Scuro in one of his loving moods went to her, put his nose down to her, and said, "Climb on me, little IstHer friend, climb on me and be warm until Annel comes back." And she did, scampering up his nose onto his head and over to the shaggy fur of his neck where she settled quietly.

Very few sounds came from the Beast Stockade. The few that did come were roars or screams. Each time they came I was forced to clench my fists and clamp my jaws, else I would have shouted in rage and in fear. Annel's absence felt forever, which added to my rising emotions. I guessed others felt similarly, but we all remained voiceless.

Annel at last came in his rippling silence from the nearby woods. He moved up to us and whispered, "Is empty. Big. no smell. Is empty. Is hiding."

"You mean it is hidden?" Tusks asked.

"Yes. Hiding. Not see."

"How far? Go now?" Tusks said.

"Near. Go now when Beasts not."

"Very good. Go now, all us." Tusks was learning Worm syntax rapidly, I thought, with a health-restoring humor. "IstHer, stay with Scuro, please." Tusks was definite.

So we went following Annel downslope. It was easy for the first stretch—no rocks, no thickets or brambles, no Beast sounds. But then it changed. we had to go into a thick forest of close-growing and scratchy trees, then through a gravelly, rocky, slip-slide stretch, and at last onto a winding trail that led us quickly to the Worm cave. From only five or six feet away it couldn't be detected by any of us but Annel. He led us to it and we couldn't see it until he took us to the entrance.

"See," he told us, "See Worms once wise—good. Worms here some of first Worms. Not bad. Soft—too soft. Too lazy." He stopped talking and pondered. We waited. "Not bad. Too soft. Too easy to make—to make slave, you say?" Tusks nodded. "So—this place—early long back—more good than ones today. Go in now, Tusks, sir? Go in now?"

Tusks nodded, "Yes, Annel. We go in now. Good work, Annel. You take us."

So Annel, eager and proud to be one of us, rippled to the dark entrance. We all followed. When we stood before it the opening seemed to lead into a lightless cavern.

"Not dark when in," said Annel. "Many lightholes. See when in. Slow."

So we went very slowly into the dark. But before we could be afraid or dissatisfied we were in a large chamber—probably a cave to begin with—well shaped and smoothed, with small holes to the outside letting in soft light. Any scent in this room was of fresh air. There were no messy or unfinished places. Other rooms opened from this one, we could see. And each one seemed like the first—fresh and tidy and livable. I could hardly believe it, but I had to. All of us responded the same way.

Tusks spoke for us all when he said, "Worms good, Annel. Good makers. You good. They good. But like Beasts, some bad. Or scared. Or no food sometime. We glad to be here. We make our place now—here—so can watch Beast Stockade?"

Everyone said yes. We all set to work. Arachne put her wondrous webbing over all openings—to protect us from intruders. Then we came together in the largest central room, the room with no outside opening. For a time we sat in silence. It felt soft and tender and contained. At last Arachne spoke.

"We are very close to darkness and evil, children. Very close. It is too easy to absorb it. It is like foul air. So we must protect ourselves in every way we can. We need enough rest, enough food, enough shared work and love to keep us well. So let us prepare together."

We very soon became a web of preparation, with Arachne at the web's center. IstHer rode on Annel's back to find fresh food if possible. Scuro, Zeke, and I were to go to the lookout place to watch the Beast Stockade. Twilight went along to take any messages back. Duo and Twist, directed by tusks, stayed in the cave to explore the rooms and do what was needed if we were to live in them.

We had a dreadful and exhausting watch over the Beast Stockade. We saw Worms being rewarded for vicious behavior and Worms smashed for frightened behavior. We saw Beasts being quite obviously flattered for cruelty to stubborn Worms. And Beasts being beaten by Beasts for not being cruel to reluctant Worms—or for not flattering submissive Worms. We could quite clearly tell Beast elects from Beast rejects. It was not so clear when we tried to do the same for Worms.

Scuro made an important observation. "Beasts are horrible or they are wonderful. Ours are wonderful. Worms are gentle—brave, like Annel—or they are blown-up soft like most of those down there, poor creatures. If Beasts and Worms want to run the Great Land, let's stop them!"

"Let's go back to the others and see what's happening and get some food," Zeke said. I was hungry too. Twilight said he wasn't, and would just as soon stay and watch. Scuro wanted to stay with him. So Zeke and I went back.

On the return I saw—again—in the pale blue sky the black bird and the golden bird flying close together. I wondered what they could be doing.

When we arrived back at our cave we found that much had been done. Rooms had been explored and put in order by Duo and Twist so that each of us would have space—small but adequate. Such supplies as we had were stored, and IstHer and Annel had found a small stand of fruit trees and had made several trips there and back with many small yellow balls to store. And they would bring new supplies when needed. When Zeke and I told of what we had seen the room was very still for a time and gloom was definitely present.

"Now then," said Arachne, "let us not see only negations. I know they are there. But we must not drown in them. No saving can come from negations. The Stockade is a very terrible thing, certainly. But we must find how to learn more about it, and when we do that perhaps we can find ways to change it." She was silent for a time. We all were. "Does anyone have ideas?"

After a wordless time of waiting Scuro spoke boldly. "What if we sent word to the bats and asked for some of them to come to us to help us. Where is Twilight? We need him to take word to Bat Land."

"I'll go and get him," Scuro said. Scuro made a proper bow of his head and was gone. "I, for one," said Arachne, "believe Scuro is right. We need the Bats to help us."

"Very much agree," said Tusks. "Always positive. Queer little creatures, Bats—gentle, soft, intelligent. I can think of many ways they could certainly help to save our Great Land."

It was evident that Bat help suddenly struck us as imperative. Scuro returned with Twilight. He flew to Tusks's head and said, "For what am I wanted, please?"

Tusks bowed to Arachne. "My lady, you are from the Old Ones and the Guardians. You know their desires. Do please state your ideas." Arachne bowed to Tusks and Twilight together. "You know as well as I know that the Great Land is in danger. The Old Ones—and the Guardians—have bidden each of us in one way or another—some for the first time, some for the second or third time—to help the Great Land. Now we know that the problem is those Beasts who want to rule the Great Land for their own purposes. Their numbers are growing. Their power is growing. Do you have ideas as to how and where you could help?"

"Twilight, what could Bats do for the Great Land?"

He was small and insignificant on Tusks's head, like a piece of ragged blackish cloth. But his high voice was clear and sure. "Arachne, I believe that a horde of Bats, if they came by night into the Beast Stockade and flew into Beast hair, Beast bodies, Beast rooms—and if they squeaked and bit and swarmed—if they did that, Beasts would be afraid and would run in panic and Bats could harry them into the river or into great caves with your webs to catch them. We could do it. We really could."

"We were blind," said Tusks, "blinder than Bats, as it were—so blind as not to see what you Bats can bring. Your plan is very courageous! We thank you. We want your help to help us make plans to help the Great Land."

All of us came to little Twilight and we thanked him and stroked him. His funny little eyes—so poor for our kind of seeing—and his incredible ears—so far surpassing ours—made his face oddly lovable. By the time we had all said our feelings, Twilight was dozing on Tusks's head. So I lifted him very gently and put him on a high shelf where he could rest until nightfall.

We talked softly but urgently about Twilight's idea. We agreed that it was good. That a few hundred Bats could overwhelm a few Beasts seemed to be possible. In truth, I believe all of us felt it was a wonderful plan. And we talked softly so not to be heard by intruders nor to waken Twilight. And while we talked we nibbled at what fruit and leftover bits from Arachne's supply was there. It wasn't much and we put aside a few tidbits for Twilight.

When he wakened he said, "If I'm going to Batland—and I am, because how else can Arachne's plan become real?—I must go. It's quite a distance."

I lifted him down and put him on Tusks's head. "How long will it take, Twilight?" asked Duo.

"I'm not sure. If it's dark outside I can go fast. I'd be back here before light comes, I suppose. And hope! If Batland is willing we could be back before the light. Or at least at the edge of light. So—is it dark or not?"

Annel rippled to one of the openings in an adjoining room and rippled back. "Get dark, Twilight. Right time go."

Twilight was gone before any of us could speak.

"What do we most need to do, Tusks?" I asked.

"Well, I say we'd better get some rest first. If the Bats come—and I'm quite sure they will—we need to be all ready to get into the Beast-Worm battle at the Beast Stockade. So let's rest."

Very soon each one of us was resting somewhere in this familiar cave. It seemed more like a huge nest, with comrades curled up here and there and wherever. We fell into a deep, listening silence. After hearing various familiar coughs and snorts from various directions, I slipped into sleep. Or something like sleep. Whatever it was it didn't last long enough.

I roused to the sound of Tusks's voice saying, "Wake up! Everyone wake up! The Bats have come! Big Bat wants to speak with us! Wake up!"

We assembled as quickly as we could—somewhat dazed, not quite totally there, but ready. Twilight and Big Bat were hanging to a shelf of rock in the big room. Big Bat spoke. "Twilight asked us if we would come. We said of course. We need at least two nights to get the Beast Stockade confused and unorganized. We want to do upsets to the worst Beasts before light comes. I and a dozen others will go now and do some beginning work. All others must rest here over day to be ready for the night's attack." Big Bat looked around at us all.

Tusks bowed to Big Bat. "We are very grateful to you. The Great Land and the Old Ones, I am sure, are also grateful. This cavern is large, with many openings. You are free to use any part or all of it as you need. We welcome you and will help in any way possible."

"And I, as a Guardian," said Arachne, "I, too, welcome you for the Guardians. And offer you all my help, including my webbing, which might be needed by you."

"Thank you, friends. I and my small attack group will go and do what we can to upset things." He paused thoughtfully. "Is IstHer in your company, please?"

"She is," Tusks replied. "IstHer, will you come out?"

IstHer scampered across the floor and sat looking up at Big Bat.

"You, little mouse, are the one who said those words we had carved in stone outside our great cave. We honor you, IstHer, for your words, your courage—and we are pleased that you are distantly related to us. If you wish, we can take you on a Bat flight before we go home—whenever that is. But now the attack group must go and upset things. And as soon as we go, the rest will come pouring in—so get yourselves to one room only. We won't come into that one."

With a few squeaks the attack group left. And all of us scurried into the nearest room and Arachne put webbing across its entry. All we heard of the bats' arrival were faint high-pitched squeaks and the flutter of bat wings. Soon all was still.

Tusks wakened us when he saw the first light. I went to one of the Bats' rooms and peeked in. I could hardly believe what I saw and I never forgot it. Hundreds of bodies covered ceiling and walls with gray-black fur. It was like one great soft beast, stirring as if a breeze moved over it. I backed out carefully, not wanting to disturb this awesome being.

Tusks called us together briefly. He had several items to present, things that evidently he and Arachne had discovered. We needed to keep watch over the Stockade—especially since the Bat attack group had been there. We also needed to get more food supplies in case of urgent hunger. So Annel and IstHer would collect food. Arachne said she wanted to explore more deeply into this cavern where we were. "It goes much farther than we have seen, and we need it," she said firmly.

"I will go with you, Arachne," Tusks said. "Two are better than one."

"Thank you, Tusks. I am honored."

After those four set out on their tasks, I went with the remainder—Duo, Twist, Scuro, Zeke—to observe the Beast Stockade to see what effects, if any, had resulted from the first visit of the Bats' attack group. When we arrived at the top of the hill we went slowly and cautiously to the edge where trees hid us. Scuro, Zeke, and I lay flat and squirmed out between trees so we could see over. Several Beasts were on the ground outside the gate. A Worm lay half outside and half inside the gate. No sounds could be heard.

"What happened?" Zeke whispered. "Are they dead?"

"No," said Scuro. "they're breathing. I'll bet those dark spots on top of the big gate are bats—some of the attack group—and they've been diving on the Beasts and Worms, I'll bet! Must have given them a bad time!"

"And the Worm? Do you think it's dead?"

"No. I can see it is breathing. Worn out, probably. Better than being killed, anyway."

Duo and Twist came nearer. With Thaddeus's eyeglasses they could see clearly now—and from their expressions it was clear that they were pleased at what they saw. As Beasts themselves, they could feel into Beasts as none of us could. As Duo explained to us, "If you're a Beast, and you don't have Thaddeus, you can't see very well—and, if you can't see very well, you couldn't see small dark bats diving at you and probably biting and squeaking and clawing at your hair."

It was evident that whatever the Bats had done they had succeeded in frightening the Beasts for the time being. We had no idea what had gone on inside the Stockade, nor could we know what would happen when all the Bats descended on Beasts and Worms. We could do no more here.

"Let's go back," said Scuro.

I was absorbed in my thoughts as to what would come next, and how we could help the Bats, and could we ever find the old tunnels beyond the Stockade, and how could we free Quatro and his lady, and could Brawn and Potens as leaders of the evil Beasts be found and captured with the Bats helping, and—suddenly we were home and Arachne and Tusks greeted us, with Tusks saying, "We found a long deep tunnel going from this cave down. Toward the Stockade, we are sure! Come and help us explore it! It may be our greatest weapon! Come!"

CHAPTER 15

I was so excited about the tunnel that I had to hold onto myself. We waited for someone to come for us. And it seemed eternal. But at the end of eternity Arachne's quiet voice spoke. "Now, my children, follow me. Very slowly. Not all of you this time. Only Maris and Scuro and Tusks. The others wait here, please. We will not be gone long. Come."

Scuro followed her, my hand on his back, with Tusks behind us. At first the way was dark. It went in spirals down, or so it felt—and seemed fairly smooth under my feet. Slowly my eyes adapted and I could see walls which obviously had been worked on. After several spiral turns the passage went straight for quite a distance. Then one last spiral down, and ahead I could see daylight, with the silhouette of Arachne moving into it. And suddenly we were—all four of us—looking out through hanging vines at a river valley! It was soft and lovely and quiet, this valley, and it beckoned.

"Do not go out, children." Arachne said. "We must not betray this marvel! It is hidden and unused—perhaps unknown by our enemies. I believe our Bat friends will find it very helpful. So let us return to our comrades and make some plans, for I feel our task grows harsher and more urgent each move we make."

Our return to our company did not take long. We walked into the big room where the others were waiting. Duo, Twist, Annel, IstHer, Zeke, and—unexpectedly, to me at least—Big Bat. Arachne said in a quiet voice, "A time will come—hopefully not too far distant—when many of us—perhaps all of us—will enter the valley below and secure freedom for the Great Land. I hope deeply for that. But not yet." She bowed—a difficult action for a spider, I realized—as she came to Big Bat, who was leaning over a shelf of rock in the cave wall and peering down toward us.

"Dear sir Bat, with all our energies we thank you and your multitudes who are here to assist. Please tell us how we can help you to help us?"

"My lady, as you already know, we Bats do best when the light is dim or absent. We did what we could to upset the Beasts as soon as the first of our trained fighters arrived—and the Beasts were disorganized and angry, but not totally so. As soon as twilight begins again we will descend upon them in fullness, be assured. There are several hundred of us here. Our plan is to swoop down on the Beasts, cling and claw and bite and fly into faces and scratch at noses. We will not injure in a deep way. We will terrify Worms also. When dawn comes we will return here and report to you and rest during the daylight hours, while your company does what it must do. If you need to go on with this treatment we are at your service."

After Big Bat withdrew, the rest of us went to get some sleep before any further action. All except me, that is, and Scuro—who sneaked after me and in so doing saved me from real disaster. I was so pulled by the delicate beauty of the valley and by an overwhelming desire to learn if we had been there before with the Starflower that I could not resist going into it. Part of me knew I was wrong to do it—but the other part waited until Arachne had gone to rest and doubtless others also. So I put away the obedient side of me and tiptoed to the place from which we entered the tunnel. I took a deep breath, knowing that I was risking much, and entered the tunnel's darkness.

Once my hand found the wall I was all right, and I could follow the turns even if I couldn't see. But very soon I could. It was smoother and richer than it had seemed before. Unquestionably, it had been cared for by beings who valued it. I marveled at the work that had gone into its making. Then I reached its end, and the soft valley and its river wandered into the muted colors of late afternoon.

Stepping out into the coming twilight, I was greeted suddenly by two birds—one black and one gold. They perched on a branch very near to me, obviously unafraid and obviously ready to talk.

"I have seen you before, I believe," I said.

"Yes. And we have seen you. Twice. With another creature. Who are you? What's your name? Why are you here? Tell us! Tell us! Tell us!"

"I am Maris. I'm trying to help the Great Land."

"All alone? You can't, you can't, you can't!"

"Why not?" I was beginning to wonder if they were enemies of some sort—so I decided to ask. "Why are you so negative? Are you spies for the enemy Beasts and Worms? Who do you serve?"

They hopped to a nearer branch, their large bright eyes fixed on me. "That should be our question to you. But we'll answer—and then you answer it." Their eyes sparkled in delight. Shoulder to shoulder on their branch, they put their heads together and recited:

"We serve the living joyful things
in darkest night and brightest day.
We serve the lost and help it sing,
and in the gloom we seek a way."

They paused, their heads cocked roguishly, and then said in unison, "You say now who you serve."

"Well, as I said, I serve the Great Land. It is in trouble because of more and more bad Beasts and Worms. I came from another land—due to an earthquake—and I experience—as I have twice before—that I fall into the Great Land and find that I am needed. So I serve the Old Ones and the Guardians.

The two birds were hopping and bouncing on their branch like delighted children. "You are Maris, then," the dark one said. "We were asked by an old friend of ours and yours—Antic to watch over you—and your comrades—in case you needed messages carried, or a little guiding done, or even a spying task. I am called Shadow. My comrade is called Light. We are at your service if we can help."

I was happy beyond measure that they connected with the Guardians by way of Antic. I said so. And then I risked. "I am not supposed to be here." I related what was going on now with our group and the Bats. And I was honest enough to say that Arachne had indicated that we should not give the secret away.

"We won't tell," said Shadow. "But it is well to be very cautious. Beasts and Worms are guarding a hidden, deep, dark tunnel-cave a distance beyond here. I sneaked into it a few days ago. I couldn't believe what I saw. There is a thin, half-starved Beast guarding a white mare who is obviously about to give birth. The Beast is alone to guard the white one. At one point enemy Beasts tried to get in the narrow tunnel, but he guarded very fiercely and the enemy retreated. We felt sorry for him but could do nothing. Maybe your company can." And they flew off suddenly.

I was stunned and startled both by their departure and the news they gave me. It must be Quatro! It could not be any other Beast. It was Thaddeus's vision. What should I do? Go on? Or go back? I knew deep inside me that I must return and tell my news, although I had broken Arachne's command. For a moment I hesitated—and then turned and started to run back. At the moment I started to run a huge Worm emerged from a dark wood on my left, slithered silently in my direction, its great mouth open.

A loud Worm voice said, "Go and get it! Show what you can do!" And a second Worm came in sight, nipping at the tail end of the first one. "If you want to live, go and get it! Go! Go!"

I started to run with all the strength I had toward our tunnel. But the Worm was fast, especially because of the harassing Worm, and was gaining on me. I was running out of breath. I stumbled and knew I was lost, and just as I hit the ground I heard a bark and a deep growl and all at once Scuro was beside me.

"Stay where you are!" He growled and bared his teeth at the Worm nearest me. "Get away, you horror! Get away or I'll tear you apart! Like this!" And he nipped the Worm's tail. "I can do much worse! Get away!"

By now the Worm being taught to harass me had fled into the trees. And the teaching Worm was learning that Scuro had sharp teeth and lots of courage. Scuro had chewed the Worm's tail thoroughly. "Now get out! I can do worse—and there are others where I come from who can do worse than that! So go and tell your Worm friends that you can't win! Get out!" And he growled and nipped the Worm until it fled into the forest.

"Oh, Scuro! Thank you!"

"Don't thank me! Thank your luck that I missed you and came after you! We'll both get it from Arachne when she sees us—because we must tell the truth. So come on."

He led me quietly back to our tunnel and up to the room where the others were gathered awaiting the dawn return of the Bat army. Arachne looked at us. "You have been breaking the rules of our company, Maris. And you also, Scuro—but for a better reason, I believe. So, Maris, tell us what your story is."

I told why I had disobeyed, and what I was concerned about, and made no excuses, and described the two birds and their tellings. I told of the Worm encounter, my fall, and Scuro's coming. And Scuro told his side of it briefly. When we had finished there was a considerable silence.

At last Arachne broke it. "Dawn is near, children. Soon the Bats will return and Big Bat will report to us. And then we will see how we proceed. I am not distressed with either Scuro or Maris for their actions. Much has been learned. Very much. But, dear children, it is better in the future for you to share ideas and thus not to run such risks. Let us be still until our comrades come."

I had never seen Arachne more kind. I had always loved her, but now more than ever. Not for being kind, but for being so rich with love. The stillness was like velvet. And it felt warm and thoughtful, and it went on for a long time, until the sighing of Bat wings opened our eyes to the coming of dawn. We could hear the rustlings from the other rooms as the Bats settled in. Big Bat came into our room and fastened to his shelf.

"Big Bat," said Arachne, "Will you tell us briefly how the night was and where matters stand, before you rest?"

"Of course, my lady. First, let me say we believe that we need at least another round of time to do our work, if that pleases you."

"Big Bat, sir, we are deeply grateful for your presences, for just as long as you feel you need to do as much as planned. I have sent out one of our company—one of you—Twilight—to see what he could do about food for all of you."

"Oh, lady, that is not necessary. We eat copiously when we are near food, and it carries us for a goodly time. And when we return home we eat again a great amount. So do not be troubled. Now permit me to rest. We will come back at sunset and tell you of our battles with the Beasts and Worms. They came out the worst. So do not be troubled." And he fluttered away to join the others.

Arachne called me to her. "Maris, I do not want to chastise. I only want to say to you that when you hear or see or guess facts that belong to all of us, please come to all of us and tell us so we can plan together. And so also we can assist and protect each other." She turned to Scuro, who stretched out nearby. "And you, Scuro, are blessed for following and saving Maris. Yet you also could have shared your worries and taken someone with you. Either or both of you could have been hurt—or killed. So let us try to be a company from here on, and not just singular individuals. Beginning now."

I never loved her more for her honest and caring self. "Arachne, I'm very sorry—and I hear you and I agree. I have learned a lot in this. I won't do it again."

"Me to," said Scuro, as he sat near Arachne. "You tell me your ideas, I tell mine to you. Always. I promise."

"From what the two birds said to you, Maris, it *must* be Quatro and his lady who were seen by Thaddeus in his vision. So we know that they are alive but suffering. And probably not too far from here. Is that correct?"

I nodded. "It seems so. Those birds are 'here-now-and-gone-again' birds—as my grandmother back home would say. But somehow they know something, and my guess is it isn't too faraway."

We were silent for a while, as if each of us was trying to see into the unknown, to conjure up visions of truth and knowing, so that our comrades could be found and rescued. I kept trying to guess where they were. My hunch was that they were fairly close because the birds had seen them. And also enemy Beasts—not too far away, I gathered from the birds—were wanting to get them. For what? To kill? To capture? To torment? Whatever it was that they wanted it wouldn't be good. I knew that.

Suddenly Big Bat flew in, and to everyone's surprise Light and Shadow followed after him.

"Well," said Big Bat as he glided into a shelf near to Arachne, "I gathered these two as they were trying to find you. Or so they said. Perch near the Spider Lady and wait until you are asked questions."

They found a shelf nearby and perched together very close, looking a bit frightened.

"Do not be afraid of us, children." Arachne loomed large, impressive, motherly, all at once. "Tell us how far away the Beast and his lady are, please."

Light spoke first. "Madame—Lady—they are not too far. A distance—maybe for others a long walk—but not too long. For us—very quick." He bowed to Big Bat. "For you also, sir—very quick. To go at night is best—and if you" —and again he bowed to Big Bat— "brought along a lot of your army, or whatever you call your group, you could hold the Beasts and Worms away from the prisoners while the rest of us got them free."

Arachne listened carefully. "Thank you. I believe it is a very good plan. Do you agree with your comrade, Shadow?"

Shadow nodded emphatically.

"And do you agree, Big Bat? Does it seem to you—who harried the Beast Stockade all night—that further attacks could get Quatro and the Lady free?"

"I do. We made a great commotion last night. It was one of the best harrying episodes I can remember." He chuckled softly. "Yes. Oh yes! It was real Bat genius. I wish you could have seen us! Every Beast and every Worm in the place was assaulted by ten to fifteen Bats. We dove on them. We clung to them where they couldn't reach us. We bit. We squeaked into their ears. We flew around their heads wildly. Oh Arachne, it was a Bat battle—and we won it! As day came closer we left exhausted Beasts and Worms all over the place. And only one of our company was hurt—but not badly. She is a fighter and always gets into the midst of things—so a day's rest and she will be ready to go."

Arachne listened quietly and with evident delight. "Thank you—and all your company, Big Bat—for your patience and your courage. And now—do you believe we can together—our group and yours—set our friends free and get them to us here? Is it possible?"

Big Bat thought for a few minutes. "Yes. My suggestion is this. As soon as the day dims we will assemble a special Bat assault group, very skilled, and go in the direction Maris went. When we find the place where the prisoners are, one of us will fly in unseen—we're very good at that—and tell the prisoners what is going to happen. We will also have other Bats going around to find enemy Beasts and Worms so they can be harassed and confused. As soon as we can create enough muddle we will get the prisoners out. At that point we will need one of the Beasts in your company, Arachne, to act like an enemy Beast who is taking the captives to another prison. I wish we had a Worm who could go along."

"We do," said Arachne. "We have Tusks and we have Annel."

Both of them nodded.

"Of course," said Tusks. "Annel, will you risk?"

"I go. Glad. Help. Yes."

"We must practice, Annel. We must act like the bad ones, the cruel ones. Mean. Angry."

"Yes," said Annel. "I make angry. Yes."

Big Bat said he needed rest before nightfall—and also time to assemble a special Bat squadron for the rescue. So he left. As did Light and Shadow. As did Tusks and Annel—to practice their acting of enemy Beast and enemy Worm.

Arachne turned to me. "Maris, I appreciate your courage. But courage becomes dangerous if pushed too far—dangerous to you and for your friends. So go gently, my dear. And go and rest until we waken you."

I wandered off into a small room where Scuro was curled up in a corner, with Bats hanging silently from walls and ceiling. I sat down beside Scuro. He roused and licked my face. I hugged him. It was good to feel his warm furry body. "Oh, Scuro!" I whispered. "How will it all come out?" I hugged him again.

"Don't fret, Maris. Be like a dog for awhile. Just do what is needed and don't jump rivers until they show up. Worry isn't rest and it doesn't help. Curl up by me. Be a dog and get some sleep."

His fur was soft and warm. So I dozed off.

I was wakened by a warm tongue licking my face, and Scuro saying, "They're here. Big Bat and his special group are here. Wake up, Maris. Wake up!"

From then on for a long, long night it was hard work, and terror, and comradeship, and woundings, and concern, and anger, and love. Our company consisted of Big Bat and what he called his Bat assault group, and Tusks, Annel, Scuro, and me. I feared that Arachne would say I should not go—but she didn't. She only said, "Stay with Scuro and obey Big Bat, whatever else you do to help. We will wait." She sighed. "That is hardest—but spiders are experts in waiting."

As we started off along the downslope of our tunnel I missed Zeke. But he was watching the Beast Stockade. Light and Shadow joined us, flitting obediently behind the Bat assault group. Tusks, Annel, Scuro, and I were following the Bats and Birds, which was not easy to do because they flittered and fluttered above the floor of the tunnel, rising and falling like small waves while we were putting foot after foot in a stumbling gait on the uneven downslope. I kept my hand in contact with Scuro's back to keep me on the track in the darkness.

Suddenly, Big Bat said, "We are near the tunnel's end. Go slowly. We must all come very close together. Shadow and Light are going out to see if they can bring information to us. If not, we Bats will see what we can learn. If we Bats go, you few who are left—*stay here* until we come for you. Is this clear?"

We said it was.

"All right, you two birds go and return as soon as you can. Quickly and quietly."

It seemed a long time, but I'm sure it wasn't when they fluttered in. The path in the opposite direction where the captives were, they said, has no visible being on it.

"Very well," said Big Bat. "This is my suggestion. I want the Bat attack group to go first. Flutter as high as you can and see as much as you can. I believe that Annel and Tusks should go next— so that if any enemy Beasts and Worms approach, you two can be—as you have rehearsed—a Beast training a Worm to be vicious. Do it well. Lives depend on your acting. Maris, Scuro—you two must stay in deep shadows—as much unseen as possible. And do not do anything—*not anything*—until and unless I tell you to. Is it all clear now? Attack group first—with Shadow and Light along. You two return with any information. Annel and Tusks, you set out now. Carefully. I will be here and there as needed. Maris and Scuro—in dark places. Quietly unless I give an order. So—go now."

For a time I thought I heard the others. Then I knew I heard only my own footfalls—and Scuro's nails as he padded beside me. It was scary. So dark, so silent. I kept my hand on Scuro's head for direction and comfort. And just as I was feeling lost in silent shadows, all sorts of cries and calls and screeches and crashes ripped the darkness apart.

"Maris! Maris? Maris!"

It was Big Bat's voice at its loudest. "Maris, we have them out! Free! You and Scuro come and lead them back! We Bats are attacking enemy Beasts and Worms, and ours are being harried also! Come!"

I grabbed Scuro's neck ruff and stumbled alongside him as best as I could. It seemed forever but it was quite soon that Scuro tugged me onto a side path and stopped. "Reach your hand out and touch Quatro, and then his lady." I stretched my arm and my hand met a warm muzzle. "Quatro? Oh, Quatro!"

"Maris!" It was his voice. "Maris, lead us home! Oh, please lead us home! Blanca and me. Please!"

Another muzzle, gentle, tentative, found my other hand. I stroked it and a soft head of tangled hair.

"Quatro. Blanca. Come home with us."

Scuro's growl reminded me that we should turn and bring them. I held the hair on each of them as we turned around. "Come as quickly as you can, but do not hurt yourselves."

With Scuro leading me, and I them, we went at a slow walk back the dark way. We could hear shouts and other noises behind us, and I was afraid for Tusks and Annel and the Bat groups but I knew I must go on to safety regardless. I did not speak, but I kept in touch with my hands as we fumbled in shadows. All this time we were surrounded with helpful Bats, squeaking and guiding us. It seemed endless darkness and endless walking.

"We're in our tunnel. Feel the upslope?" Scuro said. "Not far now." I was glad for that—for a rest for them, and freedom, and love.

When we came into the large room of the great cave a gentle fire was dispelling the shadows, and Quatro and Blanca moved together to stand in the warm light. Arachne came to them. "Dear Quatro and your white lady, welcome. We are grateful you are here with us. We have a room ready. And there is food and rest for you. Blessings on all—including the one to come. Zeke, will you escort them, please?"

He came to them—smiled at me en route—and, with a gentle hand on each of them, led them away. It was evident he was not missing the battle. He was needed here and was doing his tasks well and I was glad.

Just as I was about to ask where were Tusks and Annel, Zeke hurried in again. "Just got a report form a Bat that both Tusks and Annel were wounded and are coming here now. Shadow brought the message. Light is with them to be sure they get here. I'm going to help."

Obviously Arachne knew, because she made no comment except, "Maris, will you and Scuro take down some of my webbing to make bandages if needed? And, Zeke, do go and help."

Scuro and I got the webs and returned to the big room just as Tusks and Annel arrived, with Zeke following. Tusks had a large and bloody wound on his foreleg. Annel had a bleeding slash toward the end of his tail. Zeke and I wrapped spiderweb silk around their raw flesh. The bleeding stopped very quickly—as Arachne's webbing always worked.

Arachne came to each of them, praised and thanked them, and told them to go and rest. Tusks hesitated. "Dear Arachne, may I just greet Quatro briefly? I love him."

She said, "Yes," and let Zeke guide him. And Tusks returned limping and beaming and nodding his dear ugly head in happiness.

Soon we all slept.

CHAPTER 16

I was aroused by the fragile twittering of Bats—and as I came fully awake I remembered yesterday, or last night, or whatever it was or whenever it was—and then I remembered Annel and Tusks and their wounds, and then I remembered Quatro and Blanca and their suffering. And I knew that I must be needed somewhere by someone for something.

Struggling to my feet, I staggered after Scuro into the big room. It was filled with Bats everywhere. Annel and Tusks were present, bandaged and wide-eyed. Zeke waved to me from across the room. IstHer was on Annel's head. Arachne and Big Bat were standing on or holding onto—a large rock that had been pushed by someone to the room's center. After we were all there around the stone, Arachne spoke.

"Let us first hear from you, Big Bat, and your report from last night's raids."

"Helpers and nurturers, there is much accomplished, much to do still, and much to know." He spoke clearly. "However, I must tell you that unless we have many more large-sized beings on our side we will not win. We Bats can harass and upset big enemies—but we cannot overpower them. We need more helpers on our side, more like Tusks and Annel and Scuro."

It was IstHer, from her place on Annel's head, who spoke freely. "My Lady—Arachne, my thoughts are that we need more help from Guardians and from the Old Ones. I sneak around and ask lots of questions. When I hear that the Worm Slithers is getting more and more powerful, and the Beasts called Brawn and Potens are also—well, I think we need more of our friends to help us. Also I heard that Beasts are finding bad and mean Wasps, Toads, Bats, and are training them, in addition to Worms. We need friends like Ears, Cat, Waff, maybe Thaddeus. Or something like that."

If a spider could smile—which I hardly knew they could—Arachne did. "IstHer, if all of us could be as honest and as willing to risk as you are, there would be more truth in the Great Land. Does anyone else wish to speak? With ideas, suggestions, questions, plans?"

"Please, Arachne, I'm willing to go to the Place of Them with a message," said Scuro. "Or I could carry someone there—or someone from there."

"Thank you, Scuro. But we need you here. And a Bat can take messages faster and less obviously than any of us. I'm certain we can find Twilight and let him be a messenger—if that's our plan."

Suddenly, a Bat floated down from the mass of Bats and squeaked, "Here I am! Ready to go when wanted!" We all cheered, and Twilight bowed as releasing laughter rippled through the room. He returned to his shelf.

"Now," said Arachne, "We must make some serious choices. If Tusks is up to speaking—will you, Tusks, say how you feel we should proceed?"

He stepped forward proudly, his wounded leg seeming not to hamper him. "I agree that a message should be sent at once. The Old Ones and Guardians can best decide who to send as soon as they have all our facts. If our Beast friends were sent it would take longer—but not as long as we took, being not really sure where we were going. And, do we tell them about Quatro and Blanca?"

Arachne said, "Whoever goes—tell them. They will be joyful." She paused. Looking around at this motley gathering. "Is Twilight still here?" He fluttered down from an upper Bat shelf and landed awkwardly on the stone. "Here I am, lady."

"Now then, before night comes, choose a Bat friend and the two of you leave as soon as it grows dark. Take our message to the Guardians and they will let the Old Ones know. Together their decision will be made." She waved several of her legs, and said, "It is time for our Bat fighters to rest now until night comes. And it is also time for us daytime beings to confer."

After considerable rustling and whispering our small company gathered together. We made an odd group of all sizes and all shapes—a spider, a dog, a worm, a Beast, a mouse, and me, Maris. After a considerable silence Tusks spoke. "I believe we need to do something for Quatro and Blanca. They need peace and quietness and nourishment, of course. But I feel they also need friends and love. They must have suffered long loneliness and fear as well as hunger. I suggest that they need comrades with whom they can unburden themselves, and can talk with. And Blanca especially needs feminine support, I'd guess."

No one spoke.

"Well," said Tusks. "I guess I'll go and see them."

"Please, Tusks!" Arachne pleaded. "I didn't speak because I was shocked at what we had not done! We've been so involved in our war that we forgot their imprisonment! You are completely and totally right!"

"I sneaked in once," Scuro said. "Quatro said he was grateful. And she asked me to wag my tail because it made her happy."

Arachne spoke eagerly. "Let us ask them to join us for a rich meal! I don't know how we'll make it—but let's try! Maris, you go and tell them—for all of us. I'll arrange the meal."

As I approached their room I began to wonder what I would say, what I wanted to say, what I needed to say. I was trembling as I neared the place—trembling from uncertainty. And from shame. But as I looked into the room—it was an expansive one, and had at least two good-sized heaps of grass or leaves, and it had a basket-shaped something filled with stalks and what seemed to be heads of grain—as I looked in Quatro and Blanca were stretched out, side by side, noses touching, eyes open. I wondered if I should have come. And yet I needed to—for their sakes and mine. So I spoke, softly.

"Quatro, dear friend. You are free."

All of a sudden in a moment of timelessness Quatro's muzzle was touching my outstretched hands and his eyes, always so rich with feelings, were filled with tears. "Oh, Maris! Maris! I never thought this could happen! To be free! To be protected! To see you again! The terror has been so long! Will it really end sometime? Before the child is born? Will it end sometime?"

The best thing I could do was to stroke him until he stopped trembling. He was thin and worn, but his eyes began to be less fear-filled and anxious. And then I said, "May I stroke you, also, Blanca?"

Hesitantly, she struggled to her feet. She was small and shaggy white and needed combing and was very pregnant. I ran my fingers gently through her hair. I could see that she was beginning to trust me.

"Are you both feeling a bit safer here?" I asked as I kept on stroking Blanca's hair.

"Yes," Quatro said. "Maris, I was afraid it would never end. Never! Very little food. No sleep. But I fought them! Oh, how I fought them—the horrible Beasts—and Worms, although they were easier to bite. Oh, I hate them, the bad ones!"

I put my hand on Blanca's head. "You two will now go with me to be guests for a real meal. Please come."

Great tears were in Blanca's eyes as she and Quatro followed me to the banquet. Just before we got to the big room, I stopped. I put one hand on Blanca's head and one on Quatro's head. "Dear comrades, you have been so very long hiding in fear. Why do you not go boldly together into the room where friends are waiting? Please, Quatro. I am right behind you."

Quatro shook himself and then bowed to Blanca, and they stepped forward into the room. I followed them. They were greeted by many voices of old friends and newcomers. Everyone there was gentle, and no one was loud—but love was everywhere. The Beast friends were gentle and welcoming. Quatro presented Blacna to members of our group—beginning with Arachne, and Blanca shyly spoke to each one.

The last introduction to Blanca was IstHer, who immediately said, "Can I sit on your back, please, Blanca?" Blanca nodded in delight as IstHer climbed up into her white hair. "Are you comfortable, little IstHer?"

"You are warm and nice and it's curly here. May I comb your hair?" Blanca nodded and IstHer began combing Blanca's curls. She hummed happily as she worked on Blanca's hair with her paws. Suddenly, she said, "Oh, the little one inside you jumped! That is wonderful!"

After the meal Arachne suggested that both Blanca and Quatro needed peace and rest. IstHer and I escorted them to their room. As we left, Quatro said, "We have come home. We thank you!"

On our return Arachne, Zeke, and Scuro were talking. The injured ones—Tusks and Annel—had gone to rest and let their wounds rest as well. IstHer was, as always, bouncing with energy.

"When will we hear from Them? We need to be ready for the battle, don't we? Maybe if we each got out our feather that Thaddeus gave us, we could call him? Couldn't we?"

"IstHer, don't be impatient." Arachne was gentle. "You have a good suggestion. Those who have feathers from Thaddeus—bring them here."

Zeke and I, IstHer, Tusks, Scuro—each of us searched and found the feather hidden somewhere on us—or where we slept—and brought them to Arachne. She touched each of our feathers, saying, "I scarcely believe this is necessary, because I am certain that Twilight's message has been delivered and that plans are in the making. However, I also suspect that Thaddeus—en route or not—is tuned in to us. And also—as I recall—he said use them only when real danger threatens. And at the moment it doesn't. Let's just think of Thaddeus and the Guardians, talk with Them inside yourself for awhile."

I closed my eyes and tried to see Them, the Guardians, all standing in a row and looking at me as I looked back. I sort of saw Them—but vaguely and dimly. Suddenly, IstHer's voice broke in. "He's here! Twilight is here! Welcome back, Twilight!"

We almost overwhelmed poor Twilight with simultaneous greetings and questions—so much so that he retreated to a window shelf out of our reach. Chastened, we waited. Finally, Twilight fluttered to a place where he could see us, hear us, and be heard by us.

"Well," he said, "they are coming—Ears and Waff very soon, then later Thaddeus and Cat, and perhaps Domar and Molasses. Thaddeus brings his magic. Ears and Waff are fine fliers, and Waff is a real fighter. So is Cat." And he fluttered up to a high ledge.

There was nothing for us to do except to wait. And as IstHer predicted, Waff and Ears flew in very soon. Ears didn't get the reception that Waff got because we had seen so many Bats that one more was not at all different. Even so, I welcomed him joyfully.

Waff was something different. His large cat-sized golden body and his great unlidded insect eyes were wonderful to see again.

"Marizz! Arachne! Other friendzz! I am honored to be part of thiz company. I bring greetingz from many who wizhed to come—and who are ready if needed." I wanted to ask about everyone I knew, but I didn't. We would be informed when it was time. Waff continued. "I think that Thaddeuz and Cat will not be too long coming. Thaddeuzz izz experimenting with a new magic zomething which none of uzz underztand—juzt bang! poof! and they get there—all at onzze—did it with Domar and zcared her a lot. Molazzez loved to be flipped here and there in Time. Anyway, they're all coming at zome time. Uno, Duo, Trio, Twizt—they are planning to be here on foot. No magic. Guardianzz approved. And alzo Dag may come." At that moment there was a great commotion outside, made up of shouts, bangs, a sound of cracking and breaking. We couldn't tell who else was coming. What we saw was the floor of the cave—at its entrance—rising and cracking and breaking open. The crack widened and widened and something black and metallic bulged upward. It was a frightening scene—as if some dark and inhuman evil was pursuing us. We retreated from the terror as fast as we could.

I kept watching the black thing as it emerged. I felt we were doomed. I started to run, then my last glance over my shoulder told me the truth—because under the black monster was the dear and dirty face of Thaddeus! I burst into tears and laughter. "Dear Thaddeus, it's you!" Zeke came. Scuro came. And together we pulled Thaddeus and his kettle and his magic paraphernalia out.

"Wait for the others," he said, peering down into a dark tunnel, "They're in there somewhere."

Very soon I heard a familiar voice from the hole. "If this is what your idea of easy traveling is, I don't agree, Thaddeus. We'll be in this mess forever—and I, for one, am—"

"You're here, friend," called Thaddeus. "And I don't think you lost even one of your nine lives. Come on out."

And Cat emerged, covered with dirt of various kinds, looking totally angry and totally disheveled. I picked him up and brushed him off. And then I began to laugh at myself, at Cat, at Thaddeus, and at the others who were watching this incredible emergence. I stroked Cat and he purred.

"Dear Thaddeus," I said as I embraced him, "You are wonderful, dear friend. If you can do this, you can do anything."

Everyone began applauding in one form or another. Even Tusks and Annel applauded—wounds and all—and bats were everywhere in the air, seeing as much as they could.

In the midst of this noise and dirt and confusion, Thaddeus was calmly removing things, one by one, from his great black kettle. As usual, what was in the pot was taken out and piled without any reason of any sort. And, to the amazement of everyone, Thaddeus at last reached into his pot and lifted out the little house, Domar.

I dropped to my knees and took Domar in my hands and whispered, "Dear Domar, how wonderful to have you here with us!" I put my ear down to her door and heard her tiny voice say, "I've missed you. Soon *I* can hold *you!* How exciting life can be, dear Maris. And Molasses says, 'Yes.'"

CHAPTER 17

Tomorrow seemed to come all at once. However, I and my comrades did have a fairly restful sleep. The only one who didn't, as far as I could tell, was Thaddeus. From what I heard he had spent the remaining hours of the night lumbering quietly among the wounded creatures of all kinds, administering his magic for healing and his words for courage.

When I found him he was resting, his head leaning on his black pot, his eyes closed, his salamander feet looking sore and scratched from his night's work. I realized how courageous he was and how much I loved him. I sat down near him and waited a time.

"Oh, Maris!" His head lifted and his eyes opened. "Is something wrong?"

I stroked his head and ran my fingers softly along his curved back clear to his tail's end. "Nothing that I know of, dear Thaddeus. I'd guess there are wounded and dead Beasts and Worms, and others that are running away. At least I hope so. And not one of our company is badly hurt. Annel the most—but between Arachne and Isther, he has been thoroughly cared for. And also I love you!"

He lifted his head, stretched his funny legs one after the other, let his tail slowly swing back and forth a few times. "Dear Maris. We've done a lot of things together in this Great Land. Oh, why is it hard to have cool water and pools and love and helpfulness and happiness? Why must there be fighting and death and cruelty and envy and all things like that!"

"I wish I knew. What can I do for you, Thaddeus? Get some food, take messages, help you up, go away? How can I help?"

"Would you sort of straighten out my things in my pot for me? They've been shaken up a lot in our battles."

So for a loving time I sorted and straightened and put in order his precious black kettle's contents. I had just done the final sorting and placing when Zeke appeared—obviously in a great hurry.

"Arachne wants us to come to the big room."

"Zeke," said Thaddeus, "could you kindly and carefully take the kettle and its contents?"

"I am honored, Thaddeus. Thank you."

So we entered the great room—Thaddeus, then me, then Zeke, holding the black pot as if he was carrying a jewel. The room was crowded with creatures.

Arachne spoke first. "We have a full message from the Old Ones and the Guardians, brought by Twilight just a short time ago. It says, 'It is joyful to have Blanca and Quatro with you. We know you are dealing as well as you can with the dark powers. Owl, Dag, Da and Gada, and King Feathers are en route. Drums and chants are sounding for you and we will keep them going until the Beast evils are at least under control. Do not be optimistic about over-powering the Beasts. They are bigger and more numerous than we are. Take care.'" Arachne paused, then said, "And so let us get ready for the others to arrive." She looked around at the strange and unbelievable assembly. "As a central group, let there be Big Bat, Annel, Thaddeus, Waff, Tusks, Maris, and myself. We are not better than others, but we are representing each of the various categories. The rest can gather and talk, or sleep. We'll meet and return to you. Does that feel right, my friends all?"

There were nodded assents and "yeses" and "thank yous" as we seven went into a small side room. Annel, Thaddeus, Tusks, and I leaned against the rock walls—each of us leaning differently depending on our various shapes. Arachne, Waff, and Big Bat each found an outcrop of rock on which to stand or perch or sit. Very directly and seriously Arachne laid out the facts gathered from all available sources. There were still many Beasts in other parts of the Great Land who were cruel, warlike, ready to destroy anything or anyone in their path. They also were working hard to coerce or to force beings such as Wasps, Toads, Birds of Prey, and Worms to go as slaves or as partners in taking over the Great Land.

"These are facts," said Arachne. "When we are joined by those five sent by the Old Ones and the Guardians we will be only twenty-two. So—it is for us to be very wise, skillful, wary, and prepared for anything. Thaddeus, you are the wizard. What are your opinions?"

He laboriously lifted a front leg and awkwardly did what he called stirring his head. Then he curled around his black kettle and spoke from that posture. "It comes from a better place this way. I think there are enough of us to win. Whatever winning really means. Which I doubt. But on the other hand, we have put down the enemy in the past. Or have we? Maybe we've just covered them over and acted as if they weren't when all the time they were. Because they still are." He stopped and stirred his head again, his eyes closed.

"Thaddeus," said Arachne. "What are your suggestions?"

"Suggestions? Well . . . " There was a long pause. "Well, I believe I can make a long-lasting fire in the Beast Stockade to drive them all out. I can also make large rings of fire where Beasts can be held as prisoners. I can also make a fire that chases anybody I name. I can make big things small—like Beasts to bitsies—and I can make small things big—like Bats to bombing planes. And I can—"

"Enough, Thaddeus," said Arachne. "Your gifts overwhelm me. I am sure we can use them all. But don't try to explain them to us—or to anyone else—until they are ready to use."

Big Bat was called on next. He said at least three-quarters of his group had to return home before nightfall to keep their land safe and sound for Bats and for all friends who passed through or needed refuge. But he was leaving one-quarter of his group with Twilight in charge, to help in whatever way they could.

Wounded as he was, Annel spoke boldly when asked. "I better. I do what can do. Help and teach other Worms to be not bad. To learn. And I fight too."

"And you, Waff?" asked Arachne.

"I'll give all I can to teach my people to fight and bite and zting all enemiez, ezpecially bad Beaztz. Alzo bad Wazpz and zuch. And Birdz, if bad onez."

"We need you, Waff. And we are grateful to your help. Tusks will instruct and direct the Beasts in our company, surely. Maris will be wherever she is most needed. But please, Maris, consult me or Tusks."

Arachne continued, "I do not intend to be the director. Each of you has his or her own vital responsibility for those working with you. I suggest that each of you go and gather your group and discuss plans which need to be started—" she turned to Thaddeus "—at coming of night, or when it is complete night? Which?"

Thaddeus pondered, eyes closed. "When night is almost there but not quite. That is a deceptive time and best for unexpected occurrences. If Maris assists me we will set fire to the Beast Stockade. It won't hurt anyone—I don't make magic to kill—but it will sound and look like all things were coming to an end and all Beasts and their associates will believe it is and will panic. Then all of you can begin to harass and harry them and drive them riverward. Hopefully by then some of us will have made a sort of corral right at the river's edge, and also hopefully we can trap them in it." He paused, shaking his head. "Dear me, if it doesn't work—well—let's hope it does."

The time seemed both endless and rushing like the wind. At least for me and my working with Thaddeus, taking things from his pot, sorting them, putting them back in, testing magic wands. Just as we finished our trial rehearsals we heard Zeke shout. We rushed from our practice room into our big central room, to be greeted by and to greet a roomful of great birds—Owl, Dag, Da, Gada, and King Feathers.

I stopped in awe of them—these friends. Owl was as round, full-feathered, and wise-looking as ever. King Feathers was as regal and leader-like as ever. And Da, Gada, and their son Dag were as ugly as ever and I loved them most of all. It was a joy to see all of them and to be with them. All of us rushed into greetings and hugs and a wonderful happiness, until Thaddeus, of all the company the least likely to be urgent, said, "Come on, friends, there's work to do right away."

It is not possible to describe the events that led up to the night's incredible climaxes. IstHer rode Dag and I rode Gada—at their suggestion—so we could get an aerial view of the land. In part it was a lovely land with its meandering silver-blue river and in the distance the hardly visible benign mountains between us and the Place of Them. But in another part it was pockmarked with holes in hills and around the Volcanic Mountain, and from many of the holes came ugly smoke. When we returned to the rest of our company we were unhappy to have to tell them what we had seen.

But Thaddeus and Arachne believed that we could harry and drop things on these places and drive the residents out of their dwellings into the open. And then other divers could herd them toward the river.

"And then what?" asked Cat. "Drive them in and drown them?"

"We don't kill our enemies, Cat! We'll make a big corral near the river and drive them into it." It was Thaddeus speaking. "I've got it all ready—the corral—and as soon as they're in it I'll surround it by fire."

"When did you make your corral?" Arachne asked.

"King Feathers took me. He could fly the highest and be the most invisible and I could drop my invisible net and some Bat friends will go and lift it and fasten it to trees. After dark, of course—which is coming soon. Maris, here is the magic fire." He handed me a small bundle form his kettle. "Climb on," said Dag.

Thaddeus handed Zeke the kettle. "I'm going because I must concentrate on my magic words to be said as Maris drops the bundle. So—let us go at once. And all you others follow and be ready when the Stockade seems in flames."

We did. We were hardly settled on Dag's back when we were high above the others, and went into a long and silent glide over the forest and river. Circling, we saw the Beast Stockade in the failing light.

"Circle once and dive." said Thaddeus. "And Maris, when the dive is at its lowest, drop the bundle. Go as low as you can, Dag—but don't risk. I'll say a few magic words—and Maris will drop the bundle. And then you, Dag, go up as fast as you can."

So we surged upward on Dag's strong wings. We circled twice, high in the air—we could hardly see the Stockade—and Dag said, "Hold tight! Here we go!" It was a terrifying moment—as if Dag had dropped from under me—but I held tight to his back feathers with one hand and to the bundle with the other. Thaddeus was talking to his magic as we dove. The Stockade yard was closer and closer—and it was, as near as I could tell, milling with Beasts and Worms and other beings.

"Ready, Maris!" Thaddeus said. "Drop it now!"

And I did, and Thaddeus was muttering magic words. Dag twisted his body and soared upward as flames exploded in the center of the Stockade. I couldn't see as Dag went upward, but I could hear screams and roars from all directions. If I had not known that this was Thaddeus's magic and not a death-dealing battlefield, I'm sure I would have fainted.

Dag was turning and going lower over the Stockade. "You did it, Thaddeus! Look at them running, and all in a jumble, falling over each other and crowding each other to get out!" He swooped lower. "Wow! They're all headed toward the river! And—yes—there are our comrades chasing and harrying! Look! Cat, Waff, Zeke, our Beasts—I can't see them all, but they're in there! Oh, my feathers, what a scene!"

Swiftly we flew. But I realized that full night had come. The dark was black dark. How could we possible see anything? And I was just opening my mouth to say so when Thaddeus said, "Dag, how well can you see in the dark?"

"Not very well. I'm not an Owl."

"So how can you see the corral?"

"I can't."

"I guessed that. I brought along some special drops for night-seeing. It's good and safe magic. Let Maris put some in her eyes and in yours and then we can descend toward the corral."

It was another scary moment when I was afraid I'd miss my target. The wind blew at me and I hung onto Dag's neck, leaned over, and managed to get the drops in.

"I see the corral! I see it!" Dag shouted. "All sorts of beings are milling around in it—and outside it!"

"We'd better dive bomb it, Dag. But from the road on which they're coming from the Stockade. Dive them, to help our friends who must be chasing and pushing them."

This was the scariest moment for me. I saw the Beasts and Worms in panic, shoving and pushing each other toward the corral, and I saw many Bats attacking them, and was quite sure I could make out Zeke and Scuro and Cat attacking Beasts and Worms. We dove several times at clusters of Beasts, scaring them into the corral.

At last Thaddeus said, "Please take us down, Dag, to that dark forest edge, so we can come out on foot. If you can see it."

Cautiously, Dag descended, alighting in silence and darkness near the road. We all made our way silently until we stood behind some trees beside the road. Beasts, Worms, and other enemy creatures were pushing each other in haste to get to the corral, and we could just make them out in the growing darkness.

Suddenly, there came a deep, low, and loud "hoo-oo" from the night, and I could just make out Owl flying a bit above the terrified Beasts and Worms. He was literally hooting them into the corral. And then Twilight landed on Thaddeus, saying, "Most of the Beasts are inside the corral. We can harass the others into the corral. Some of us are on the watch. Could the flames around the corral be lighted? We can chase the others tomorrow."

"Very well, Twilight. Dag, will you carry Maris in a circle above the corral walls? Maris, you will pour out this powder as Dag circles. Start at the entrance and end at it. As soon as you have made the circle of powder, come back to me at once. Go!"

We went. It did not take long to do it—only great care in the dark that every inch of corral was covered. We came back to Thaddeus, where a tiny fire glowed. As soon as we landed he said, "Stand back! Stand way back!"

There was a whoo-oosh of fire, and almost instantly the great corral was surrounded by leaping flames. The Beasts inside roared in terror and backed away from the edges. I almost felt sorry for them, although the fire would not injure them.

"This will last for several days," said Thaddeus. "Who will watch tonight?"

Cat, Twilight, his Bat group, and our Beasts all volunteered. The rest of us went wearily home.

CHAPTER 18

After they had witnessed the strange arrival the Bat company—except Twilight, of course—returned to their daytime resting places led by Big Bat. And we—the old friends—clustered together. It was a joy to see Waff sitting on Tusks's willing head, and Cat curled against Scuro, and IstHer on Annel's back. And more wonderful and absurd than all else was the usual and unique scene of Thaddeus and his pot and his magical mess getting prepared for something.

Thaddeus bowed to Arachne. "My Lady, may I let Domar be herself again? Various ones of us have benefited by her guardianship. When I learned about Quatro and Blanca I thought that they should be in Domar's care. And I have put as much protection as I know into Domar." He bowed to Arachne. "Can they live in Domar?"

The great Spider was her most benign self. "Of course, my dear Thaddeus, of course. There is a large and very hidden room in this great cavern of ours. So let us go there—you and I and Domar—and see what can be done. The rest of you, please stay here to watch over things, and welcome our own Beasts whenever they come."

So much had happened so fast that I had difficulty trying to remember who was where. IstHer scampered onto my lap. "Do you suppose sometime I could go into that little house when it gets bigger?" IstHer asked.

"I think so, IstHer. That little house has a large family when it grows big. You will see. And—"

My sentence halted as I heard a shout, and shouts, and we spun around to be met by a procession of Beasts following Annel. They were weary and dirty and obviously thirsty, with tongues hanging out. Cat and Scuro wakened and Waff called, "Uno, Duo, Trio, Twizzt! Welcome! You arrived!"

Annel said, "They lost. Need eat. Good friends, I say them. Bring here to Tusks, sir."

While Zeke and I greeted them and hugged them, IstHer climbed onto Annel and the two went off for food. We waited until they brought some, mostly leaves and fruits, and the Beasts devoured it. Meanwhile, Cat and Scuro had come to greet them, standing beside Tusks. When our Beasts had eaten all they could Tusks led them to a side tunnel to get a rest.

After the Beasts had departed and Twilight had gone to his ledge to "get ready for the next fight," the rest of us—Waff, Scuro, Cat, IstHer, Annel, Zeke, and I—quietly distributed ourselves in various resting positions. For a time nobody spoke. We needed to gather ourselves into a readiness for what was to come. We were very still. I guess we were inwardly preparing for the conflicts that we knew were ahead for us if we were to save the Great Land. "It is so beautiful," I thought to myself as I rested, "so beautiful. Why do creatures want to destroy their lands? How terrible to steal and destroy what cannot be remade? We are monsters." I fell into a disturbed and hostile and dark unconsciousness.

I wakened, weary and confused but ready. What I saw first was Thaddeus—and Domar full-sized—and then our own Beasts, all of them, standing beside Domar, and all of the rest of the company except Big Bat. No, Tusks was missing. But before I could ask, Arachne spoke.

"Quatro and Blanca are safe in hiding—safe from all enemies, we hope. Tusks is with them. And Domar will be. Thaddeus has given them lots of magic food. Then plans will be made to get them away—back to the Place of Them with us. We hope the plans will work. Hope and courage is what we must abide by."

She let her gaze travel from one to another to another of us. And when a Spider does that it is very compelling and impressive. "Tonight, children, we are going to put all of our power—inner and outer—into trying to confuse and outwit the evil Beasts and their slaves and cohorts. If we can do it even in part we will have a chance to save the Great Land. Killing and destroying is not the way to freedom. It is the way to despotism and ultimate despair. Life is to live and to love, not to deny and destroy!" I could not avoid her great spider eyes as she spoke to us.

One by one, by twos and threes, and all together in a single monumental gaze, we said a silent and then resounding "YES!" I shall never forget that enormous reply. And we lived in it after that. And some lived in it perishing.

"What do you propose, Big Bat?" Arachne asked as the night came and the Bat troops were awaiting orders.

"My Lady Arachne, I believe my people should go in as fast and as roughly as they can—harassing, screaming, biting, clawing, scratching—and not only attacking the evil Beasts but also their underlings—weak and evil Worms, Wasps, Toads, and a few renegade Bats."

"Thank you, Big Bat. We honor you and are filled with gratitude for your work. Now, dear Tusks, will you say your plans and hopes, please?"

Tusks bowed with dignity. "We are now five Beasts. We have fought before and we will fight again. My suggestion is that we must act first as if we belonged to the evil Beasts and were on their side. Annel, our loyal Worm comrade, will go with some one of us Beasts and act as a weak Worm being trained to be mean. So he can bite and harass as much as he likes, and can keep things off balance—I believe we can terrify—and hurt, if necessary—enough evil Beasts to force them to begin to give up. I hope."

Arachne thanked Tusks. "Dear Thaddeus, what are your plans? Yours are the most strange and, usually, the most helpful."

"Well, you see I've got some new magic—worked on it quite a bit recently—like I reduced my friends to very small sizes—like Cat and like Domar—and we could crawl through the dirt and get out—you saw us—and I'm sure I could get any—or all—of us in these small sizes so we could tunnel out."

"Out of what?" Arachne asked.

"Whatever we're in. Like trouble. Attacks, etcetera."

"But Thaddeus—we are trying to overcome the evil Beasts, Worms, and Toads. How does your plan fit in with this?"

"Dear Lady—if our enemies could be made small we could capture them and retrain them and then restore them. Or we could become very small and could natter away at them—like your IstHer does, or can do, I'll wager. Maybe that would be best—and more exciting! Just imagine being IstHer's size on the back of a Beast or a Worm—the evil ones, I mean—and being able to hide in Beast fuzz or in Worm wrinkles—it would be like a cosmic flea biting every available inch of a monster."

Arachne hesitated, a small smile on her face. "Dear Thaddeus, because I trust your magic always and never understand it, I leave it to you. What do we do now? Night is here. Decide quickly. The Bat troops are ready to go."

"Let us be small and ride a Bat into the night's work. Return here as soon as a green flame comes into the night sky. Now each of you touch the inside center of my black pot, climb on a Bat, then do your task and return as dark ends. Watch me." He reached into his black pot and touched the center—and a very small salamander emerged and climbed onto the back of a waiting Bat. All of us present followed, and most of us I guessed were as scared as I was.

To find myself clinging to a Bat's fur, my arms around its tiny soft body, and hearing it say to me in its high voice, "Hold tight, little friend. When I dive on a Beast you drop from me onto its back and, while I keep diving and biting, you pinch and kick its ears and nose. "I'll come and pick you up."

With those meager instructions I was airborne into the darkness. Very shortly I knew we were dropping down toward the Beast Stockade. Then I could see lights in the stockade—lighted flares and fires illuminating a large square filled with Beasts and Worms, outcries of anger, screams of pain. And then I saw our Bats—so small compared to Worms and Beasts—diving, biting, clawing, harassing. I wanted to cry for their courage. I stroked the fur of my Bat.

"Watch out," it said. "We're going in to a Beast who is torturing a Worm. Kick its nose and ears. Hang tight to its fur and keep kicking. I'll come for you. Ready. Go."

Suddenly, I was on the head of a foul-smelling Beast, holding tight to its fur. My Bat was gone and it dived at the Beast's eyes. I pulled the Beast's hair. I managed to kick its nose very hard. And I screamed into its ear the loudest I'd ever screamed. My Bat finally came, let me climb on, shouted, "Hold tight!" and dove at least four times at the Beast's ears, nose, neck until it was stumbling away from the Stockade into the darkness. "We've done that one very well," said my Bat carrier. "You were great! That one won't pick on others for quite a time. Maybe never again, I hope. And do you mind if we rest a bit? It's hard work."

So we rested on the top of the Stockade—not very restful, because Bats kept resting and leaving and resting. But at least I got the feeling of what vast energies these hundreds of Bat comrades were giving freely to help the Great Land restore itself and find its balance, and I was deeply thankful for them, for all other helpers, and that I could be there with them. Before the night ended my Bat and I had heckled and disrupted and driven off at least eight or nine Beasts, separated them from Worms—and from a Toad who was being tortured—and heard one exchange between two Worms who were deciding to get out of all this "bloody torment" and to try living in "a more friendly way."

The green flame eventually flared in the night sky and as dawn came we returned to our many-roomed cave, tired, dirty, but with some sense of accomplishment. We were returned to our normal sizes by Thaddeus. The Bats went to rest—all except Big Bat. He met with us in our central room, although we were a weary lot after a sleepless and tiring night. But that did not stop Arachne. Together we all discussed what we had done, and not done, and needed to do. Generally, we agreed that many more Beasts and Worms—and even some of the lesser and weaker creatures—were on the verge of quitting.

"What is our task now, my friends?" Arachne's voice was softly urgent. "Have we made enough trouble? How can we make it more certain?"

Big Bat spoke first. "I must send at least half of my company home before long. However, I'm sure that if we all joined forces we could destroy the Stockade, especially if Thaddeus helped us with his magic."

Thaddeus nodded happily. "Of course. I've got some very new magic for such an occasion. It has to do with expanding and compressing. I think—If I practiced a bit—I could make the Stockade and everything in it very small. And we could just pack it up and send it by some flier—to the Place of Them."

Arachne suggested/commanded that Thaddeus get to work to carry out his plans. "And you, Tusks? What do you suggest as a next move?"

"Well, what occurrred to me, Lady, is that I'd like another night with every Bat, and every one of us, to go into the Beast Stockade shrieking, yelling, shouting, banging things, biting creatures, driving everything in the Stockade out and toward the river and into the river."

"And let them all drown, Tusks?"

He paused. "Well—no, I guess not. But get them out if they promised to be peaceful and helpful. I think some of them might—"

"Might what?" asked Arachne.

"Might want to be peaceful and helpful."

"Why?"

"Well—I'd guess they're tired and lonely and want to begin to relate to peace and beauty—at least they must have some feelings about such things, I should think. I hope so."

We all rested a while. It wasn't rest for me. I kept seeing and hearing the evil Beasts and Worms of the night hours, and how they snarled and quarreled and hurt each other. I slept a bit—at least I dreamed of the bloody sights and sounds of the Stockade— only to be pulled awake by Big Bat shrilling, "Come on, all of you! Night's work is calling us! Come to the center!"

Arachne spoke first. "I want you to know that Domar has been flown back to the Place of Them, carried by a special Bat group. She is her small size—and inside her are Molasses, Blanca, and Quatro, in their small sizes. For safety, Thaddeus sent all the instructions for returning them to their regular sizes if anything should happen to him—although he doesn't believe it will. Nor do I. Now, are you ready? We must go fast. Go on the run, aggressive, shouting, mean!"

Thaddeus said, "Force them toward the river. Fast! Nip and push and shove. Arachne will stay here with Twilight in case she needs any message sent to us or to Them. So—here you go. I and my pot must stay here to keep watch. Go!"

We went at a fast pace into the darkness. From then on it was nightmarish. We were surrounded by Bats fluttering themselves and us forward. Zeke and I stayed within reach. And as soon as we neared the Stockade it was evident that Beasts were—at last—really afraid. Afraid of each other, of us, and therefore in blind flight. We kept after them, shouting, pushing, banging against them when we could do so without starting a fight.

Soon after we left the Stockade we saw Cat and Scuro, side by side, nipping at Beast heels and Worm tails. It was evident—or as much so as we could see in the night—that the Stockade was being abandoned, at least for now. That would mean, I was fairly sure, that Beasts and Worms would have to be confronted anywhere and everywhere and would have to become decent citizens of the Great

Land or be dealt with. For now they were being cleared from their fortress and forced into an open forest and a river valley.

Zeke and I went carefully, guided by Bats, and we had the good fortune to encounter and to argue with—and sometimes prove to—fleeing Worms, or Beasts, that they would be better off if they cared more for others than for their own wants. This, we soon learned, did not help much because right now the fleeing Beasts and Worms were lost, afraid, turned out of their terrible Stockade where their cruel treatment of each other and of others had poisoned them. We were sure they had to learn a different way. They were angry, upset, put out of their fortress, wanting to be the powerful ones who could rule the weak.

"Do you feel sorry for them, Zeke?"

"Not really. But they're missing their meanings by wanting power over everyone. I almost got into that. My Dad has power and wants—or wanted—more. It's not good."

At that moment Zeke's Bat swooped to him saying, "That Beast is dragging an injured Worm by its tail. It's badly hurt. I'll help you to free the Worm. Get the Beast by an ear and pull hard until it lets go of the Worm. I'll handle the Beast. You two care for the Worm."

It all happened so fast that we couldn't take time to be scared. Zeke grabbed the Beast's ear, pulling it and biting it fiercely. Instantly, the Beast let go, turning toward Zeke. Zeke ducked neatly and kicked the Beast. Meanwhile, I reached for the Worm as the Beast let go. It was bleeding profusely from its mangled tail—and then I realized its head was also bleeding from raw wounds. And then I recognized the Worm.

"Annel!" I cried out. "It's Annel! Oh Zeke, help us! Please!" Zeke turned, saw the situation, hit the Beast twice, downed it, kicked it fiercely in the head. It lay inert. Zeke's Bat said, "I'll handle it. Friends are coming to help me. Take care of your friend."

We worked over Annel as fast as we could—taking off our worn socks to use as bandages to stop the bleeding. It took a time. And Annel hardly breathed. We rubbed his body as well as we could without touching the wounds. Tears were on my face because he was so brave and frail.

"Will he die, Zeke?"

"I don't think so—look—*look*, he's trying to speak—lean to his face and listen—I'll care for the wounds—"

I put my ear near his odd Worm mouth. His eyes were closed, his long, legless body seemed lifeless. But I listened closely and could hear, "Ist—not here—Ist—she OK?—Ist, Ist—"

Then I heard. Of course! "Dear Annel. You are with us—Zeke and Maris. IstHer is all right. We take you home, Annel. Don't try to talk. We take you."

We looked at each other. How could we carry a shape like Annel? Zeke ripped his worn shirt off, tore it in half, and bound the two wounds. "They'll heal. You take the tail end, Maris, it's the lightest. I'll take the head end. And we've got Bat friends who will open the way for us. Here we go."

Zeke was loving and efficient as I had never seen him. He guided the Bats, he kept me from too much worry, he saw to it that Annel was comfortable. And after what seemed an endless time wandering in darkness we reached our cave home to be welcomed by everyone—including Arachne and IstHer. Thaddeus got some magical potion and put it on Annel's wounds.

Our exhausting day ended as Annel at last opened one eye and said, "Can help. Good. All well." He shut his eye and murmured, "See tomorrow."

CHAPTER 19

The next few days had to be a beginning recovery period. The great corral kept its walls of flame, replenished from time to time by Thaddeus's wizardry. The captive Beasts and Worms were somewhat subdued. our squadron of Birds dropped vegetable and fruit food to them occasionally. We rested off and on in the woods, or stayed home and got ready to act.

There were a few dead Beasts and one dead Worm—all found along the road from Stockade to corral—and we dug a place (with great difficulty because we had no tools) and we buried them sadly. As Thaddeus said, "It could have been us."

Our major question was what to do now. The message from the Place of Them did not suggest any plan. So after a few days we gathered together in a grove out of sight of the Beasts.

We were all present except Big Bat. The day was comfortable. We could hear the river. A small breeze stirred the forest. We formed a circle of twenty-one beings!

Arachne climbed onto a high stump so she could be seen by all of us and we banded up close to her. She looked at us for a quiet period. Then she spoke. "Dear friends, I wish I could say that our work is finished. But you, as well as I, know that it isn't. In times past, as our Beasts and Maris remember, many Beasts were killed but many escaped to this part of the Great Land to establish a counter Kingdom. We have disrupted the counter Kingdom but we have not destroyed it. What might we do to change it? Let our own Beasts speak first. Tusks?"

He bowed. "My Lady, I have been pondering that. There must be some in the corral who could be—or are—ready to change. Not all, of course. But some."

"And how would we know them?"

Thaddeus stepped forward. "It might be done. I can't say for sure, but it might. I have some special powder which, if eaten, turns eyes red if the person lies and leaves the eyes natural if truth is told. I've got quite a stock of it."

"We can try it if nothing else works. But—can we think of anything that would insist on truth without magic?"

"I can, Tusks," Isther said from her place near Annel. "What we must gather in the dark, what we must save and heal, what we must fling into the light—not power but our caring—neither rage nor laughter but a golden river of peace. I don't know exactly what I meant—or mean—except that some Beasts in there may be like our Beasts, may want to join our Beasts and us. How can we know if we don't ask?"

Tusks replied, "IstHer may have a real point. But I think that we would also need Thaddeus's powder. If Beasts in the corral are first offered the powder—told it is life-giving or something, and then are asked to agree to IstHer's words—if they say 'yes' and have red eyes they are kept in the corral. If 'yes' and no red eyes, they are freed."

"And just what does freed mean?" asked Arachne. "There must be a condition—like traveling blindfolded to the Place of Them with our Beasts as leaders and helpers. How do you feel about that—you Beasts who have just come from Them?"

Duo ventured his opinion first. "After all, I was a mean Beast until the humans and their comrades helped me to love and to help others. Maybe we could help some of them in the corral."

Tusks sounded excited, which he usually didn't. "I'm willing to go with you—maybe only two of us first, quietly, to talk to them through the corral mesh. I don't quite see how we get Thaddeus's powder and IstHer's words into the plan, but—"

"I do!" Twist sounded excited. "We could put a bowl of powder inside as a friendly gift. Then we'd know, when we finished, who honestly wanted to go to the Place of Them."

So Thaddeus put his golden powder in a large and elegant-looking copper bowl. As best as I could, I printed IstHer's words on a large but light rock. Then Thaddeus and I and our three Beasts went slowly and gently toward the corral with its flaming wall. The prisoners roared and screamed and backed away as we approached.

When we neared the barrier Thaddeus went up to the wire, touched it with a green stone, and the fire ceased in an area of ten feet or so. He stood in that flameless place and waited. Very hesitantly and fearfully one Beast approached the wire. Thaddeus slowly slid the bronze bowl inside, and stepped back. Tusks stepped forward.

"Friend," Tusks said in a soft voice, "I am one of you—a Beast. And others are with us. Here is healing food. Try it. It could lead you to freedom. Please trust me."

Tusks stood very still. The Beast moved slowly, slowly, and very cautiously, toward the bowl. When he came to it he sniffed, lifted his head, and looked at Tusks, then at the bowl. Then he came to the bowl, lowered his head and pulled it back several times. Tusks and I remained very still. Finally the Beast, with a suddenness as if his life was at stake, lowered his muzzle into the bowl, licked the powder once, then again, and then raised his muzzle—yellow, sniffing, and apparently pleased with the taste.

Tusks said nothing. But he put his own muzzle to the wire. "It is good, isn't it?" he said.

"Yes! Oh, yes! It all feels better already! Oh thank you! Thank you! Can I tell some others?"

"Certainly! Please do!"

To our amazement the Beast did just that. It didn't rush into anything. It just wandered about among other Beasts, said something, and moved on. It even spoke to several Worms. Almost before we knew it the copper bowl had become quite desirable. Not all of the imprisoned Beasts and their helpers—mostly Worms— were coming. But certainly more than we expected.

Eventually the copper bowl was emptied. The prisoners who had not eaten were grumbling, growling, harassing each other. Duo and Twist went to talk to the ones who had eaten and to say that more was coming.

It worked. By the time I found Thaddeus and reported what was happening—and by the time we got back with more golden powder, more Beasts were waiting. So Thaddeus patiently put in more and the Beasts ate it until it was gone.

At last Tusks and Thaddeus stood before the non-fiery section of fence and asked for silence. The prisoners were quieter than I had thought they could be—but most of the near ones had eaten the powder and seemed to want something from us.

Tusks took command quietly, but with authority. "Friends, I have things to say to you. You must have some idea of why you are here. Do you?"

After an uncertain silence a few voices came from the crowd, saying things like, "We hurt others" or, "We wanted more than we had" or, "We wanted to rule everyone" or, "We got hurt so we hurt others" or "We wanted to be the top of all creatures" —or a variation of all these, plus minor complaints and poor excuses. There were many who said nothing.

I regarded this milling crowd with some despair. Could we possibly trust any of them? And risk letting any of them go free? I could tell from Tusks's face as well as Thaddeus's that they had questions also.

Tusks spoke to them. "The Old Ones of the Great Land—living at the Place of Them—desire peace and equality, not war and torturing and killing. They desire Beasts—as well as other creatures—who are open, friendly, willing to serve the Great Land and all its inhabitants. They will protect and honor all Beasts or Worms or other beings who will work with and for the Land." A quiet pervaded the near Beasts. Those in the back areas were muttering, with a few rumbles coming from those farthest back. Thaddeus and Tusks nodded to me. I took the folded paper from my pocket.

Tusks spoke again. "Beast friends, will all of you who ate of our gift of golden powder please come near to this mesh barrier in just a moment."

Suddenly, startling us as much as the prisoned Beasts, King Feathers in all his majesty soared over the barrier and alighted in the space separating the Beasts who had eaten our food and those who had not. The two groups separated from each other widely, with King Feathers between them.

Thaddeus stood near King Feathers and spoke to all the prisoners present, Beasts and Worms together.

"Those who have eaten of our healing food will—when the Words of the Future have been read—pass before us, and look at me directly. We will then know who among you can join with us to save the Great Land." Thaddeus turned to me and nodded.

I read—and without fear.

"It is lovely as nightfall and golden as day—what we must gather in the dark, what we must save and heal—what we must fling into the light—not power but our caring—neither rage nor laughter but a golden river of peace—"

For a held breath nothing responded. Then a few jeering roars came from the background. King Feathers, from a place near the non-eaters, spread his great wings and screamed. The Beasts were silenced. And then, one by one, the near Beasts who had eaten the golden powder moved slowly in between the great eagle and Thaddeus. With only two exceptions, Thaddeus chose nineteen Beasts, looking carefully into their eyes and nodding to them to stand beside Tusks.

When Thaddeus finished, he turned to the cluster of newcomers outside the prison. "I know that you trust the words you heard, and that you will, from here on, go with our Beasts to the Great Land to help us establish the golden river of peace. We are grateful you are with us. Please follow Tusks." He turned to the ones who had not come out. "The rest of you will be held inside the fire wall until you are ready to be healed." And with that he touched a stick to the non-burning space and suddenly the corral was again completely walled in by flames. A roar of anger and protest filled the air. But the Beasts who had honestly said "yes" were following Tusks and Twist and Duo out into the night.

When at last Thaddeus made sure that the corral wall would keep aflame and secure, we all went wearily homeward. Some progress had been made by King Feathers and he went with Tusks, Duo, and Twist, and the freed Beasts, to be sure none of them tried to run away. (I learned later that one did—and that King Feathers swooped down on the Beast, lifted it into the air, and carried it back to the fire-guarded corral. When Tusks told me about it, he said it was the best thing that could have happened, because it taught all the others a needed lesson.)

We reached our cave home before dark. Our herd of converted Beasts met Arachne and most of the others of our company. Our own Beast comrades shepherded them into one of the large rooms of our cavern, fed them again, and at the meal's end Thaddeus came to them. "Friends, do rest and sleep now. Tusks, Twist, and Duo will stay with you to look after you. Waff is going to Them to report your joining. Good night to you all."

Zeke shook me awake. "Everything's all right, Maris. It's only that Arachne has word from Them. They want Duo, Twist, Da and Gada to shepherd the new Beasts—blindfolded—to Them."

Tusks and Thaddeus—sort of like concerned fathers—wandered among the Beasts, spoke to them, fed them more of Thaddeus's golden food. The Beasts seemed receptive and responsive. From the black pot all sorts of items came out and eventually melted together. They became weird eyeglasses—thick and dark—and each Beast was fitted with a pair. Surprisingly, no Beast complained.

"Let me explain what you can see," Thaddeus spoke to them. "You can see the ground and your feet. That is all. It is enough. You will be carefully guided. The Guardians and the Old Ones are waiting. Love and concern for your well-being is with them."

One Beast, a smallish one, spoke in a surprisingly firm voice. "I thank you and your company for kindness and concern. For me it is wonderful to feel that I'm going somewhere to do something helpful rather than being mean because others are mean. So I'm happy and I trust and I'm glad I'm going wherever I'm going."

"Do you have a name?" I asked the Beast.

"No name. Never."

"What if we named you Glad?" Said Tusks.

"Oh! I would be a new Beast! I'm Glad! That's my name! Glad! Thank you! Thank you! I've never been happy in my life! Now I'm Glad!"

Glad stood there in his blinding glasses, his head held proudly, his Beastiness close to some of our loved Beasts. Tusks went to him and rubbed his nose against Glad's. "Welcome, Glad. I predict you will be one of us, serving Them."

We were quite surprised and delighted at the behavior of the Beasts. At least half of them were willing to talk, and to describe the ways of their cruel Beastmasters. Most said some words of gratitude or hope.

The smallest of the group was obviously very frightened, although it had chosen to go. Duo gently touched its back with his nose and said gently, "We love you, little one. We want you with us. You have been much hurt. From now on you shall be called Giant because you are brave." Giant bounced up and down in a frenzy of joy—as a small goat-kid would do in a spring field. "I've got a name! I've got a name! I am—I will be—a Giant!"

Tusks, in his kindly and loving father-self, told them that for the rest of this day and through the night they would rest and eat, keeping their eye covers on to get used to them. "Duo and Twist will be with you—and Da and Gada. In the early morning they will lead you to Them." Glad and Giant called goodbye.

It was almost four days before we had word of them. Although worried about them, we also had to meet often together to find ways to work with the stubborn and negative Beasts in the flame-walled corral. They were growing hungrier each day. We were doing all we could to find plants and fruits for ourselves and for them. They were becoming more and more irritable—not only with us but with each other. The one thing that seemed positive was that they were not at each other's throats in a killing way, although as all residents or prisons, they were angry and wanted out.

At last, in desperation, we all met together to decide what we could do to change the situation. We knew we couldn't keep these Beasts and Worms imprisoned forever. Nor could we just turn them loose. After we had discussed and argued and come up with absurd solutions IstHer, from her favorite place on Annel's back, said, "Thaddeus, don't you have any special magic that you could use to make them all my size? If you were my size in a world where almost all other beings were at last eight or ten times bigger—you would be very careful about what you did, where you went and how you went, wouldn't you?"

"Yes, IstHer," said Thaddeus. "If the Beasts were smaller—at least for a time—I'd guess they'd have a different idea of how to treat others."

"If you can make Domar go from big enough to hold quite a few of us to small enough to hold in my hand," said Zeke, "you sure could do it to Beasts."

"I have," said Thaddeus. "Not too long ago—for Quatro and his lady. Yes—I can do it probably. Of course if someone wants it, there's no resistance. If they're fighting the magical self inside, then it's harder. But I'm willing to try. Shall we? Tomorrow?"

Before we could answer there was suddenly in our big room a large flying form. And then the wonderful voice of Owl boomed against the walls.

"All is well. The traveling Beasts are almost to the Guardians, who are eager to have them come. The Old Ones are following

194

every step taken by you to save this Great Land, and love you all. And their message is that all of us Birds will come for you at the river somewhere." He paused, looking around at us with his great eyes. "The other message is that Quatro and Blanca have a child. He is golden white and has a small horn growing in the center of his forehead."

CHAPTER 20

I could not sleep that night for thinking of the golden white child with a single horn, and of its parents safe with the Old Ones and surrounded by love and food and Domar. When day began to filter into our cave I walked out into it. To celebrate the little unicorn—as I was sure it was—I bowed to the spreading light and asked it to care for the child and the Great Land.

"Maris," Zeke's hand startled me as it touched mine. "Maris. I wanted to honor this day, too. I feel it will be filled with many doings."

"I'm glad you're here, Zeke. I'm excited and afraid all at once. Are the others awake? With plans?"

He nodded. We hurried back to our comrades. I felt nearer to him than I ever had. He had grown out of boyhood—almost—and I trusted him. In our large getting-together-for-plans room were all ten—me, Zeke, Annel, IstHer, Tusks, Waff, Cat, Scuro, Thaddeus, Arachne—plus Owl who, as messenger, also said he was staying.

"Now," said Arachne, standing beside Thaddeus, "IstHer and Thaddeus will make the corraled Beasts small enough to handle. Tell us your ideas, Thaddeus, if you please."

He scratched his head with a large hind foot—and this meant he was almost ready. Then he turned to IstHer. "Come and stand beside me while I tell our ideas." She came and put her small gray-furred body against his brownish, hairless, loose-fitting skin. What a wonderful, unbelievable pair!

"Dear friends, hear our ideas. Maris will help me go through all the things in my pot so I can get the very best combination of magical size-changing. We will mix it in with food that the Beasts like. Then IstHer will ride on Owl and scatter food over the whole of the corral. Then we'll see what happens. Does that seem possible, Arachne?"

She nodded. "It seems well planned. I do have two questions. Does the corral also shrink? If it doesn't, then won't we have dozens and dozens of tiny escaping Beasts to try to capture?"

"I'm sorry, my lady, I forgot to say that we are asking you to spin a web to cover the exit to the corral. We will see to it that the one exit—which is now closed by the flames—will be flameless when you arrive there."

"And when does this all begin?" Arachne asked.

"As soon as I can get all my magic sorted and in order. It has fallen out so many times that it's all very confused. But Maris can always get things straight. And IstHer will help. I hope we'll be ready before the day is too far along."

"Thank you." Arachne nodded. "We will all go to gather food supplies while you three get the magic ready. Come, my friends."

The next period of time—as always when dear Thaddeus sorted—was total confusion. IstHer was naturally adaptable and relaxed. So when we finished being sorcerer's apprentices, Thaddeus had what he wanted laid out before him. Slowly and thoughtfully, he asked one or the other of us to "bring that" or to "put that back in the pot." Eventually, what he wanted was in its own order before him and he mixed this with that and that with this in his usual seemingly confused way. Then he said some words, there was a puff of smoke, and before him was a large pile of silver dust.

"Now I need mashed fruit and the package that has some of the leftover Beast food I made. Get it quickly."

I asked IstHer to see Arachne and get Annel's help and gather fruit. I went off to find any leftover Beast food. I found Tusks. He had found a moderate-sized package of the golden food. Soon after that we returned to Thaddeus. Then Arachne, Annel, and IstHer arrived with quite an amount of fruit, mostly carried on Annel's undulating body.

"Splendid!" Thaddeus turned to me. "Please bring the black pot, Maris."

I pulled the pot to him. Then, at his instructions, we put in the golden food, the newly made silver food, and, last, the picked fruit. "Stir it all together, Maris, with my black prayerstick." Once found, I stirred vigorously and, as I watched, the golden food, the silver dust, the fruit, all blended into a simple greenish gray mash.

"Splendid! Splendid!" Thaddeus was beaming. "Now let's make it into packets—so Owl can carry them as well as IstHer. Meanwhile, I hope Annel can take Arachne and her web and enclose the opening. Flames are there now. However, Annel, if you will carry this—" and he handed Annel a green prayerstick. "Hold it in your mouth and touch the flaming opening. Arachne can ride on your back and can fling her web over the opening and you can retreat a distance."

Arachne and Annel looked at each other solemnly. Then Arachne smiled. "I've never ridden a Worm. It will be an experience."

"My lady," replied Annel in his learned speech. "I've never carried a Spider. I am at your service, with pleasure."

I was excited and afraid, wanting to be present and not wanting to. What were we going to do with all these hostile and tiny Beasts milling about—or trying to get out of the flaming corral? I said that to those present.

Thaddeus scratched his head. "Sorry. Hadn't though of that. Oh, dear. What can we do?"

Then Arachne spoke. "I can made a series of enclosed webs rather than only one—that is, webs made into a sphere with emptiness inside so there is a series of balloon-like webs, each with an opening. When the furthest is filled to capacity it closes. Then the next one the same, and so on up the line until the first one is filled and closes. An ancestral Spider thought of that idea for catching swarms of insects. Now we try for Beasts. And I have a sense that it will work."

"Yes," said Thaddeus. "We must not do anything in haste. Arachne needs to make her series of balloon webs. IstHer needs to finish the packets of food to be dropped from Owl's back. Annel will take Arachne and her nets to cover the exit. Let's call in the others so everyone is ready to help."

It was clear what Annel, Arachne, Owl, IstHer, and Thaddeus were to do. "But," I asked, "What about Tusks, Cat, Scuro, Zeke, Waff, and me? Aren't we also involved?"

"Of course you are!" Thaddeus said. "We're all involved. Just had to plan the difficult details first. I suggest that Tusks, Cat, Scuro, and Waff stay by the exit. Accidents can occur—like a web thread breaking, or like some Beast not eating and staying large and trying to escape, or some Beast or Worm coming from outside the corral. And I believe that Maris and Zeke are the ones who could most frighten and keep the Beasts at bay."

Thaddeus looked around at his strange company. He shook his brown salamander head. "In case you forgot, I too am part of the company. As a matter of fact, I am going first to the edge of the woods from where I can look over the corral and see where everyone is—or isn't—and can use my magic if necessary. So—you all know what you are to do. The day will not go on forever, although a lot of it is still left. Maris, will you assemble my belongings, and then put my pot on my head?"

This I did as quickly and as much in order as I could. Thaddeus departed, looking like some sort of a serpentining military machine. We let him get a good start. Very soon Arachne returned with Annel. "I was afraid I had forgotten how to make serial webs," she said, "but I hadn't. So I and Annel will go and attach them to the exit after the fire is out. The webs are almost invisible, so they won't be noticed. And I will join Thaddeus in the woods." Tusks, Cat, Scuro, and Waff had already left. IstHer had finished her food packets to be dropped and was waiting for Owl.

Zeke looked at me. I looked at him. "What do we do now?" I asked. Zeke said, "What Thaddeus said. Remember? He said we could frighten and keep angry Beasts at bay. Remember?" He laughed.

"Yes. Now I do. It isn't what I'd have chosen—but let's go."

He grabbed my hand and off we went down the corridor of our cave and out into the late day. It was light still, with sharp shadows. We took a path we knew and very soon could see downslope to the Stockade-corral. The fire was inside, beasts banging heads against it and retreating. An occasional chorus of shouts swelled and stopped.

"Look over there, Maris! In the near woods. It's Owl! And IstHer is climbing on his back with the packages! Oh, hold tight, IstHer! Hold tight!"

We watched them as they circled the corral. The Beasts looked up as Owl went lower and they began to run around, shouting and roaring. Owl calmly soared over and over and around and over until the Beasts quieted. Then he came soaring in and IstHer dropped a large package, which broke open—as it was obviously intended to do—and the greenish mixture scattered.

The Beasts sniffed, backed away, came forward, sniffed at it again. Finally, one Beast took a bite and another and another. Others followed. They were really hungry. At that moment I felt sorry for them—poor, angry animals!

While Owl was circling for a second run, Annel and Isther came to the one place left open in the corral but still fire-covered. Annel did what Thaddeus had told him to do. He held a green prayerstick in his mouth, put his ugly face almost into the flames, and they went out. Before any Beast could move to it, Annel turned so that Arachne was directly in front of the opening. She leaped—as only Spiders can—to Annel's head and flung the web over the opening very accurately. As they went away from it, one round web opened into another and others until five round, webbed "rooms" —like a transparent tunnel—went from corral to freedom. The last one before freedom was closed to the outside.

"We'd better get near to the webs, Maris! Zeke pulled me out of the woods toward the cleared space where the series of round web rooms extended. We're supposed to deal with escapees, is that correct?"

"Yes. But not alone, remember. Look, there come Tusks, Scuro, Cat, and Waff. Each one of them could harass Beasts trying to escape. So we join them, I guess."

We did, and decided to spread ourselves along and around the web cells. So far no Beasts had tried to get out—and yet many seemed to be eating the packages of food that IstHer and Owl were dropping into the corral.

"Look there!" said Zeke. "Look where that bunch of Beasts is! Gobbling the food! And one of them—no, two, three of them—they're getting smaller! Wow, what a magician Thaddeus is! Look!"

I did. It was amazing. They ate and slowly they diminished in size until they were only a bit larger than IstHer. None of the eaters realized what was happening until one of them—more perceptive than the rest—dashed over to the opening where the series of spiderweb nets began.

"No fire! Fire's gone! Can get out!" It climbed into the first spherical web, explored around frantically, discovered the opening into the second web, climbed through, and proceeded to the third, fourth, and fifth web net. Then, in typical uneducated and untrained Beast fashion, it went endlessly around and around and around the last web trying to find a way out.

Meanwhile, IstHer and Owl made their final trip to drop all the rest of the food bundles. As we watched, it was very clear that Beasts were, as a group, more like uneducated adolescents. Those in the corral were, for the most part, greedy and brutal, gobbling the food, pushing others away. We saw no Worms, and wondered if the Beasts had killed them all, or penned them up. Also the Beasts in the corral did not yet seem to be aware that the eaters shrank as they ate, or that the little ones were climbing out of the corral—at least as far as they could go.

Zeke grabbed my arm. "Look at the last round web! I can hardly believe it! Look!"

I did. It was incredible. It was a bulging ball of little Beasts. "Zeke, we've got to get someone to carry that ball away. Scuro could carry it."

"Good idea," said Zeke. Scuro came at once. He went up to the bulging ball of little captive Beasts. Very gently he took the exposed side of the web in his teeth, taking care not to bite into Beast or web. Very slowly he pulled on it. The small Beasts inside were terrified, I could see by their expressions. So while Scuro pulled slowly, slowly, I talked to them about not hurting them and caring for them and things like that. I really felt sorry for them and hoped they could become like our Beast comrades.

When it came free Scuro carried the full web off into the forest where Thaddeus and Arachne were. When he finally came back he said that Thaddeus and Arachne felt that, until Owl could carry them to the Guardians, they should be protected. So Scuro carried them to one of our small rooms, accompanied by Cat and Waff who would watch over them.

By the time twilight came, four full webs had been taken to our place. And we prepared to take the last ball of little Beasts. But we did not dare it until Thaddeus and Arachne came to where we were beside the fifth web. We needed Thaddeus to send the fire forth as we loosed the last web of tightly packed little Beasts.

Slowly, we pulled it free, and immediately Thaddeus touched the free space and flames roared upward to complete the corral's fire wall. We stepped back from the flames. At that very moment Tusks joined us. "Owl is making five round trips to the Place of

Them, carrying these Beast bundles. He has already gone with the first. What is happening in the corral?"

"We've hardly noticed, I guess," said Zeke. "I guess we've been so concerned with what has come out that we've not attended to what has stayed in."

"That's all right. Let's check our friends inside. First, however, where are IstHer and Annel?"

"We're coming." It was IstHer's voice. "We got some fruit. After Owl's last flight with me."

We went singly and silently to the wall of flames, each of us—according to our height—trying to find someplace where we could see inside the Beast corral in order to learn what had happened. It was a dismal picture. The Beasts still inside were angry, confused, and sad to see. It was as if they were thrown completely off their balance. Their numbers had truly diminished. They went back and forth restlessly, coming toward the fence and glaring at us, then going away. Part of me hated them and felt they deserved what they were getting. But another part of me pitied them. There was goodness in Beasts. In our friends. In those who had chosen to come with us, and were now with the Guardians and Old Ones—and, hopefully, in all those who had shrunk and were being transported to the Place of Them.

"Why don't we see any Worms?" I asked.

"Well," replied Annel, "all hurt or killed, or got away." He sighed. "My people sad. Hope can help them. They my people."

CHAPTER 21

I awoke remembering all the webs of dwarfed Beasts and, despite weariness, was glad that they were by now in the care of the Guardians in the Place of Them. Glad also that Waff and Cat were with Them.

We struggled up when daylight came, like beings who had been in a catastrophe and were safe but somewhat dazed. Even Arachne seemed not her usual balanced self, as she started sentences and let them fade away unfinished. Thaddeus went to sleep again for a time. Tusks seemed to be in a meditative mood, gazing up at the cave's ceiling.

Zeke and Cat broke the mood by beginning to chase each other around the cave room in a burst of the delight of children. Very quickly Isther and Annel joined them, followed by Scuro with Waff on his back.

Suddenly Thaddeus came awake. "What's all this joy? Why—of course—we need it! Come, my friends! Arachne! Tusks! Maris! Let us all dance! Come!"

And it happened—like a birth—that in a moment of time we moved from serious and weary stupor into delight—chasing, teasing, laughing, even singing—until, one by one, we dropped to the cave floor in relaxed and happier states of being.

"Wonderful! Wonderful!" Tusks looked at us all. "You see how we can dance into joy! I really didn't know that until now! Thank you, dear Thaddeus!"

"Don't thank me, Tusks. Thank those whose ways lead us into the eternal child in ourselves. It cures us of the poisons of the power-desiring Beasts."

And for the time being—quite a time being—the eternal child reigned. It was a deep need, deeper than I could have guessed. For so many days and nights we had seen only hatred and viciousness

and cruelty centered around the Beast Stockade. And we were weary—deeply weary—but with a bright undercurrent of joy. Because the unicorn child had been born and safe. Because we knew that in the Great Land the Place of Them was being well tended, and had many new inhabitants who were, we hoped, glad to be there and learning to help in creative ways. And also just because we needed to let feelings come. So we danced and danced and laughed and teased until, one by one, we curled up together in a tangle of bodies of assorted shapes and sizes. We slept deeply.

When I awoke I could see that my comrades were yawning, stretching, and slowly getting to their feet. We had just gathered ourselves together when, in a silent arc of feathers, Owl came before us. Arachne, Thaddeus, and Tusks moved to Owl first, and bowed and greeted him. Then the four of them turned toward the rest of us.

"Owl," said Arachne, "we welcome you. How is the Great Land?"

Owl gazed at us with his rich shining eyes. "It is good. The small horned one is doing well. Very well. And his parents also. All three are loved—and loving. The small one loves Domar and stays in her as much as he can. Also—so far every one of the first group of Beasts we took from here—glasses and all—are happy, learning fast, helping with all kinds of work. And as for the bundles of dwarfed Beasts, they are all set free into a large fenced yard. We are going to watch them carefully. If they can learn to be tamed, learn to trust, learn to love and be loved—well, we can work with them, I hope. They do seem to be wanting to be useful somehow. And Giant and Glad are trying to find ways to tame them by loving them."

Owl bowed. "Now I bring a message—perhaps it is a command—from Them, the Old Ones. They ask you soon to return to the Place of Them by going on foot part of the way. Then They may send the Birds to carry you. That is not yet decided because many Beasts are still trying to be conquerors. The Old Ones will give further instructions soon." Owl smiled—or at least I saw a smile on his round face.

Tusks spoke then. "Friend Owl, what do you believe is halfway from here to the Place of Them? Do we climb mountains, go through wilderness, swim in water?"

At that moment I pulled my courage together and asked Tusks if I could speak. "Of course," he said. "What troubles you, Maris?"

"Dear comrades—including Owl. I am afraid for all of us. Some have already been injured and weakened. And we have given our utmost, I believe. Why must we go on —hungry, hurt, weary? Why? It seems to me more than we can give. Why can the Old Ones not send the big Birds to carry us to the Place of Them and from there let those of us who are strong enough help to get the Bad Beasts and help heal the wounded? Are we so bad that we have to be punished all the time?" I was trembling as I finished, and prepared to be reprimanded by Owl or by Tusks.

But to my surprise, Tusks spoke firmly. "I agree. We have labored, climbed, fought, gone hungry, harassed the enemies—all because we love the Great Land. I feel as Maris does. We cannot continue to wear ourselves out. I know we are ready and willing to battle for the Great Land. But we must have some rest to recuperate."

Owl bowed deeply. His great eyes shone. "Dear comrades, I hear you and feel with you. I shall take your message to Them and get word to you very soon. Bless you." And he lifted silently into the air and was gone.

"Well," said Tusks. "Hadn't we better talk of where we could go to meet the Birds—if they are sent—and also should we not—at least some of us—explore the Beast and Worm situation now. We need to see what the conditions are. Do you agree?"

Our waking joyfulness had been dampened by Owl's message—but because we had taken a firm stand we felt stronger and willing to explore. After some discussion we agreed that first we needed small Bird comrades to give us some ideas of where we could meet the big Birds. And all unexpected, Light and Shadow fluttered in, singing a poem:

"We serve the living joyful things
in darkest night and brightest day.
We serve the lost and help it sing
and in the gloom we seek a way."

It was wonderful to welcome our bird friends and to hear their reassuring song. They explained that Antic—however he had learned our plans—had told them to help us. At that moment he sailed in, filled with greetings and joy and bounces, and his first message was one of excitement.

"Greetings, my comrades. The way we are going is very beautiful—but be sure you are ready for possible hazards. It's a rich valley and a beautiful river. We are going to someplace to meet the big Birds from Them and will be flown to Them. If They agree."

"What place will you go to? To the river valley? Can I help?"

"Yes, you can, Antic. You and your two friends, Light and Shadow."

So we all went into the morning light and made our way to a lovely hollow near the river quite protected from the raw land. The dawn sky above the hollow was silent and beautiful. After a time, we gathered around to plan where we could go to meet the Bird carriers. I knew that Tusks agreed regarding where we would gather to meet the Bird carriers—assuming that the Old Ones would heed our wishes—described by Antic.

"I remember that lovely stretch of river from where you can see an island—and the river is wide there—and you can see the Mountain of Them in the distance—and I believe that is where the Birds can find us." These words burst from me unbidden.

Scuro said, "Yes. I remember. Let's go there. It's a great road."

Everyone assented. We couldn't go until word came from Them to Tusks. And we also needed to watch the Beasts. So we went—some of us—to see if Beasts were in battle. They were not. They seemed weary and slow and afraid. None were roaring or fighting. It was a sad scene.

"Wait a minute," Zeke protested. "We can't just pull out and leave the leftover Beasts to starve inside the corral's fire walls! Can we? We can't just treat them their way!"

"Zeke is right," said Tusks. "We cannot. But, on the other hand, to set them free would be against all we're struggling for."

After a long and very silent pause, Thaddeus spoke. "We are caught in our own magic trap. I can—I hope I can—make them small and we can enmesh them and send them separately—separate from us, I mean—to the Old Ones. By way of Owl. With a warning to Them to keep this batch of captives imprisoned for the time being. We could leave them to starve or to eat each other. We, then, would be as bad as they. They must be hungry. Some of you go and try to collect food and bring it back here."

The next piece of time was filled with work. Some of the company went off to find food and some went for herbs. I found a stream of water, filled Thaddeus's pot, and—wonder of wonders—built a small fire and set the pot to boil. Soon the herbs were in the pot. Then Thaddeus and I found what we wanted, put it in the pot to boil along with the herbs and the edibles that had been gathered.

When the cooking fire burned low, Thaddeus blew it out. As it cooled, he stirred it so that sweet smells came from it and reached the hungry Beasts.

"This will fill you and help you, my friends," said Thaddeus to them. "Come and eat. And to help you to trust, I will eat with you. Come." He put a front foot into the pot, lifted out a large glob of food, and put it in his mouth. "Good! It is good! Come!" And he pushed the pot inside the corral.

One Beast came, then two others, then several. Hesitantly, then eagerly, then hungrily, all of them were crowding around the food and eating ravenously. Soon the dish was empty, and soon after that all the Beasts had curled up together and gone to sleep. As we watched them in this peaceful relaxation, they slowly and gently diminished in size.

"How will these be taken?" I whispered to Thaddeus.

"Watch the fire walls. I'm going to turn them into a web. I hope. Then Owl can gather up the sleeping ones to take to the Place of Them."

Thaddeus moved to his pot, gathered various items, and handed them to me to put one place or another. Then he recited a long sequence of unknown sounds, sang a strange tune in strange words, and suddenly grabbed his tail and began spinning around and around. And the fire walls sank into the ground and disappeared. Slowly and gently a meshed web grew from the earth under the sleeping small Beasts until it went well beyond the perimeter of Beasts.

Suddenly, Owl was there. And quietly Thaddeus gathered the sleeping Beasts into the web, fastened it, handed it to Owl. And they were gone, Owl and the nest of Beasts.

So that left us. Suddenly Antic, who had gone off on some duty, flew in. "Dag came and left a message from Them. It said, 'Owl and others will come to the riverbanks near the island and will

carry all of you back to the Place of Them. Be ready by tomorrow morning. We await you with joy.'"

This set us into a fury of moving forward along the river's shores. As we walked over and over we were planning our travel and what might meet us on the way. Nothing did. Antic told us when we were near the island. It was dusk, but we cheered the island in whispered voices. Surprisingly, we all fell asleep quite soon.

CHAPTER 22

After only one or two hours of rest—and some sleep—we were all wakened in the dark by Tusks.

"Come, children! Come! Now!"

Scuro began to bark, and to call out, "Up! Up!" between barks. Zeke awoke, quickly for him, and began to gather us out of sleep. Then, bless him, he rushed off and found some fruits we had cached in a hole. We all had something—not much, but something—and also some of Thaddeus's awful inventions for food—tasteless, but it helped. Soon we were gathered together.

Zeke, in an unusual state of awakeness, made a brief, unexpected speech. "Exi said to me once that the Great Land is what lives under and within all other lands. It is sort of a pattern of patterns. What happens here can alter what happens in other lands and countries and also in people. That is what he said. And we, I guess, are part of a pattern that we can make whole or upset. Is that right?"

Tusks looked at Zeke lovingly. "So now, all of us must get ready to meet Da, Gada, Dag, and Great Owl, or whoever of them comes. They will take us to Them."

We were willing travelers—eager, even if tired. We stumbled over rocks, almost fell into the river, called softly to each other to know each of us was present. Tusks and Arachne went first. Annel's wounds were healed by Thaddeus's magic, and Annel had IstHer riding. I followed them. Scuro came along very near, just behind the company as a good shepherd. We pushed ourselves hard in order to reach our Birds. And we got there in time to have a meager rest until the delicate day began. It was lovely. Suddenly, we saw against the porcelain sky the four great Birds circle and descend! It was what we had been waiting for.

I resisted hugging them, although I wanted to. But I kept myself in hand because I knew that we longed to return to Them—and also that our carriers had other work to do, and that the Birds would give us directions. We could not help greeting them and stroking them because we loved them and they loved us. Arachne and I climbed onto Da. Zeke and Scuro settled onto Gada. Great Owl took Tusks. And Annel, with IstHer on his head, rippled onto Dag. Such wonderful carriers, these Bird friends, as they lifted us into the rose and apricot sky. And Dark, Light, and Antic all of a sudden were flying around us and greeting us and adding a joy.

It was not a long flight, compared to other flights of dangerous explorations for enemies. It was clear that the Old Ones were having us delivered close to home. It seemed a quick flight as we climbed down from our carriers and thanked them and they rose into the air, headed for their nests and some sleep.

"Let us rest a bit before we move toward Them." Tusks followed his own idea and settled on the earth. We all did likewise. It felt good to me as preparation.

I was in the midst of a nightmare of blood and battle when I was wakened by a great noise. I couldn't get my eyes opened and I kept trying to and not succeeding. And then I heard Tusks's voice shouting me awake. I struggled to get my eyes open, but it was like they were glued shut. And then Scuro's voice, right next to my ear, said, "Take your hands off your eyes, Maris! Take them off your eyes!" And then I felt Scuro's tongue on my face, pushing my hands away.

"Open your eyes, Maris! A friend is here!" It was Tusks's voice, excited and loud. It must be some helper or other. So I managed to waken fully and opened my eyes and looked up.

"Quatro!" I cried out. "Is it really Quatro?"

"It is," the voice said. And the loved face came down to mine and a nose, soft and gentle, touched my face. I started to cry, and then I staggered to my feet, and then I threw my arms around him and kissed his head and he licked my face again.

"You look strong, Quatro." Tusks gazed at him with joy. "And how are Blanca and your son?"

"Splendid. They have had so much care and love from the Old Ones and the Guardians and Domar and her family that they are healthy and filled with happiness. And our son is a happy child and his name is Uno because of his single horn." He paused and looked at us all. "Oh my friends! What a joy! And I was sent to shepherd you, Tusks, sir—and everyone here. The Old Ones sent me to take you to them."

It was comforting to follow Quatro in warm light and green earth. I breathed the fresh air. Though it was a steep path we climbed, it was rich with a fullness of life and a possibility of overcoming darkness.

When at last we crested the green sloped hill it was like a birthday for everyone. We came into the lovely field of green with its clumps of dark green trees and a few patches of blue flowers. There they stood, my beloved beetle Exi, my dear ant friend Grandan, Arachne, and Thaddeus. And behind the Guardians a light was glowing from Domar's window and door.

It was so joyful and so unexpected after the long, dark, fearfilled days of Beast battle that tears ran down my face in relief and happiness. I touched each of the Guardians gently, and risked giving a quick kiss to dear Thaddeus. And then I went to Domar's door. "Oh, Maris! Maris, how wonderful to see you all again! My family has grown larger, and now we can be together—but you can see and hear about all that later. Now it is just greeting all of you and being happy that you are here. Owl will come later."

"And now," said Arachne, "you will come with us to a place of rest. And then meet with the Old Ones."

So we were taken to a dark and sweet-smelling chamber. We stretched out gratefully, and I guess most of us slept. How long I was asleep I could not tell. I only knew when a voice awakened me that I was Maris.

"Now let us go to the grass where you can be refreshed," said Exi. "Follow me." It was joyful to follow after Exi's blunt black beetle body to the soft green meadow where food of every kind was laid out on the grass. And we all came happily together—Worms, Beasts, Human, IstHer, Birds, Cat, Dog, Insect.

Exi stayed with us until we had eaten. Then he said, "It is time for the Old Ones to be met. So please come with me." And we followed him to the great square. The drums sounded. Owl entered and moved toward the center, and then, very quietly, in came Dark

Fire, Grandfather, Grandmother—from three directions—to stand
together near Owl.

"Go to the Old Ones, my children," said Exi. "They want to
speak with you."

It had been so long, so very long, since I had heard the
mysterious chanting of the unknown singers to Grandmother. And
now, into this twilight of a strange day, came those hidden voices:

Grandmother . . . Grandmother . . . Let night be gentle
and let these children
help us and themselves
with a tender courage and fire
to defend the Great Land.
Oh our Grandmother!
Give these children gratitude
for their difficult journey
and for their concerns and labors
for the Great Land.
Give them night for their resting
and our love for their peace.

As I looked toward the hidden voices I saw Her, Grandmother, as I had seen Her before—and she was as mysterious and
austerely magical as ever. Perhaps more so now that I was more
mature and more conscious and felt more deeply the meanings of
the Great Land as the undergirding of all lands and all people. She
stood tall, in robes of shifting colors, and her wrinkled face in the
mysterious light was as if it was our earth, all earths, wherever they
were. And her eyes were like skies of rain and snow and unlight all
together, and her eyes held the wounds of the universe. Her crin-
kled face was more beautiful than it had been before.

"My children—ones that I knew before and ones that are here
for the first time—all my children—I thank you for your love and
sacrifices which may once again save the Great Land. You are tired
now. So eat and rest. Owl will watch over you. Tomorrow morning we meet together for plans."

She faded into the darkness.

For a time nobody spoke. The wonder of Grandmother was so
great that silence always followed her departures and arrivals, I
remembered. Then Owl came to us, his great eyes shining.

"Children, you are asked to greet Grandfather and Dark Fire before you eat your meal. And Domar has asked you to dine with her and her family. So come with me to Grandfather and Dark Fire.

It was like a dream as we followed Owl across the twilight-shadowed plaza of Them, to be introduced to and to bow to Grandfather and Dark Fire, and to be bowed to by each of them in a magical silence. Then Owl led us across the plaza and down the velvet grass slope to where Domar's light glowed.

As we drew near I wondered how many beings were in Domar as her family. Was Uno there? Blanca? In addition to her earlier family of Molasses? Perhaps Isther. I realized that when this whole group arrived—and all of us stood around her—Domar would not believe it. But I was wrong, very wrong, and once again had to give Domar full credit for wisdom.

I went behind Owl and the rest followed. Owl deposited us in the glowing light from her door and window. Owl bowed to her, saying, "Your loved friends are here, Domar. May you all be blessed. And I was told by Grandmother that all of you may sleep on this ground some way or other. Good night, friends and helpers. We will see you tomorrow." And he lifted himself on his silent owl-wings and was gone.

"Oh dearest Domar!" I stood before her and I could not keep tears from my eyes. "What a wonder that we have come back to you. It is not believable, but it is!"

"Yes, my loved friends, yes! Yes! It is the most wonderful event I could dream of! And it isn't a dream! It's true! And please, my dears, at least look into me and greet my little ones."

So one by one we peered into the small, cozy room. IstHer was seated in the window where she could look out or in, and she called out to each of us as she saw us. We called back. Beside her was Molasses in her moisture dish. She squeaked something I could not hear, but Domar said, "She's happy. That's what she is saying. She's always happy, and it's nice to have someone like that. So it's a dear family in here. And a dear family outside—my good fortune."

"Domar, Domar, we love you deeply," said Tusks. "We want you to be our guest at dinner. I planned it all myself, so everyone present is my guest." He looked upward and let out some kind of a call, and almost at once a flock of little Owls came down among us, carrying in their beaks small bundles which they placed before us and then flew away. Each one of us had a bundle—including Molassses and IstHer.

After the Owls had gone we thanked Tusks thoroughly—so much that he was embarrassed—but we meant it. Then we sat on the grass in a warm and loving half-circle so that everyone could see everyone. Molasses and Isther sat in Domar's door, and were asked to spend the night. It was a soft, warm, loving time. When we finished our meal, Tusks called the little Owls and they carried away the empty bundles, hooting softly as they disappeared.

Darkness was gentle and silent, and for a brief time we sat in the silence as if it had asked us to. After an unmeasured period Tusks spoke. "We must rest now, my children, because as soon as the light returns we will be bidden to talk with the Guardians about the state of the Great Land and our responsibilities."

We said a good night to Domar and her residents, and her lights went out. I found a soft hollow in the grass and Cat and I curled into it. Scuro and Zeke found a larger hole, and we were all soon asleep as much as I could tell from the soundless darkness.

When the light came over the mountain and fell on us sleeping travelers, we wakened slowly and in our own ways. I came alive very early and had the delight of watching my comrades come into the day.

IstHer was earliest—after me—and was sitting in Domar's doorway. Annel slept nearby. After a time they left the doorway and wandered over the grass. Tusks was awake and had moved away from the sleepers. He stood on a hillock talking to himself in a low voice. Zeke, his arms outstretched, slept deeply, his head on Scuro—also sleeping—and with Cat snoring softly in the bend of Zeke's arm. I looked around for our birds and couldn't see them anywhere and began to worry until I turned to Domar and there they were, perched in her window, heads under wings.

I wandered about a bit more, and then climbed carefully into Domar, whispering, "It's Maris. I wanted to be with you a while." And I stretched out, silent and at peace, and drifted into a doze.

CHAPTER 23

I wakened to the sound of drums and then to IstHer poking me and pulling on my hand.

"What's wrong? What's happening? Is a battle coming?"

"It's just all of your old friends—waiting for all of you to talk about the Great Land and what it needs."

With IstHer's busy assistance we soon had everyone up and moving towards the meeting place on the great green, with Arachne, Grandan, Exi, and Thaddeus nearby, and Blanca and the child with them.

Quatro stepped forward. "I am the speaker for the Beasts. First, however, I present Blanca, my wife, and Uno, my son. I am deeply, deeply grateful to all of you, my friends, for having protected us after we escaped. We love you all so much, so very very much." He seemed formal, but very present.

To my surprise the beautiful Blanca spoke. "I too thank you for your saving me and our unborn child. Now I—and I'm sure Uno also when he grows up—I will give the very best I have to the Great Land."

She paused, looking clearly at Zeke and me. She spoke to us particularly. "I too—as well as you, Zeke, Maris, Scuro, and Cat—I too fell into the Great Land during an earthquake. Longer ago than yours—but I was lost and lonely and fleeing from strangers for a long time. So I understand both worlds."

Quatro, close beside her, spoke to us again. "Let me say to you who are from other worlds what needs to happen—in fact, what must happen—before you return to your land. What you have already done for us is beyond gratitude. The Beasts who were sent us after you captured them—and the Worms we now have with us—are a splendid addition to us. They are helping our land to have more streams and lakes, more beauty, more laughter.

"Our deepest problem is that of the desire for power on the part of those Beasts and those Worms who are still wanting to rule the Great Land by militant force."

Tusks said, "May I ask a question or two, Quatro?"

"Of course, Tusks."

"Thank you, Quatro. Are most of the enemy Beasts and Worms in one area, or are they scattered all over?"

"Sort of both. Mostly they are in the less green and less lived-in areas. They are gathered together too tightly and we need to break them up. Do you have ideas of how?"

Tusks thought for a few minutes. "Well, it may sound absurd to you, but I would send for the Bat squadrons, and some of us—like myself and Scuro—and probably Maris and Zeke, who wouldn't be left out for anything, and all our Birds and Thaddeus's magic, and—"

"Slow down, Tusks. I hear you. Your ideas are great, and I know you all want to help. How would it be if we met with the Guardians and shared this idea with them."

We did just that. All of us went to the Guardians, and Quatro repeated to them what the suggestions had been.

"I believe it's a good plan," said Exi. "Particularly the Bats. I know many and they are wondrous. And we must include Thaddeus. He can turn doomsday into a triumph."

"I agree," Arachne said. "I would add the Vulture family as well—for transport and for attack."

"And I," said Grandan, who was usually quiet, "I would suggest using some of our new, wonderful, reeducated Beasts. They are anxious to help, eager to be used."

"May I," Quatro asked, "may I go to the newcomer Beasts and share with them, in part at least, our ideas and learn what they feel?"

"Of course," said Exi. "Of course. And we will give all our tentative plans to Them right away. So let's all of us do what we can and then come together at dark."

Antic took off for Bat Land, and would see the Vultures en route. Exi went to the Old Ones. I asked if I might go with Quatro to see and talk with the transformed Beasts. Grandan's reply was, "Of course. And take Scuro with you because both of you were together when the first Beast struggles were going on. Remember?"

And suddenly I was flooded by memories of that first time in the Great Land. I recalled Arachne's words: "Power, and power, must be united by the small." And I remembered all the conquered Beasts tangled in the sticky webs, being carried off like ugly bundles of anger. And also the canyon trap with eighteen Beasts, wounded, angry, ready to fight.

"We are near to the place where the newcomer Beasts, the helpful ones, are getting their training." said Quatro. "With only one exception—and he is learning—they are growing into splendid citizens of the Great Land." Quatro pointed to an opening in the hill. "We'll go down there."

What I saw when we entered was unbelievable. Here were all the Beasts we had helped to get into nets at the Beast Stockade—all those who had eaten Thaddeus's food and had diminished in size, and all those who had chosen to go. To my amazement and joy they called greetings to Quatro, and shouted the various names we had given them. It was obvious that they were happy and that they loved and respected Quatro as their teacher. As I talked with them, and heard their excitement because they were being trusted, I had a deep insight into what trust and love and honesty and a willingness to share difficulties could do to bring peace to all worlds. Including the one I came from.

"Remember me," said a Beast nearby. "You all named me Glad and that's who I am! I can work! I can learn to fight if it's needed! I am Glad, and I thank you!" He put his nose in my hand. And I kissed his head and patted him.

"Blessings to you, dear Glad. Protect this Great Land for us all."

Quatro stood among them. It was obvious that they loved and respected him because he had helped them to learn what it was to love and respect others.

Then we went to the Guardians. Only Exi was at their place but he went and gathered all but Grandan . . . even Thaddeus—which wasn't always easy.

"I'm here," piped Antic from a grassy rock. "The Bats will come with their assault squadron tomorrow."

Quatro went through his plans quickly. "We need to rush into the volcanic barrens and scatter the enemy Beasts in several directions to where there are comfortable cave corrals—really sort of temporary prisons—and hold them and domesticate them. If they refuse they remain prisoners. This will be only a temporary solution. We hope to change some of them into free and helpful Beast friends. Others, I am sure, will be renegades. Some will be injured or will die. These are truths. We must face them, and soon. The Old Ones, as well as the Guardians, believe we must act."

"We agree," said Exi. "And Grandmother, Grandfather, and Dark Fire say the work is up to us. Thaddeus will be our magician and consultant. So we believe, Quatro, that the sooner we act the less wounding there will be."

"I am with you." Quatro spoke emphatically. "The sooner we act the lesser will be the wounds. So I suggest we move fast. I suggest Da, Gada, and Dag be summoned to join us. I suggest Antic meets and hastens the Bat squadron. And that I go to the temporary training centers and learn how many reformed Beasts are ready and able to work with us."

Light and Shadow volunteered to go to the Vulture trio.

"Maris, why don't you and Zeke go to our big rooms of Beast comrades and tell them what we are preparing to do and find out if they agree."

For the next hours we all took up our tasks, going from place to place and group to group, telling all the eager beings of various kinds what would probably happen and where they needed to be when the drums of the Old Ones sounded. All had been given the plans by the time Da, Gada, and Dag arrived in the great central field. All of our Company was present. Thaddeus was there, complete with his magic paraphernalia. Quatro and Tusks stood together quietly—doubtless making plans. Suddenly, there was a dark cloud across the light and all at once came a large contingent of Bats. They rose and fell and rose as they came to join us, like a huge veil being waved in the air by a god. We greeted them joyfully. Big Bat alighted on Zeke's head, saying, "Here we are, dear friends! We need to rest until twilight. Then we do our best work."

The Bat squadron was escorted to one of the underground rooms where they could rest and be ready for the displacement of the rebel Beasts. The rest of us spent the night and the early dawn hours in visiting and planning with Beast newcomers. We helped them to see how they could attack and rout the enemy without hurting them, or risking their own lives.

At dawn we all gathered in the great central place. The Guardians were all there. Thaddeus had his black pot of magic on his head. The large company of helpers took a considerable space. Worms—with Annel at the head; Beasts—with Quatro and Tusks as leaders; the Birds waiting for their passengers; and we from another land. We all stood silently on the grass as the light grew.

Suddenly there came the roll of the drums from under the earth. This meant get to work. It came so fast that I didn't feel afraid as I climbed onto Dag's feathered back with Cat. Scuro rode on Da and Zeke on Gada.

It was exciting to up and up, over the Mountain of Them and over other mountains whose names I couldn't recall, and then to soar over lakes—one I was sure was the one we had swum in—and then along a river for a short time. Finally we came to the raw, rocky land where we could see at least three barren volcanic cones, each with wisps of smoke coming from the cone. It was here we were to go.

We circled slowly, the three Birds keeping close together so Da could give orders. "Take the big cone first," he called. "It's the biggest one and probably has more inhabitants than the others. We'll land in the barren flats nearby. All three of us. Let us be fierce vulture enemies. While our passengers are walking about we must act as if we would kill at any moment if anyone harms our passengers. So follow me."

We landed and waited, making no sound. Before long a Beast came out, saw us, scrambled back inside. After a few minutes several Beasts emerged. One, bigger and evidently more sure of itself, came toward us. "What do you want? This is our place. Get out!"

"We come peacefully." Zeke was amazingly composed in his way of standing and speaking. "We come from the Old Ones who would be very pleased if you would become part of the Great Land and work with Them."

The big and evidently tough Beast snarled. "We hate Them and we're going to have our own Kingdom and before you know it we're going to run the whole Land! We've got other Beast centers ready to join us here! So get out before we attack!"

Suddenly, Da spread his great wings and let out a terrifying screech and took a step toward the Beast.

"I didn't mean it!" The Beast looked frightened and at a loss. "Really I didn't! Please sir!"

Da folded his wings. "Thank you, sir. We are here to help, not to hurt."

And so, to our amazement, Beast after Beast after Beast emerged from the ragged cone and balked and then came to talk with us. Those who came were of the same opinion as the first one; namely that they didn't really want a hot and miserable Beast Kingdom and they mostly wanted peace and wanted to belong to the Great Land. And they really meant it—to our surprise and delight.

"Why don't you come with us and visit the Old Ones and the Guardians?" Zeke was being amazingly wise. "You'll find a lovely land, and trees and grass, and friends like you, and food. Why don't you come?"

There was a long silence. We waited. Then the Beasts began to talk among themselves. We were quiet.

Finally, the big tough Beast came to us. "We would like to go to your city and talk to your masters."

"We have no masters," said Zeke. "We have the Old Ones and the Guardians and all the rest who work together to keep the Great Land always in balance. We don't have masters or slaves. We work together. Do you understand?"

The big Beast scratched his ugly head with a hind foot. "I think I do. I really think I do. Quite a lot of us now believe we want to go. I guess we're lonely and useless out here."

"Do you know the way?"

"I think so. Some of us do anyway." He paused to scratch his ear.

"Watch our flight path," said Da. "That will give you the correct direction. And we will tell the Old Ones and the Guardians that you are coming."

We called farewells as we lifted into the sky, and the Beasts waved at us.

The next turn was mine and Cat's. It was a smaller cone and a smaller group of Beasts and Worms. And they were not hostile. They were unhappy and confused, and hardly knew why they had come there. It wasn't hard to convince them that to be protected and loved was good.

So when we met with the Guardians we agreed that Bat squadrons were not necessary. Any minor revolt could be handled by Da or Gada and one of us. And slowly, but without question, the renegade Beasts and Worms began to migrate back to the green lands of grasses and rivers and lakes and trees. They were near to the Old Ones and the Guardians, and when they needed anything they asked. And they did ask, usually. And they were helped.

One afternoon Zeke and I were stretched out on the soft greensward, eyes closed, resting. Suddenly, Zeke said, "I'm homesick, Maris. Real homesick. Do you ever feel that way?"

I thought a minute. Then I knew. "Yes. Yes, I am homesick. I hadn't thought about it. But I am."

"What do you suppose happened to our homes and friends and family? Were they wrecked? Hurt? Or killed?"

"Oh, Zeke! Let's go home!"

"I haven't any idea of how. Do you?"

"No."

For a while we were very quiet.

Then I thought of Thaddeus. "Let's ask Thaddeus if he could get us back."

So we went to him— Zeke and I, plus Scuro and Cat, and told him our wish. He was in his magic room near his deep pool under the great grass field when we came to him.

"Dear Thaddeus," I said. "I love you so! We've done so much together."

"Yes we have! We have! this is the third time you and your comrades have helped us regain our balance in the Great Land. And you have been so patient and so faithful and have given greatly. And you remember what Exi said: 'The Great Land is what lives under and within all other lands. It is a sort of pattern of patterns. What happens here can alter what happens in other lands and countries and also in people.'"

Thaddeus looked at us four with love in his bulgy eyes. "Yes, dear children, I believe I can get you home—all four of you. Be prepared, however, for difficulties."

"What difficulties?" I asked.

"Dear Maris—and Scuro and Zeke and Cat—you all arrived in the Great Land because of an earthquake in your land. Probably because the pattern here was being upset and shaky. Or the other way around. And it doesn't matter. We all touch each other." He rubbed his bulgy head.

"Maris, I want on Old One and a Guardian. I'll go and get them. Will you please sort all my magic items and lay them out on a cleared floor."

He went his slow side to side walk up the incline from his pool and his underground home, headed for the surface.

I asked Zeke to help me gather and sort, while Cat and Scuro rested. It was cool and very quiet in this precious cavern. Zeke and I enjoyed putting all Thaddeus's magic items in a proper order on the ground by the pool.

Thaddeus returned with Arachne and Dark Fire—a pair I wouldn't have expected. But when I thought of it, I guessed each of them was magical. And they knew all the items Thaddeus asked for, and before I was prepared he said, "All is ready, children. Please come to the pool." We obeyed. Cat was scared, I could tell, so I held him in my arms. Scuro stood between Zeke and me.

"Arachne, put the webbing over them all."

As it fell over us I began to tremble. Cat and Scuro pressed close to my sides. Zeke was right in front of me. I put my hands on his shoulders and he was trembling as much as I.

"Now, children, follow me to and into the pool. I will swim ahead of you until the upward tunnel. You are safe, all of you. The webbing, the water, and the magic will take you. We love you all. Remember us and the Great Land. Farewell."

Once into the water tunnel, Thaddeus left us. The tunnel grew into a twilight river going upward. For a time there was some light and then it was dark. Zeke kept reassuring Cat and Scuro that it would be OK. But they were frightened—and so was I—as it grew more and more murky and scary.

"Will we die here, Zeke?" I asked as I grew more distressed. "Will we, Zeke?"

"Thaddeus wouldn't do that, Maris. Trust him."

And at that moment we emerged from the water. I guess I fainted or something. When I came to consciousness I saw a nurse and my mother and father, and I was in a bed and I started to cry.

My father held my hand very tight. He bent and kissed me. "Scuro is home and all OK. We took a cat home, too. Nice cat. And your friend Zeke is in another bed here and nothing is broken in either of you."

My mother bent and kissed me. "Our house is all right. Only a cracked window. Now you rest, dear Maris. In a day or so you'll be home."

"And the tree?" I whispered.

"It was felled. And the tree house is gone, dearest."

They left quietly, kissing me goodnight. And I lay in my bed seeing—in my mind's eye—the Old Ones, the Guardians, all my friends, especially Domar with IstHer and Molasses. And I could hear drums. And I said aloud to myself, "Please let us keep our pattern clear and open and loving so that it can never harm the Great Land! Please!"

And I went to sleep.